"Nothing is ever going to happen with me and Sean."

"Why? Seriously, why? You don't stop loving someone overnight, Jill. It doesn't work like that."

"It wasn't overnight."

"One night we're plotting your first kiss, and the next you barely say a word to him. You aren't your mom. You don't have to give up on Sean just because your mom gave up on your dad."

I started to feel ill, listening to Claire. "Is that what you think?"

Claire lowered her voice. "You won't talk about it, so what am I supposed to think?"

If Claire had spoken to me in anything less than the gentlest tone known to man, I might have been able to deflect her.

"I just woke up, okay. Sean is my friend and that's all I want from him anymore."

Claire quietly stared at me until I started painting again, then with a deep sigh, reached for her own brush. "Okay, but are you sure that's all he wants from you?"

Books by Abigail Johnson

If I Fix You
The First to Know

IF I

FIX YOU

ABIGAIL JOHNSON

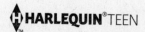

Recycling programs
for this product may
not exist in your area.

ISBN-13: 978-0-373-21249-1

If I Fix You

Copyright © 2016 by Abigail Johnson

HARLEQUIN®TEEN
™ www.HarlequinTEEN.com

Printed in U.S.A.

For my parents

Dad, I finally get to return the honor
and dedicate a book to you.

Mom, you taught me to love reading and gave me the world.

PROLOGUE
FEBRUARY

Mom left on a Tuesday. I remember because Tuesdays were taco night and Dad and I to this day don't eat tacos. Also because that was the night I fell out of love with Sean Addison.

Winter was old and wheezing by late February. The lingering chill in the air still bit at my skin after sunset, making it hard to remember that in a few months it'd be hot enough for the soles of my sneakers to stick to the asphalt.

Tourists from back East flocked to Arizona during the winter months, so the snowbirds, as we called them, were still thick on the roads and in Dad's auto shop. I'd personally changed enough oil that winter to fill a swimming pool, and that particular Tuesday was no different. I was drowning in motor oil. The plastic smell of it clung to my hair and coated my lungs when I inhaled. My red coveralls were smeared with the same greasy stains that turned my hands that ineffable shade of zombie gray.

But all of that was okay, because I could change oil in my sleep, which left me free to dream about the only thing I'd ever truly wanted: a 1967 Triumph Spitfire Mark III convertible with Sean Addison riding shotgun.

The sports car I'd wanted ever since I had helped my dad

rebuild one when I was eight. It was creamy white with tan leather seats and the original chrome bumpers (which federal safety regulations didn't allow on later models). The budding mechanic in me had swooned over the one-piece front end that tilted forward for unparalleled engine access, and the exhaust that sang like a siren to my ears. I'd been saving to buy my own for the past eight years.

The boy I'd wanted from the first day of kindergarten. He took in my coveralls—which I insisted on wearing every-where back then—and instead of teasing me like the other kids, asked me if I could fix the tire on his fire engine. As we got older, I started liking him for more than his good taste in mechanics. Beyond the fact that his eyes were the exact shade of my favorite blue jeans, he could always tell when I needed to laugh after a night spent listening to my parents fighting. Sure, Sean was more likely to high-five me than kiss me these days, but I planned on fixing that.

"Jill?" Dad's voice echoed around the garage bay and stalled my car-and-boy-fueled daydream.

"Under the white Civic." I rolled out on my creeper, sat up and spun to face him in a way that still made me grin like a four-year-old. I didn't even mind that the momentum made my dark blond braid slap me in the face.

Dad and I had been nearly the same height for the past year, but what he lacked in height he made up for in girth—and not an ounce of it fat. He could lift a midsize car with his bare hands. He used to joke that that was how he'd got-ten Mom to marry him.

Dad was already pointing over his shoulder, but I cut him off, a premonition making me narrow my eyes. "If it's another oil change, I'm calling Child Protective Services."

Dad considered me. I was half serious, which made him smile. "How about a clogged fuel intake—"

"Deal." I'd reek of gasoline by the time I was done, but it'd be a welcome change from motor oil. Plus I happened to like the smell of gasoline. I scrambled to my feet.

"—and an oil change."

I sank back down and cocked my head at him. "I can't tell if you're kidding or if you just hate me."

Dad tossed me a screwdriver.

"So the latter, then."

Dad was halfway across the bay when he turned back in a much-too-casual-to-be-casual way. "Oh, did I mention it's a '69 Plymouth Road Runner?"

That caught my attention. Big-time. Dad knew I had a weakness for muscle cars. "Seriously? Does it have the beep-beep horn?"

Dad shrugged. "Are you willing to get your hands dirty to find out?"

I held up my hands. "Dad." I needed to say only that one word. The telltale line of grease was visible underneath all ten of my fingernails. It would take a solid twenty minutes of scrubbing to get it out, and weariness beat vanity most nights. Dad didn't even bother anymore. Drove Mom nuts. At dinner she'd stare at the pair of us over the table and make little comments about dirty hands. Never mind that it wasn't dirt, just a little clean grease to show how hard we worked.

I'd spent my days at Dad's auto shop every summer, and even some school nights, since I'd learned how to hold a wrench. Seriously, I knew how to change a tire before I could tie my shoes. Dad still had my first tiny pair of cover-alls hanging in the main garage.

I wasn't afraid to get my hands dirty, especially if it meant working on a true classic.

"Ragtop or hardtop?" I asked, hurrying to join Dad by the door.

He dropped a kiss on my head and ushered me ahead of him. "If it was a ragtop, I'd have sent you home early and kept her all to myself."

"Sure you would." Dad once took me out of school in the middle of chemistry class when we got a 1964 Shelby GT in the shop. Because he couldn't wait two hours to show it to me.

"Should we order pizza, make it a night?"

As awesome as that sounded, Dad had obviously forgotten one important detail. "Last night you told Mom we'd be home early for dinner."

Dad's smile died. "You heard that?"

I curled my fist tighter around the screwdriver, hating the way his shoulders hunched when he felt like he'd let me down. Lately, they'd been fighting more. Sometimes Mom would be waiting for Dad at the door and would lay into him before he could get inside. The only semisolace I'd been able to find night after night was climbing out my window up to the roof, but even there I could hear them. Sometimes I'd swear she was trying to make him hate her.

Sometimes, I wondered why he didn't.

Acting as a buffer between my parents was not high on my wish list, but I'd rather she snipe at me than yell at Dad again. "Do you want me…to call her?"

Dad shook his head, strong shoulders still hunched. I vowed silently not to give him any more grief about oil changes for at least the rest of the week. Hopefully, the inevitable blowup with Mom would have cooled in a few days.

Dad's tight-lipped expression told me he wasn't nearly as optimistic as I was.

"I'll take care of it. Why don't you finish up the Civic. We'll start the Road Runner tomorrow."

"As in Wile E. Coyote?"

Dad and I turned to see Sean come strolling into the garage. My mood skyrocketed at the sight of him. Yes, he was blue-eyed, blond-haired and all kinds of pretty, but he actually looked even better on the inside. It was the combination that brought that euphoric Christmas morning smile to my face.

"Little late for a walk-in, Sean."

Sean was used to Dad's less than warm demeanor—which I was going to optimistically attribute to fallout from having to call Mom—so he answered with a smile. "Hey, Mr. Whitaker. I was in the neighborhood, and Jill keeps offering to change my oil."

My eyes closed slowly and I could feel Dad's stare. It wasn't like this particular cat was still in the bag, but Dad getting so much concrete proof of my crush felt like I'd gotten caught driving a Prius.

Fortunately for me, Sean didn't notice the awkwardness and kept up an easy conversation with Dad. He even attempted to tell a car joke, which admittedly, did not go over well, but he still tried. That was the kind of friend he was.

I nearly dropped my screwdriver gazing at him.

Dad clapped his hands together, making me jump. "I tell you what, Sean, why don't you show me your little Nazi buggy and *I'll* check your oil."

Sean cocked his head. "You know, I'm pretty sure the fine folks at Volkswagen decided the name 'Nazi buggy' was too regional when they released the Jetta."

Dad shrugged. "It's still not a real car. It's like…"

"A neutered, asthmatic poodle?" I said.

"Whoa." Sean slid a step back from me like I'd insulted his manhood.

Dad grinned as if proud that I still had my priorities in order when it came to boys and cars. "Then I'll leave it to

Jill." Catching my eye as he left, Dad added, "Don't let him distract you."

My cheeks flushed. "I'll get everything done."

Sean watched Dad leave the garage and I headed to the slop sink to wash up. Well, that, and so Sean wouldn't see the blush still heating my face.

Sean leaned against the wall to my left. "You like my Jetta." It was half question, half statement.

"I like your Jetta—"

"Right? Right."

"—I'd like it better if it went from zero to sixty in 3.5 seconds."

"Does that mean you're too cool to ride in it when you get off?"

I splashed water at him. "No."

"Good, 'cause I'm starving."

"Me too, but I've still got cars to finish, then I have to sweep and use the auto scrubber on the floor, and replace the ceiling light in the corner. On top of that, I need to grab a quick shower and change before we go anywhere."

"Whoa, whoa, whoa." Sean held up his hands. "I can help with most of that, and I think you're seriously underestimating how hot you look in a one-size-fits-all jumpsuit."

I laughed. No one looked good in a one-size-fits-all jumpsuit, except maybe Mom. "Really, you want to help?"

Sean picked up a reciprocating saw and raised an eyebrow. I turned the handheld saw right side up in his hands. "I was testing you."

"Sure you were."

Sean eyed the rest of the equipment around him. "Maybe I'll start with replacing the light."

"Good call." I pulled out a new bulb from a cabinet and offered it to him. "There's a ladder in the closet."

Sean looked toward the closet then back to me. "Too far." He bent, wrapping his arms around my legs, and lifted me up, way up, considering I was already pretty tall and Sean made me look short. "I'm better than a ladder, right?" He gave me a bounce that had me clutching his hair.

"I swear, Sean, if you drop me…"

He grinned and bounced me again. "That's your problem. You lack follow-through. If you're going to threaten me, be specific."

I switched out the bulb, shot the broken one into a nearby trash can and made a swish sound. "How's that for follow-through?"

"Not bad." Sean pulled his arm to one side and caught me around my back with the other, carrying me like the fireman he planned to be. The way he was smiling at me… *I* started to feel like Christmas morning. My arms tightened around his neck.

"Time to leave, Sean."

Sean and I whipped our heads toward Dad. I hadn't even noticed him come back. "He was helping me change the lightbulb." I elbowed Sean, and he grunted before putting me down, then pointed to the light overhead.

"Yeah, but since I'm not paying either one of you to do that…"

"Are you offering me a job, Mr. Whitaker?" Then Sean elbowed me back, tickling me right between the ribs. "Jill, tell him what a mean ladder I make."

I couldn't tell Dad anything while I was laughing. Dad thought Sean was a reckless flirt. I thought Sean was reckless perfection. Dad didn't appreciate the distinction the way I did. That was another thing I needed to fix.

"He's leaving."

"I am? Aren't we hanging out?"

"Yes," I said, making it more of a question than I wanted as I met Dad's eye. He gave a slight but reluctant nod and I turned fully to Sean. "My house in an hour?"

Sean paused, and a tiny frown appeared between his brows, but then it was gone. "Don't be late." He lightly knocked my shoulder with his fist, waved at Dad and left. He might as well have said, *See you later, my totally platonic pal.*

I drew a finger across my throat and let my tongue drop out to one side, then I zombie shuffled toward the cars that would probably keep me busy way past closing.

And what do you know, they did.

On the upside, I didn't have to wait for Dad. Whatever conversation he'd had with Mom, it was bad enough that he "decided to work late" and sent me home alone. If I were going to see anyone but Sean, I'd have let that knowledge affect my mood.

When I got home and spotted his Jetta, I was practically giddy to the point that I ignored the ajar front door, which made the contrast all the more devastating when I walked into the living room and found...my mom and my... Sean.

It was like one of those optical illusion pictures where all the lines cross and intersect but don't seem to originate from anywhere. A trick. There was no other explanation for seeing Mom curved on the armrest of Dad's favorite chair, legs crossed, leaning over Sean so that her blouse gaped open and skin and lace spilled free.

I watched her toy with the button on his shirt, trace the edge with her fingernail. My vision shrank to a pinprick when I saw her lips moving toward his ear.

When her free hand slid to touch his thigh, it was like the world exploded. All at once there was a rushing sound in my head and my bag slipped through my fingers, hitting the floor with a dull thud.

I'll never forget Sean's eyes when he jerked his head up and his gaze met mine, wide and utterly devoid of the warmth it usually held for me.

Ice and fire burned inside my chest in the split second before he shot out of the chair and bolted to the door, leaving Mom holding his jacket in her hands. He said something to me, words that ricocheted off the dead thing inside me and fell to the floor between us. I couldn't hear anything until the door shut behind him.

He'd just been sitting there, not leaning in or touching her back. Later I wanted that to mean something, but there was no killing the insidious and relentless thought that slithered around in my head, refusing to die no matter how many times I stabbed it:

Sean didn't leave until I showed up.

And Mom. My mother.

I didn't know that betrayal was a thing. I didn't know that it could paralyze while it quietly devoured light and sound and the air itself.

She was still holding his jacket. She was still sitting in Dad's chair.

Dad.

And it started again. Only it was his pain on top of mine, crushing and constricting, and I made a noise that wasn't a word.

I stood there with my fingers twitching, longing for the feel of my bag and the ability to move backward in time. Not just before this night, this moment, but months and years. Back to a time when she loved us enough not to annihilate everything, only my memories dissolved before I found it.

I had no defense against her words, nothing to shield myself with. She could have pierced my heart with a single syllable. But she didn't, and that was worse.

She didn't even try.

Mom slunk silently into her room. Her final words to me were scribbled on a Post-it note I found on my pillow the next morning. My eyes blurred so much while reading it that the only thing I noticed was, she spelled the word *suffocating* wrong.

CHAPTER
1

JULY

Falling was such an elastic word. It was basically horrible. People got hurt and died, falling. There was force and pain and fear, if the height was great enough. Even sometimes when it wasn't. The terror of not finding something solid underfoot was just as real for half a second as it was for twenty.

Yet *fall* was the word most often coupled with love, falling in and falling out of. How was that even possible? They couldn't be the same. One *fall* ushered in delirious, stupid happiness; the other *fall* expelled those euphoric emotions with blood and tears and scars. Bliss and agony. Fall and fall. It wasn't the same. There should be a better word.

Above me, a falling star shot across the sky. Except it wasn't a star. It was a piece of rock burning up as it entered Earth's atmosphere. It was beautiful as it flared bright against the night and died.

But it was too hot to be thinking about anything burning up, even beautiful things.

And it was too quiet.

Five months should have been long enough to acclimate to the silence, to embrace the thing I'd sought for years. It was mine now. Silence so stark that it wriggled under my skin.

Stretched out on my roof, I was searching the sky for more stars when all-too-familiar sounds punctured the silence. For a moment I thought the fighting was coming from below me. I shot up like the shingles had shocked me, but the voices weren't coming from my house.

It was so messed up that that realization disappointed me.

I drew my knees up and rested one heat-flushed cheek on them. A prickle of perspiration needled across my skin as I studied the nearly identical house beside mine. All the houses on our street looked the same. Ranch house after ranch house, with drab beige walls, barely pitched roofs and graveled yards. I hadn't given much thought to the moving truck parked next door yesterday, but it was hard not to pay attention to the rising voices.

I'd gotten good at eavesdropping on fights. Not a skill I'd ever wanted to master, but I hadn't wanted to still be an A-cup at almost seventeen either. The new neighbors were amateurs. They'd left their window open. A few more minutes and Mrs. Holcomb across the street would be calling the police. She'd probably still be up watching her "stories" from the previous day.

A tiny part of me died inside because I knew that. The highlight of my evening was watching an old woman watch TV.

We didn't get nearly enough stars over my particular patch of Arizona, and I needed to watch something.

A tiny breeze puffed warm air over me, causing the loose strands from my bun to tickle my cheeks. I pushed them back, focusing on the open window next door. The blinds were lowered so I couldn't see much, but I heard enough, and it was nothing I hadn't heard before. She was miserable and angry. He was frustrated and angry. It was his fault; it was her fault. Rinse and repeat. It wasn't an even fight. He got quieter as she got louder.

Things got more interesting when they moved and I saw their silhouettes through the window. She was much smaller than he was, and shaking with rage.

"Explain it to me then," he said. "I don't understand how you can blame—"

His head snapped to the side as she slapped him. He took his time turning back to her and when he did, I was almost positive she spit in his face.

"They should have arrested you."

Whoa. And yep, spit. He wiped his face. "You don't mean that. Mom, look at you!"

Mom? That was…interesting, except that wasn't the right word. There wasn't anything *interesting* about someone getting slapped and spit on. Still, if he was some kind of criminal and she was scared of him…but so far, she was the violent one. He hadn't so much as lifted a hand to defend himself. Not that I had tons of experience, but that seemed decidedly uncriminal to me.

She screamed incoherently at him after that. They moved back out of view and I heard a crash, like a lamp breaking against a wall, followed by him grunting. And all the while she was shrieking, until more crashes drowned her out.

I was up on my knees at that point, eyes wide, ears straining. This was so much worse than anything I'd heard from my parents. They'd yelled, sure, but that was it—words. The fighting next door was bad, like someone-getting-hurt bad, and from the sound of it, not the petite woman with the wicked arm. Where the hell was nosy Mrs. Holcomb?

More silence, then another crash. "Throw anything you want," he said. "I'm not leaving you—"

"You stay away from me." Her voice quivered.

Surprise colored his words. "When have I ever hurt you?"

"You arrogant little..." Her voice lowered into a hiss I couldn't make out. "If I had any choice, you think I'd be here?"

"You'd be dead if you had any choice. Just stop. It's over. I'm not the one in jail."

Which meant somebody was in jail—the wrong somebody, according to the mom. But she was the one hurting him, while he thought he was saving her life...? Either way, I couldn't just sit there and hope her arm got tired before she hit something vital.

Half turning on my roof, I squinted in the darkness, looking for the unopened can of pop I'd brought up with me. I heard yet another crash seconds before my fingers brushed against the cool aluminum.

I crouched down as close to the edge of the roof as possible and hurled the can across the ten feet or so that separated our houses.

I figured the sound might distract them.

I hadn't figured on how badly my aim might suck in the dark.

I'd been trying to hit the side of their house. Instead, the sound of shattering glass filled the night as the can broke right through the kitchen window.

I clapped a hand over my mouth and flattened myself to the roof just as the back door banged open and a guy who really didn't look all that much older than me shot into the yard.

His hair was black in the faint light, and long enough that it fell over his eyes when he moved. Gravel crunched as he stalked around. It didn't take him long to realize his postage-stamp-sized backyard was empty.

Don't look up. Don't look up. Don't look up.

Leaving seemed like the best idea I'd ever had. I could turn away, slide off the edge of my roof and through my bedroom window. I could do it without a sound too. But I didn't. Instead I stared. I watched.

It was totally stupid on my part. He could be dangerous, or at the very least angry that I'd broken his window—a fact he was sure to realize if he spotted me. But for some reason I wasn't scared. Not really. I'd done what I wanted. I'd stopped the fight. His mom hadn't followed him outside, and he didn't seem to be in a hurry to go back in—not that I blamed him.

That was one seriously enraged woman. I was half-surprised he wasn't limping, based on all the stuff it had sounded like she threw at him. Why hadn't he left? And if he belonged behind bars like his mom said, why hadn't he…stopped her? He was easily twice her size, and I could practically see the anger steaming off him. He was physically capable of stopping her, yet I'd heard him grunt with each impact and ask her to stop instead of making her.

He dropped his head and stretched out his hands to lean against the small wooden shed in the far corner of the yard beside mine. He bounced a palm off it once, twice, then straightened and slammed his fist into the door over and over again until the wood split with an audible crack.

I sat up, shivering in the hot air, and watched him back away. It was unnerving, but still—better a piece of wood than a person. My new neighbor had enough self-control to take hit after hit—and spit—and walk away. I doubted I could say as much.

When the clouds parted, I saw something dark drip down

his knuckles a second before he bent down. The shard of glass he'd picked up glinted in his hand as his head tilted up.

The newly revealed moonlight cast a perfect spotlight on me.

CHAPTER
2

My eyes went wide as they met his, and all I could do was stare. At him, his bloody hand, the broken glass from my stupid, stupid pop can.

"What the hell? Did you break my window?"

I flinched like I'd been hit. My stomach teemed with slimy snakes as I stared into a pair of royally pissed-off eyes.

"I'm sorry. I wasn't trying to hit your window."

"No?" He stood, turning the glass over in his hand. "What were you trying to hit?" Glancing toward his house then mine, he tracked the distance between them, between the fighting and me. When he hunched his shoulders in realization, the stance was so much like Dad's that any trace of fear I'd had vanished completely.

"I was trying to distract you, or really, just your mom. I thought something banging against the wall might bring you outside, or her, and things could cool down." I said that last part as I was literally sweating from every pore on my body. I exhaled. "I didn't think it through. I just didn't want...anyone to get hurt. I'm sorry. It's not any of my business. And I will pay for the window."

"Forget it."

Maybe all the years spent listening to my parents fighting had anesthetized me to clipped and angry speech, but the slimy slithery feeling in my gut was dissipating.

"At least let me—"

"I said forget it." His anger was fading as quickly as my unease, but I preferred his initial hostility to the defeat that hung heavily from his limbs as he started walking back to his door. "Don't bust any more of my windows, yeah?"

"Wait."

He paused and looked at me over his shoulder.

It hadn't been long enough yet. I knew from experience that if he went back inside, she'd more than likely be waiting for him. Whenever Dad had tried to walk back too soon after a fight, Mom got her second wind. With Neighbor Guy's mom, I didn't want him to find out what her second wind might entail.

I was betting it would hurt a lot more than a thrown lamp.

"Don't go back in yet." I swallowed. "I mean, I'll go inside. You can stay." I swung my legs off the edge of the roof and was preparing to roll onto my stomach when he stopped me.

"Hey, don't." He held up his hands as he approached the wall dividing our yards and tripped the motion lights on the side of my house. "Just stop, okay?"

I stopped. The shifting clouds had kept most of his features in shadow, but in the harsh, unforgiving floodlight, I got my first good look.

The cement block wall was close to six feet high, and he could have rested his chin on it. He was also older than I'd initially thought, though his age was hard to pinpoint since he looked several days overdue for a shave. But more than anything, I noticed the reddened outline of an open palm on his cheek.

Seeing the mark on his face made the fighting more real than the moving shadows and sounds had earlier. His mom had hit him…a lot. I didn't care how old he was; that wasn't okay. Especially since it was obvious to me within a minute of talking to him that he wasn't going to hurt anyone. He was visibly distressed by the thought of me, a complete stranger and admitted vandal, jumping off a one-story roof.

It's not okay.

I mentally shook that thought away when I realized that the shadows that had abandoned him were no longer surrounding me either. And his eyes were trailing just as freely over me, my too-small old gym shorts and faded Jim's Auto Shop tee, up to the tangled mass of dark blond hair piled on my head.

I tried to imagine the view from his perspective and hit the brakes when the picture of a vagrant twelve-year-old formed in my mind. A feeling of inadequacy wrapped around me like a sweaty hug and I almost jumped down just to get away from it. And him.

"What are you doing up there anyway?"

I doubted he could see the dark sleeping bag I kept up there, so he couldn't guess that I slept on my roof more nights than I slept under it. More important, he didn't need to. "I like to look at the stars sometimes."

He looked at the sky and then back at me. "Stars? Seriously?"

I didn't bother looking up. There weren't any stars that night. The sky would have looked blank if not for the moon, although even that was in the process of being swallowed up by clouds.

"I said sometimes."

"And the other times?"

"I just like to get out of my house. It's quiet up here."

He smiled. "You mean usually." It wasn't a big smile. More of a quirk of his lips on one side, a brief flash of teeth. It was the weak smile more than his words that brought me right back to feeling awful for him.

I bit the inside of my cheek and tugged at the hem of my shorts, trying to cover more of my legs. Then I sat on my hands to keep from pulling my stupid bun down.

His eyes flicked down to track the movement of my legs. He took a step back, then half turned before facing me again. "You can't go around jumping off roofs, okay? You'll break your leg or something."

I bristled at his words and let them fuel an equally flippant response. "As opposed to my hand?"

I couldn't actually see his injured hand with him standing that close to the wall, but I saw his shoulder lift and assumed he was flexing it. The muscle in his cheek—the one that was still red from being slapped—twitched. I immediately felt responsible. Not just for a thoughtless comment, but for reminding him of what I'd witnessed.

As easily as if I'd called them, the snakes slithered back inside.

Neighbor Guy nodded, to himself or to me, I didn't know, and left without another word. He didn't go back inside, which relieved me to no end. Instead I stood and watched as he walked around the side of his house and got into a navy Jeep parked in his driveway. With an urgency that rocked his vehicle, he backed out and hit the brakes hard before he turned and drove off, a grinding noise echoing behind him.

The solace my roof usually provided abandoned me after that. I no longer felt like I'd helped him, not in any substantial way. Uselessness gnawed at me for hours before I moved to the flat part of my roof, which covered the patio, and drifted into an uneasy sleep.

The grinding noise roused me sometime before dawn. I didn't function well at that hour, but as I watched him park and enter his house, something occurred to me that was so obvious, I wondered how I'd slept at all.

I slipped silently off my roof—without breaking either of my legs—and through my window. In my room, I pulled open the bottom drawer of my desk and found a stack of coupons wrapped in a rubber band. Mom had designed them back when she'd decided all the shop needed to thrive was a little advertising. She said people still had to drive, even in a bad economy. Coupons, flyers, we'd even done a commercial…it was pretty awful, but she'd been so happy the day we shot it. The advertising did help, but her enthusiasm had waned when the business didn't boom the way she'd anticipated. We hadn't seen a coupon all year.

I thumbed through the stack and pulled one free. Before I lost my nerve, I scribbled a few words on the back and hurried out the window so Dad wouldn't hear the door.

I knew what that grinding noise meant. He needed new brake pads like, yesterday. Probably not the most important problem in his life, but it was the one I could fix.

I walked up to the Jeep and clamped the coupon underneath his windshield wiper.

I did owe him for the window, after all.

CHAPTER 3

The sky was beginning to lighten as I climbed back through the window. My T-shirt snagged on the latch, jerking me back, and I kicked my desk lamp trying to regain my balance.

The lamp didn't break, but the accompanying *crash* as it hit the floor was loud enough that I wasn't surprised when my bedroom door swung open and Dad burst in brandishing a baseball bat.

"Jill, what…?"

Under different circumstances, a father catching his daughter sneaking into her bedroom in the wee hours of the morning would be followed by a lot of yelling. Dad took one look at me crouched on my desk and sighed. "Still with the roof?"

I could hear the weariness in his voice. He didn't get enough sleep as it was without me waking him up early. He worked all the time, partly for the money—stupid Pep Boys had opened a shop two blocks from us and we were starting to feel the pinch—but also so he wouldn't have to think about Mom leaving him. Leaving us.

"Sorry, Dad." I closed the window behind me and hopped off my desk.

He raked a hand over his wild mess of dark, bent tangles. It was getting long in the back. Mom always had him keep it neat and short, but it was starting to brush past his collar. "You can't keep doing this. Not at five o'clock in the morning. Only serial killers get up this early."

I didn't try to follow that line of logic. "Or cross-country runners. You remember which one I am, right?"

Dad yawned wide enough that I could count the fillings in his teeth. He shuffled farther into my room and set the lamp back on my desk. "Didn't Dahmer run track in high school?"

"Ha-ha. You're funny at five o'clock in the morning."

"I should be catatonic at five o'clock in the morning. *You* should be catatonic at five o'clock in the morning."

"I'll be quieter next time," I said. "Promise."

Dad made an odd growling noise as he yawned again and arched his back until it cracked. "Mmm…would it kill you to sleep in the house again? It's gotta be ninety-five degrees and the sun isn't even up."

I didn't care how hot it was. I wasn't ready to come back yet. I watched him, waiting for him to say it, to bring up Mom.

But he didn't.

He never had. Not in the five months since she'd left. Not a word, like it was totally normal for us to wake up one day and find her gone. Had he known she was leaving? Did he know why? Did he want to? I didn't know the answers, and I really didn't know how to ask the questions. So we lived like that. We pretended and ignored the little and not-so-little reminders of her that we inevitably encountered every day.

Slowly but surely she was disappearing from our house just as she had from our lives. Sometimes I'd notice a picture missing, or a pillow. We were both doing it. Purging her. Last month I took her favorite coffee mug up on the roof with me and dropped it on the driveway to watch it break apart. If Dad saw the pieces, he never said anything. I was going to break her reading glasses next. Maybe back over them with Dad's truck.

But she wasn't gone yet. There were the things I couldn't get rid of as easily as dropping them from the roof.

The things I saw in the mirror.

Sean.

"It's not that hot," I said. Which was comparatively true when we considered how hot it would get, but not really the point, and we both knew it. I could tell by the pinched frown on Dad's face that he wasn't happy with my response. Neither was I, but sleeping inside wasn't going to change that. The utter silence in the house at night crawled under my skin like tiny fire ants biting and stinging whenever I tried. And sometimes I'd hear Dad pacing at all hours. Maybe he wasn't able to sleep in their bed alone. Maybe the quiet ate at him too. Either way, I couldn't stand to hear it. Or not hear it.

I pulled a smile onto my face. I didn't want Dad to have to worry about me any more than he already did. "And I promise not to ritualistically murder and eat anyone this morning, no matter how great the temptation is."

Dad's own smile took longer than I would have liked to match mine, but it got there. Better. I needed to find a way to keep it there.

"You want me to make you something—" he yawned "—for breakfast?"

I raised an eyebrow. Mom was the cook, which maybe explained why I'd never wanted to learn. Dad's culinary skills were only slightly less hazardous than mine, which meant we were on a first-name basis with all of the take-out restaurants within a fifteen-mile radius of our house. Still, he tried. Or at least, he offered.

In response to my undisguised skepticism, Dad half smiled, half yawned and then stared again at my still-made bed. He let out a soft sigh and looked at me.

I held my breath.

So did he.

But all he did was sigh again. "I'll leave the cereal box on the counter for you." Then his face scrunched up. "I forgot to get your Froot Loops. Sorry, honey. We've got some choc-olate-sugar-cinnamon things though. You like those, right?" He kissed the top of my head and disappeared down the hall.

I shut my bedroom door and leaned my palms against it.

We were never going to talk about it.

Why she left.

CHAPTER
4

My dark red Schwinn was parked in the garage next to Dad's current project. I eyed one with disdain and the other with enough desire to make my mouth water. The truck was a big, beautiful beast. Large enough that I had to hop up when I got into it. Driving it was like trying not to get bucked off a wild animal. No power steering and the brakes were a tad temperamental. Little by little it was becoming street safe, but not, according to Dad, daughter safe yet.

Details.

The bike was the same one I'd had since junior high and I took it as a deep, personal insult that I still had to ride it most mornings even though I had a driver's license and a revolving supply of vehicles in varying stages of drivability at my disposal.

Dad had yet to agree. I'd keep working on him.

The wheels clicked softly as I rolled my bike out of the garage. At least the temperature hadn't reached lethal limits yet. The wind that whipped my ponytail around didn't feel like a hair dryer in my face. That fun would come on the bike ride home.

I turned into my high school parking lot ten minutes later and saw a lone figure jogging around the track by the canals. Her hair was pulled back in a French braid with a few wispy curls escaping around her face. She looked like she'd stepped out of a toothpaste commercial with her big blue eyes, white-blond hair and matching smile.

She'd been my best friend since the day her family moved in down the street from my old house. She'd knocked on my door with her mom in tow and introduced herself to my mother. "Hi, I'm Claire Vanderhoff. Do you have any kids I can play with?"

She'd been six at the time and was still every bit as forthright at sixteen.

She waved and hurried to meet me.

"Hey! Look at you almost being on time." Claire bounced in front of me, her body in perpetual movement. "Be careful, waking up this early is addictive. I alphabetized my entire pantry already this morning, and tried out a new juicing recipe. Here."

My hands were balancing my bike as I walked it to the rack, so I had no choice but to tip my head back when she lifted the thermos to my lips. The blackish-green liquid that hit my tongue tasted like super bitter—and chunky—grass. I mostly concealed a gag.

Claire rolled her eyes and took her thermos back. "That's your body crying out for more than milk shakes."

"Do I look like I pedaled through a drive-through on my way here?"

"No, but that's probably your plan for the ride home."

She had me there. "What did I just drink anyway?" I nodded toward her metal thermos.

"Wheatgrass, kale and gingerroot."

I grimaced. "Seriously, Claire?"

"What? It's supposed to help detox and give you all this energy." Claire took a whiff. "I found the recipe on this diabetes website that's pretty good."

I noticed she was quick to put the lid back. "You need to start your own site. You could make something a million times better and it wouldn't have to taste like grass and dog piss."

Claire widened her eyes, uncomfortable with anything that even hinted at crude language. She did brighten at my compliment though, which was completely true. In the two years since her type 2 diabetes diagnosis, Claire had transformed from an overweight spectator to a rather impressive athlete with an ever-expanding nutritional knowledge base.

"I've been thinking about starting something...maybe." She smiled at me. "I could definitely make a better juice."

"And I will definitely watch you drink it."

"So," Claire said after I chained my bike, suddenly very interested in a rock by her foot. She nodded toward the end of the parking lot where a forest green Jetta was idling, its driver fast asleep behind the wheel.

Sean.

Unlike Claire and me, this was the end of his day, not the beginning. He came to the track straight from his summer job—the night shift working security at his dad's construction site—so someone usually had to wake him. I kept waiting for the morning when the simple question "Do you want to get him today, or should I?" wouldn't swirl misery through my gut.

We'd been running together for five straight weeks, and I still didn't know why Sean had agreed to run with us when Claire told him she wanted to go out for cross-country. There were days when I barely knew why I did.

Actually, that wasn't true. I knew exactly why.

Sean had been sitting on my front porch the morning after my mother left, eyes as bloodshot as mine, waiting for me before I left for school. I hadn't been surprised to find him there. He'd been calling and texting all night until I shut off my phone. He wasn't the kind of person to give up easily. Growing up with four older siblings, he couldn't afford to.

But it had hurt, the sight of someone I used to love mired in a memory too fresh and painful to bear.

He'd been wearing the same clothes from the night before, wrinkled and slept in; he hadn't even fixed the button Mom had undone.

"I don't want to talk to you," I'd said, in a voice that sounded stronger than I'd felt. I'd shut the front door behind me and kept a death grip on the knob.

Sean had jumped up, never taking his gaze off me. "You don't have to talk but I need you to listen."

I'd shook my head, feeling tears pricking my eyes as he drew closer.

"I'm sorry."

And they'd spilled over, streams running down my cheeks. I'd wanted him to deny what I'd seen the night before. I'd needed him to make me believe my own eyes had lied. To tell me something, *anything*, that meant I could keep him, keep us. *I'm sorry* was a confession disguised in an apology.

I'm sorry I was with your mom.

I'm sorry you found out that way.

I'm sorry I couldn't love you back.

I'm sorry you can't tell your dad why his wife left him.

I'm sorry your family was destroyed.

I'm sorry.

"I shouldn't have left you last night," he'd continued. "I panicked and I ran." He'd taken a middling step forward. "I need to tell you what's been going on. Your mom—"

"Is gone." My chin quivered. He was so close I'd had to look up. "And she's not coming back."

His brows drew together then smoothed, and that easy acceptance had galled me. When he opened his mouth, I'd cut him off. My lips curled back. "Don't you dare say you're sorry again."

He hadn't. He'd shook his head and reached out a hand, brushing the back of his fingertips against mine. "I didn't know. She said some things last night, but I didn't know."

I'd pulled my hand back, breaking the contact with his skin. "I'm not talking to you about this." I'd lowered my voice. "My dad is a mess and he doesn't even know—" bile rose in my throat "—what I saw. That is the only reason I'm out here and not inside."

The muscle had tensed along Sean's jaw. "That's the only reason?"

I hadn't answered him; I didn't have to. My cheeks were wet and my chin kept twitching.

"I am sorry. It shouldn't have happened. I should never have let it happen. But you have to believe that I—"

"No!" I pushed his chest, but he'd caught my hand and kept it there, eyes unblinkingly focused on mine. His heartbeat had been wild beneath my palm. *Guilt would do that.* I'd pushed again and yanked free. "I don't have to do anything."

I hadn't push him hard, I hadn't had the energy, but he'd staggered back a step. His eyes wet and welling up by the second.

"How long have you known me? How long have we been—" he'd swallowed "—*us*? You won't let me explain?"

I'm sorry.

He'd already said it. Nausea rose fast and high, forcing me to press a fist into my stomach. "My mom is gone and my family…isn't anymore." That bald admission had scraped at my throat and fresh tears needled my eyes. I'd dashed them away and blinked hard to keep any more from falling. "She was practically on your lap the moment it happened and there is not a single thing you can say to change that."

He'd bit both lips, nodding first at the ground and then at me. "Nothing I can say now or ever?"

I couldn't imagine a time when his words would change what had happened or the way I felt, but the anger and the sadness had burned through me and in their wake I was numb and done. "If I say I don't know, will you leave?"

He hadn't, not right away. I'd watched the internal conflict flit back and forth across his features and expected him to rally for round two. But for once, Sean had done exactly what I asked, and like a masochist, I'd watched him leave.

I wish I could say I hadn't cried over Sean after that day, but I had. Like, *Alice in Wonderland*–level tears. I'd flooded my entire house and street and every place I'd ever stepped. I knew all the so-called stages of grief, so between pathetic bouts of sobbing, I'd waited for anger. I'd begged for its cleansing rage to overtake me and break me free from the fetal ball I reverted to whenever I was alone. I'd wanted to get to the stage where I burned things and cut his face out of photos.

Where I dropped his things from my rooftop.

But it never happened. My stage of grief over Sean was singular. I'd cried a lot until I didn't.

And it was all his fault.

If Sean had been like Mom, he'd have switched his schedule at school so that we wouldn't have any classes together. He'd have moved lockers so his wouldn't be next to mine anymore. He'd have found a new lunch period, let alone a new table.

He'd have completely blotted himself from my life, left

those shattered, splintered shards of my heart to fester whenever I thought of him.

Unlike Mom, Sean didn't do any of that.

He kept up his attempts to talk to me, to explain something that was unexplainable. I shot him down again and again and again. How could I do anything else when at home Dad still started every time the phone rang or someone came to the door, thinking it might be Mom?

Claire didn't help either, not the way I wanted. She'd always been Team Sean where I was concerned. She knew something had happened between me and Sean the night my mother left, but she had restrained herself—barely—from prying too much. It wasn't a story I was eager to remember, much less tell, and even though it killed her not to know, Claire could see I wasn't ready to talk about it. For about three weeks she left well enough alone, which was about two weeks and six days longer than I'd expected.

"I need to tell you something," she'd said, linking her arm through mine after school one day. "You're probably not going to like it, so I'm holding on." She drew in a deep breath, the kind that almost always precipitated a speech of some sort, and I braced for impact.

"I don't know all the facts, and that's okay," she'd added when I tensed. "I understand that you don't want to talk about it. What I do know is that three weeks ago your mom walked out and you've barely been able to look at Sean since." She let out a gust of breath and dropped her bomb. "I know there's a connection."

The blood drained from my face. I actually felt the sensation, and it left me light-headed, unable to protest when Claire led us to the field before tugging me down to the grass beside her. I'd been fending off Claire's increasingly probing questions, dreading and yet somehow feeling like this mo-

ment—the moment when Claire would connect the dots—
was inevitable. It was almost a relief to get it over with. Until
Claire started talking again.

"I'm not going to speculate wildly here, I know who's involved and that's enough. On one hand, there's your mom.
I don't want to say anything bad about her, but I'm struggling to find anything good to say. She's made you cry a lot,
I'll leave it at that."

My eyes were dry at that moment, but only because I'd
already cried that morning.

"Then there's Sean. He's been the guy to pick you up
when you're hurting over her—sometimes literally—and get
you past it. So if something bad happened with both of them
on the same night, I'm not going to look at Sean afterward,
I'm going to look at your mom. And if you can't tell me why
I should do otherwise—" she held up her hands when my
head jerked to face her "—and I understand that you can't
right now—then I have to believe it was her and not him."

Her and not him. As if it were that simple. As if I hadn't
replayed that night over and over again, looking for ways
to exonerate him. Because I missed Sean, I did. Seeing him
had always been one of the best parts of my day, and now
that was gone.

Claire shifted onto her knees. "Think about it. Your mom
has been gone all this time without a word. Whatever she did
and whatever damage she caused, she doesn't care enough to
wade back in and try and fix things. Whereas Sean has done
nothing but try to fix things, and I don't see him stopping
anytime soon. You of all people should see that for what it
is. Something is broken between you two, I'm not denying
that, but if there's a chance that it can be fixed—and he really seems to want to—how can you of all people not try?"

To fix me and Sean.

She didn't have all the facts, but I couldn't argue with the ones she did. Everything she'd said about Sean and my mom was true. Historically, Mom was the one who hurt me and Sean was the one who helped me heal. But that one night had changed everything. Sean was there. He'd stayed. He'd said he was sorry.

Maybe Sean and I *could* be fixed. Maybe the damage could be buffed out, repainted, polished until it hid something only the two of us would ever know about. But that wasn't the question. The question was...did I want to? Did I want to forgive him for the role he'd played in Mom's leaving? Could I look at him and not see the ghost of her wrapped around him?

There was no going back. Despite the often-conflicting signals I got from my heart and my head, I couldn't love Sean anymore, but I didn't want to hate him either. I didn't know where that left me, and I wouldn't know until I tried.

So I did.

Ssssllllooooowwwlllyyyy. And trying was predicated on one very clear but unspoken rule: Sean and I would never talk about that night.

At first he was just there, a presence floating around in my peripheral vision, a nod when we passed in the hall. When I stopped flinching every time I saw him, he moved to short conversations and even an awkward high five when I aced a test. After that, I didn't freeze when he smiled at me— though there was a tension around his mouth that had never been there before. I didn't move away when he sat next to me or hesitantly bumped my shoulder with his. Slowly but steadily, I was acclimating to something I never thought I'd be able to accept again, much less enjoy: him.

And when summer came and we started running with Claire, shoulder to shoulder, mile after mile, I stopped torturing myself with flashbacks. Because I decided that Sean and I could be fixed. We weren't an *us* anymore; we became something else. And we did that because he was right there next to me, not giving up—never giving up. Cautious but determined to fix us.

That was the thing about me and Sean Addison: I wasn't in love with him anymore, but if I was, it would be entirely his fault.

CHAPTER
5

I kept my steps slow and even as I closed in on Sean's car. Each time it was a little easier. I hadn't felt completely at ease around Sean since puberty anyway, so I told myself this was just about exchanging one kind of discomfort for another.

I no longer got flustered or felt that overwhelming sense of euphoria when he was around. The one that made me say stupid things and get caught staring at his eyes. None of that happened for more than a heartbeat or two before I was thrown back to that night in my living room.

I halted several feet away and bit down on the inside of my cheek hard enough to make my face throb. I wasn't doing this again. I focused on that pain and pushed all thought of that night into the dark recesses of my mind, and vowed for the hundredth time to finally let it die there.

I was fixing us; *we* were fixing us.

I chanted that with each step and was relieved when I didn't have to force a smile as I reached the Jetta.

I approached the driver's side door of Sean's Jetta and saw his head tilted back and his mouth open, exhausted but there because he wanted to fix us too. Like a balloon releasing, that knowledge eased the pressure in my chest.

It was getting easier. As long as Claire was close enough to keep between us.

I slapped the window and bit back a laugh when he jumped awake, his hands flying up to the steering wheel.

Sean grunted as he got out of his car. He wasn't smiling, so the dimple that used to spike my blood pressure was noticeably absent, but I caught a hint of it when he turned to me. "That's low, Whitaker. I was having this awesome dream where I got to sleep without a small blonde girl yelling at me to—"

"Hurry up, you guys! Those miles aren't going to run themselves."

Sean scrubbed his face with his hands. "That. Exactly that." He eyed me sideways. "Tell me you don't find her energy level offensive?"

"I can hear you, you know," Claire called out, already warmed up and bouncing from foot to foot. "So, I've been doing some thinking."

I gratefully turned my attention to Claire, almost not caring that her ideas usually ended with me sweating a lot.

We joined her on the track and I casually moved to place her between me and Sean before sitting on the grass to stretch. "Spill it."

"I think we're ready for phase two. What would you say to adding a half hour of bleacher sprints each morning and a ten-mile bike ride on Saturdays?"

Sean's answer was a colorful decline.

"I can lend you one of my brother's bikes, Sean," Claire said.

I choked on the water I'd just sipped and tried not to laugh.

Sean focused a slightly deranged look at Claire. "You think I said no because I don't have a bike?"

Claire's eyebrows drew together, as if she couldn't imagine another reason for him to object.

I reached out to tap Claire's calf. "Offer to loan him a bike again."

Sean half bent to rest his hands on his knees and started laughing. It still caught me off guard when he let go so completely like that. I both envied and resented him for it.

"I'm just trying to make you a better athlete," Claire said. "Trust me, the other guys are training like this."

"Other guys?" Sean straightened up and gestured his arms around the track. It was empty apart from a pair of silver-haired ladies power-walking in matching purple sweat suits. One of them appeared to be listening to a Walkman. "Who are you talking about?"

Just then the duo walked past and we all stopped to wave.

"Look, I know this doesn't mean as much to you—either of you—as it does to me." Claire glanced in my direction. "But I know we can be better. I can be better."

Sean's irritation slipped away as he moved to stand in front of her. "In case you haven't noticed, Claire, you're already awesome. I mean, look at you. You've worked really hard to get healthy and you're doing great—"

She was. It was more than all the weight she'd lost. Claire thrived on working out.

"Jill and I look like *The Walking Dead* after running—"

"Thanks," I said.

"—but you, you barely get winded. Maybe you can do more, bleachers and biking and all that, but this is my limit. Neither the flesh nor the spirit are willing." That earned him a small smile. "Hey, you need to do more? Go for it. But, Claire, and hear me when I say this…" Sean lightly gripped her shoulders and widened his stance so she wouldn't have to look up to meet his eyes. "I will never, never, run those bleachers with you."

Another smile, slightly bigger than the one before it, crossed Claire's face. "Yeah, I guess. I mean, I didn't really expect you guys to agree."

"This is just me talking. Jill is probably totally up for it."

They both looked at me and I froze, a water bottle halfway to my mouth. Sean winked.

"What? No, my flesh is way weaker than his."

Claire spent our first mile once we moved on to the canals trying to convince me, but fortunately I had the perfect thing to distract her.

Sprinting ahead, I turned to jog backward so I could face them both. "I committed an act of vandalism last night that heroically ended a fight between my new neighbors." I relayed what happened, omitting the mom's more violent outbursts. I wouldn't have wanted those details shared if they were about me.

"Were you scared?" Claire asked.

"Well, yeah, that's why I threw the can."

Claire matched her pace to mine, letting me face forward again while Sean hung a few strides behind us. "I mean when he caught you. A potential criminal goes psycho on a...a..."

"Shed."

"—and then turns on you? I'd be scared."

Sean came up along my other side, close enough that our arms brushed a few times. "Claire, you get scared watching animated kid movies with your brothers," he said.

I shot him a tentative smile while pressing closer to Claire. "Besides, he wasn't the scary one. He was...normal, nice. He wouldn't even let me pay for the window."

Claire had tried and failed to defend herself on the movie

front several times, and wisely chose not to renew her case. Instead she said something equally asinine. "Are you sure you're not maybe overidentifying with him because of your mom?"

I came to a sudden halt. So did Sean. I bent forward, resting my hands on my knees and panting while sweat dripped into my eyes, making them sting. All my physical responses were eerily similar to that last night I saw Mom. I looked at Sean, and that immediately made it worse.

Claire stopped several feet away and turned back to us with wide eyes. "That came out wrong. I just meant maybe—"

"Seriously, Claire?" Sean shook his head, and then placed a hand on my back.

"Don't." My voice came out harsher than I'd intended, but it wiped the sympathetic look off Sean's face, so I didn't regret it. How could he, of all people, look at me like that?

Claire walked back to us, slowly, hesitantly. Unlike me, she was barely out of breath. "I'm sorry. I completely turned off my friend brain."

"Yeah, you did."

Claire's stepdad was a psychiatrist and she used to spout analytical stuff like that constantly. It got so bad that we came up with our own way of identifying it, "turning off her friend brain." She'd gotten a lot better about it but still sometimes slipped. Her psychoanalyzing me was usually only mildly irritating or something I could tease her about, but when it involved my mom…it was a lot harder to shrug off.

"For the record, I'm not identifying with him because of my mom. I saw something I could fix, so I did, okay?"

Claire was quick to nod. "Okay."

"Is your friend brain back on?"

"Yes, super on."

"Then let's go."

The last mile was awkward, but by the time I collapsed on the grass back at the school, I was too tired to care.

Claire cared. She made me promise we'd hang out that night.

"I want to run again after dinner, but I'm free after." She picked up her water bottle and started jogging backward toward her mom's minivan. "Call me when you get off work."

I shot up, hoping she'd see the panic in my eyes at the thought of being left alone with Sean, but her back was already toward me. I could call out, but that would only draw more attention to the situation.

From the corner of my eye I could see Sean lying in the grass a couple feet away with an arm thrown over his eyes. I felt a strong urge to slink away, and also the urge to reach out. The conflicting impulses were not mixing well with the remains of Claire's energy drink, and there was a good long minute where I could have thrown up.

I decided it was because of the running.

Just as I became moderately sure I wasn't going to vomit, Sean sat up and tugged me to my feet.

"Come on, I won't be able to sleep until Claire's energy drink wears off. Let me give you a ride."

And because my father didn't raise a coward, I said, "Okay."

CHAPTER 6

The walk to Sean's Jetta felt like my own green mile. The idea of being alone with him in a car with barely two feet between us brought my nausea trickling back. We hadn't done that yet—been alone.

I cast Sean a furtive look while unlocking my bike, trying to ascertain if he was as uneasy about the prospect as I was. But after one fleeting expression, he took my freed bike and started walking it to his car, defaulting to an easy tirade on the evils of running while we wrangled my Schwinn into the backseat of his Jetta. We knew from previous experience, even if the Jetta occasionally forgot, that it would fit, but only if you got the angle perfect.

"I think it needs to go to the right. I can't see, am I hitting something?"

Sean squatted down. "Tilt it left."

I tilted, and the bike slid in.

Sean straightened, a grin on his face. "And you doubted me."

Yeah, I kind of had. But his smile was light and I found

myself matching it, releasing the breath I'd been holding since Claire left.

Until his smile changed as his eyes moved past me. I turned and saw Cami Gutiérrez waving at us from across the parking lot.

I should have been relieved at the sight of another person to put between me and Sean, but that wasn't my first thought, seeing Cami. Or my second. Or my third.

Not because there was anything off-putting about Cami—the opposite, actually. Just looking at her, you could tell Cami was the kind of girl who dotted her *i*'s with hearts and rescued kittens from trees. She'd transferred to our school at the end of last year and already had more friends than I did.

Not that I was bitter.

And I was used to noticing girls noticing Sean, both before and after I stopped loving him. Sometimes he noticed them back, which unfairly sucked just as much now as it had before.

With her soft brown hair and matching skin, and the dimple that was nearly as legendary as Sean's, Cami got a lot of notice. I almost felt like I needed to duck when I got caught in the cross fire of their combined dimples. I gave the edge to Sean though. I still had a hard time not getting a little dizzy when he smiled at me, and I'd had years of practice. Cami had only recently moved to Mesa and was therefore totally defenseless.

"Cami G," he called when she reached us.

"Sean A." She let the sounds run together so it sounded like *Seany*.

My stomach prepared to sour at the hug I knew he was about to give her, but he surprised me by high-fiving her instead. Cami didn't register the omission like I did; she beamed at Sean, then wisely broke eye contact before she did something stupid like fling herself at him. Smart girl. She turned to include me in the conversation.

"So how's cross-country? Did Claire convince you guys to go out for the team yet?"

Sean launched into the many reasons why hell would be hosting the Winter Olympics before that happened. Cami hung on every word, laughing. She had a great laugh.

I looked back and forth between them, noticing the way she touched his arm, and the way he fed off her laughter. It wasn't nearly as hard to watch as it used to be. Good on me.

"I don't understand why you don't just quit then?" she asked.

Sean's gaze slid to me, but I didn't meet it. He never explicitly said it, but I knew why he worked an eight-hour night shift and then ran five miles with Claire hounding his every step. On bad days, I told myself it was penance.

"Because then he wouldn't have anything to complain about," I said. "Plus he gets to verbally torture Claire every morning and she has to take it."

"Poor Claire," Cami said.

I felt Sean's gaze linger on me a second before renewing the role of Claire's long-suffering friend. He waved a hand in front of Cami's face. "Poor Claire? Did you just say poor Claire? Try running with us sometime and see how sorry *you* feel for her."

Cami's eyes lit up. "I would if I didn't need to practice." She hoisted her duffel bag higher and pushed her still-damp hair over one shoulder. "You could maybe try swimming with me." She flushed and rushed on before Sean could answer. "Speaking of, I have this awesome pool at my house. You guys should come over sometime." She looked at me. "Claire too."

I nodded, knowing Claire and I were an afterthought, a

genuine one, but an afterthought all the same. She wanted Sean, and from where she was standing, I couldn't blame her. I also couldn't watch their love connection unfold two feet from my face. I'd rather brave the car alone with Sean.

I moved to the Jetta's passenger door. "Guys, I need to get going. My dad keeps threatening to fire me if I'm late again."

With effort, Cami pulled her gaze away from Sean. "Do you need a ride? I'm going past your shop so it's no prob—"

"No way." Sean cut her off a second before the opposite response rushed to my mouth. "I'm not loading that—" he tapped a knuckle on the back window toward my bike "—into another car."

Cami shifted her feet. "Oh, sure. I'll catch you later." She took a few steps backward and the distance between herself and Sean did wonders for her confidence. She pointed at both of us. "I'm serious about coming over. I'll text you guys next weekend, okay?"

We said goodbye and I opened the passenger door, watching Cami walk away and hating that I checked to see if Sean was watching too. He wasn't. "Did she convince you to go out for swim team?"

Sean shrugged. "I'm not looking for a new sport."

I gave him a look. "You know that's not why she asked you."

"Well, I'm not looking for that either."

Once upon a time I'd have lived off a comment like that for weeks, trying to read more into it than was there. I didn't do that this time. There was no point.

Inside the car, Sean reached across me to grab his sunglasses from the glove compartment. I inhaled before I could stop myself, and let my gaze stray to the stubble lining his jaw. It'd be rough and scratchy if I touched it. I curled my hands into fists and gazed out the window. He was saying something, and I felt his words drift over me like he was running the back of his fingers along my arm.

And then he was running the back of his fingers along my arm.

I jerked away. "What?"

"I said you can pick the music."

I hit the first preset and didn't change it when a commercial for life insurance came on. While he drove, I focused on the view out the window like it was my job to catch every detail. I berated myself for caring if Cami's crush on Sean went both ways, for reacting in the wrong way to his closeness, for wanting to bring him nearer instead of pushing him away, for forgetting—however briefly—that we were broken.

I slammed the door a little harder than necessary when I got out at my house.

"Watch it!" Sean killed the engine and followed me.

"The door's fine. Besides, I'd just fix it if it wasn't." I didn't add that it was just a Jetta, but I thought it.

"The thought of you in coveralls does good things for me, but that's not the point. And, hey." He darted in front of me when I turned to get my bike. "What did I miss? We were okay like two minutes ago."

No we weren't, but I didn't say that. Every day was a struggle not to swing wildly from one emotion to the other, a pendulum that he controlled whether he knew it or not. I couldn't slip back into the way we used to be as effortlessly as he could. It was like trying to put on an old coat that no longer fit. I felt sweaty and constricted whenever I tried. And then I'd get angry, because he didn't seem to have the same problem.

"I'm just exhausted from not sleeping great and all the running. Sorry for slamming the door. I'll be nicer to the Jetta, promise." I petted his car.

Sean exhaled, and it ended in a laugh. "That's funny, you talking to me about being tired. Check out my eyes." He caught my hand and tugged me close—real close—and it was all I could do not to step back. "I look like the biggest pot-head on the planet. I'm pretty sure my mom is secretly drug testing me even though she knows I work nights."

I should have been able to dismiss a casual touch from Sean as easily as he did from me. Not that I was able to casually touch him yet, but that was the goal.

The casual part, not the touching.

I freed my hand without effort. "They are pretty red." But still that same achingly perfect blue.

Through the windows of the garage, Sean noticed my dad's truck was gone. "I thought you were kidding about your dad firing you for being late." Sean gestured with his chin toward the garage. "That a bad sign?"

"No, I woke him up climbing through my window this morning, so he was going to go in early. It's cool, I'll just ride my bike."

"I didn't know you were still doing the roof thing."

I saw my own discomfort mirrored in his eyes and realized his comment had reminded us both that we hadn't talked much in months, and never about anything of consequence.

"I don't mind dropping you off at the shop," Sean added.

"You're forgetting I just saw up close how exhausted you are." I tried for a smile. "Really, it's fine. I need to take a shower and everything. Go home. Get some sleep."

Staring straight ahead, Sean said, "You hate that bike."

So I did, vehemently. And he knew I was choosing it over him.

He shook his head. "I can't believe I'm saying this, but Claire makes it better, doesn't she?"

My smile came easier that time. It wasn't wide, but it was honest. "Yeah."

"So we have to be sweating at the butt crack of dawn, just to be around each other? Awesome."

"We're around each other now." And it was only half as hard as I'd feared.

He glanced at the still-lightening sky and fingered the edge of my damp T-shirt. "Kinda my point."

He meant it to be a joke, based on the way he cocked his head at me, but laughing was the furthest thing from my mind. I didn't want that. I wanted to be able to hang out with him sans buffer. Claire did make things easier, but she also kept things stagnant, and we wouldn't fix anything if we stayed like that.

I looked through his window and saw my bike crowded into the Jetta's backseat. I did hate it. "Help me with it?" I meant the bike, but more than that too. I envied him and his godlike power of pretending things were okay. He made it look so easy. Smile, tease, flirt, repeat. I was still struggling.

My head was always clearer when my hands were busy, and I needed clearer. Things with Sean could get murky if I let them. I moved to the back door to pull my bike out. Without comment, Sean stepped around me, and between the two of us, we got it out without undue bloodshed. A triumph on any other day, but that day it wasn't enough.

I entered the code to open the garage and rolled my bike in, pausing with my back to him. "Maybe I will take that ride."

"You sure?"

I was. I hoped I was. "Yes."

In the blink of an eye, Sean changed. The stiffness in his posture relaxed, the shape of his mouth lifted, even his eyes seemed to change. It wasn't until that change washed over him that I realized how much he'd been holding back, how I'd been missing him even when I saw him almost every day. He flashed a dimple and held his arms open.

If I still loved him, in that moment, I'd have known exactly why.

"Sweaty hug on it?"

My eyes darted from his arms to his eyes and back again. He was asking me to accept more than a ride. A lot more. It was starting to feel like too much, but I wouldn't know if I didn't try.

I stepped into him, my cheek pressing against his damp T-shirt.

"Wow, you sweat a lot for a girl."

My heart was steady as I smiled into Sean's chest, silently thanking him for saying the exact right thing to keep the moment light and easy. When he seemed reluctant to let go, I stayed in his arms a second longer, relieved that hugging him didn't hurt. Not much anyway.

CHAPTER 7

After taking the world's fastest shower, and Sean taking the whole yellow-lights-mean-slow-down law as merely a suggestion, I made it to work on time.

Sean waited until I pulled the door open and waved him on before driving away. I watched him go, lowering my hand slowly. We'd done that a million times, and I remembered the rides that had ended with me dancing through the door when he was out of sight. Today my feet stayed firmly on the ground, but I did watch for longer than I should have. He had to have been nearly home by the time I walked into Jim's Auto Shop and let a blast of frigid air and the dark, dank scent of motor oil embrace me.

I inhaled deeply and smiled, relieved to leave Sean and the past outside. For some people it was fresh-baked cookies or apple pie hot out of the oven, but for me, the shop smelled like home. Unfortunately it sounded like home too.

Dad had a thing for Hall & Oates, and since I was like two seconds late, he already had the band blaring. Once the music was set, nobody else in the garage could touch it. Shop rules.

When I entered the main garage bay, Dad was in full-on awkward dance mode half-hidden behind the crumpled hood of a Land Cruiser. He spotted me and grinned while lip-synching to the chorus of "Private Eyes" and he pointed to the dry-erase board on the wall.

The work board. I always approached it with an addictive mix of fear and excitement, like Jigsaw or Santa Claus might be waiting for me. Sometimes Dad would banish me to the office for a morning spent chained to the desk, or assign me to endless oil changes. My favorite jobs were the unknowns; the vehicles that came in with serious emotional problems that hid behind odd growls or unexplained shakes.

And of course the shinies, the head turners that we humble mechanics never otherwise got to drive.

My feet began to drag the closer I got to the board. "Come on, really?"

Dad shimmied my way and told Hall & Oates to take five by turning down the volume. "You got something against Acuras?"

"I do when they aren't Mustangs, which we also have in the shop today." I tapped it on the board. "You haven't even assigned it to anyone, unless you hired..." I squinted at the tiny figure Dad had drawn. "The devil in a golf cart without telling me?"

Dad straightened. "That's a speed demon." He was always drawing little figures, leftovers from when he wanted to be a cartoonist.

I leaned closer. "That's actually pretty good, but seriously, where are we on the Mustang?"

"The Mustang isn't a rush, but I tell you what. The toilet is backed up, so if you'd rather I start on bleeding the cooling system on the Acura, we can swap."

I slumped forward on the counter and rested my chin on

my hands. "Do you ever worry about spoiling me with such a glamorous life?"

Dad laughed long and hard and reached out to rub my cheek with his thumb to show me a smear of grease that I'd somehow managed to get on my face already. He had the most contagious laugh.

"You want the Mustang?" he asked.

"Yes, please."

"And what do I get?"

"I'll close tonight so you can catch the game."

"What game?"

"I don't know. Some team somewhere is playing a game on TV. That one."

Dad made a big show of caving. "All right. You can drive the new flip home."

"The truck?" Oh, sweetness. The Mustang *and* he was going to let me drive the truck! I was doing a decent moonwalk over to grab the keys when Dad nodded his chin toward the back of the garage.

"Try again."

We always had a car or two in the shop that Dad got cheap at auction or online. The newest flip was an ugly-as-sin Mazda that had decent guts but needed serious cosmetic work. It was the kind of car that turned heads—just not in a good way.

Dad cued up more Hall & Oates, forcing me to yell over the music.

"How about I stay late dutifully clearing out the storage closet, while you take the Mazda and leave me the truck?"

Dad's answer was to smile and turn up the stereo as "I Can't Go for That" started playing.

After Dad left, I reclaimed the stereo and spent way too much time trying to decide if I was cheating on my imaginary Spitfire when I called the Mustang *baby*. I was fairly certain I was in the clear when I heard something worse than the din of "Rich Girl" blaring through the garage: the unmistakable grinding screech of Neighbor Guy's Jeep.

I shot out on my creeper so fast I nearly took out a tool chest. I spared a glare at the Mustang for completely eclipsing last night's nocturnal activities from my mind, then grabbed a rag to clean my hands before hurrying to the front office.

My steps slowed when Claire's comments from that morning reemerged alongside the knowledge that I was alone in the shop. I hadn't been scared last night, but Dad had been a shout away and there'd been a wall between us. What if I had glossed over Neighbor Guy's potential danger because of my messed-up relationship with my mom?

Stupid Claire. Stupid Mustang.

Stupid me?

My sneakers squeaked loudly on the checkered linoleum as I crossed to the counter, but when the door chimed, admitting him, any lingering trepidation flitted away.

My first thought when I saw him was that it was actually possible for some people to look good in fluorescent light. Not Sean I-descended-from-Olympus good, more I'm-definitely-not-going-to-strangle-you-and-look-how-well-I-fill-out-this-T-shirt good.

I smiled; Neighbor Guy did not.

"What are you, like, the only girl in this city?" His dark eyebrows drew together. "Do you actually work here, or is this some kind of stalking game you're playing?"

Blood rushed to my face and my jaw jutted forward. A litany of profane words in the most offensive combinations my short-circuiting brain could think of slammed into the back of my teeth. It was only respect for Dad and his shop that kept me from freeing them.

"Nice seeing you again too. I'm Jill, and this is my dad's shop. I'm the one who left the coupon on your Jeep so you wouldn't end up wrapped around a streetlamp when your brakes went out, but yeah, it was mostly so I could stalk you." I might have let one totally non-customer-sensitive word slip after that.

He didn't respond. At. All. I shook my head and leaned over the counter to grab the coupon he was holding, but he jerked it back. I placed both hands on the counter. "Look, I've got other people to stalk today."

He rotated his jaw and looked fractionally less like a condescending jerk when he said, "Can I take back the stalking comment? I didn't expect to run into you. Again. You're kind of everywhere."

"Yeah, my house, my work—that *is* everywhere."

His hands mirrored mine on the other side of the counter, flattening the coupon between us. "How was I supposed to know you were the one who left this?"

I unzipped the top of my coveralls. Underneath I was wearing one of the many Jim's Auto Shop T-shirts that I owned. It was identical, if in slightly better condition, to the one I'd worn on my roof. "I wasn't trying to hide it from you." I pulled the coupon from under his hand, brushing his skin in the process, flipped it over and read aloud what I'd written. "'Free brake pad replacement. Welcome to the neighborhood.'" I looked up in time to see a ghost of a smile on his face.

"Yeah, I, ah, didn't notice what the shirt said before."

I could feel myself turning the same shade of red as my T-shirt. I vividly remembered his eyes passing over me last night. Not for reading purposes, apparently. I gave in to the impulse to zip my coveralls back up.

"Look, I'm sorry. You caught me off guard... Jill." He focused on my name stitched onto my coveralls. "I'm Daniel. Or did you overhear that from your roof?"

I could tell he was trying for a less hostile tone, and I decided I could do the same, since I was more embarrassed than offended at that point. "No." My eyes dropped to the bandage on his left hand. He'd wrapped his knuckles, but there were still raw-looking abrasions visible below the gauze. I forgot about him checking me out. "Is it broken?"

The smallest shrug. "It's fine."

"Are you sure?" I stepped out from behind the counter. "Did you get an X-ray? It might be—"

"I know what broken bones feel like. It's fine."

I was about a foot away from him, my hand still outstretched toward his injured one. I was totally in his personal space, close enough to see a sliver of a scar in his right eyebrow and catch something lemony/minty coming off him. It made me want to lean in. Instead, I looked away, but not before noticing another scar disappearing under the collar of his T-shirt.

The lemony/minty scent grew stronger when he leaned closer, causing me to step back, but all he did was slide the coupon from my hand and hold it up between two fingers. "Why'd you leave this?"

I blinked and felt stupid for practically leaping away from him. He wasn't staring at me like I'd done anything wrong though. He seemed genuinely curious. Daniel. I could stop mentally referring to him as Neighbor Guy.

"I meant it when I said you could forget about the window."

Yeah, he had. But I couldn't. And it went deeper than just owing him because I broke it.

Dad had tried to explain to Mom once why he was happy "just being a mechanic." It wasn't that he lacked ambition or aptitude or anything like that. It certainly wasn't because he was content with "mediocrity." He loved to fix things. To take something broken and neglected and make it new again. It wasn't a glamorous job, and he'd never be rich enough to own half the cars he worked on, but he made things better. He said there was more satisfaction in that than anything else he might do. And whether Mom liked it or not, I was exactly like my dad.

I just liked to extend the practice beyond the garage when I could.

It was why I'd thrown the pop can. And why I'd left the coupon.

But that answer was way more than I was willing to give someone I just met, no matter how nice he smelled.

"It's the mechanic in me. I might have exaggerated with the streetlight comment, but that grinding noise your Jeep makes when you stop? That's not a happy sound. You really shouldn't be driving it. You'll end up having to get the brake rotors machined or even replaced. That's a lot more expensive than new pads. And I'd have to break more than your window to give out coupons for that."

He might have smiled. Maybe. His mouth definitely twitched.

"I don't have time to replace them before we close today, but unless we're crazy busy..." I glanced down the street at the three grinning idiots on the Pep Boys sign. "I can get to you tomorrow before lunch."

"Tomorrow's fine." Daniel fished his keys out of his jeans, pulled one off and gave it to me.

"Hey, if you don't mind hanging out for a bit, I can give you a ride home."

Daniel turned back to me just as his hand touched the door. "I'm good, but thanks. And for the Jeep."

With a last nod, he was out the door and gone.

CHAPTER
8

I expected to find Dad scrounging for dinner when I got home, but the kitchen was empty. I was starting to wonder if he was sick and had gone to bed early when I heard his voice.

Dad was a big guy and he had the voice to match. I could hear him clear across the shop even when all the machinery was running. But at home he'd learned to tone it down. Not quiet, exactly—I don't think he knew how to be quiet—but not his normal thundering volume either.

But this, this went beyond loud, beyond booming. I remembered this voice like it had been carved into my bones. I knew who he was talking to before I heard him say her name.

"What do you want, Katheryn?"

I backed up until I hit a wall, not that Dad could see me through his bedroom door, but it was an instinct I couldn't control. It was only a small comfort to realize she was on the phone and not actually in the house.

It was like being doused with ice water, knowing she was talking to him. He was so big and strong, whereas Mom was such a small thing, and yet she destroyed him, destroyed us, as if she were a giant.

After months of nothing, what could she possibly want? She was never what I'd consider maternal, so I doubted custody was an issue at this point. I'd be eighteen in just over a year, and it wasn't like she'd tried to take me with her before.

And yet, what else could it be? What else could she want? The house? The shop? She'd hated both of them. Whatever it was, Dad was more upset than I'd heard him since the day she left.

"You are unbelievable," Dad said. "No, you don't. You haven't been here, watching her walk through the house like a ghost, and that's when she can stand to be in it!"

I backed down the hall into the kitchen as Dad's half of the conversation still thundered through the house. The words I couldn't hear were chipping away at my bones like an ice pick. I lifted the kitchen phone from its base and pressed it to my ear.

Dial tone. He was on his cell phone, then.

Something about this one-sided conversation was so much worse than the months of fighting before she left, and it took me only seconds to figure out why.

They didn't know I was there.

Dad didn't know.

As horrible as their fights had been, there must have been some part in each of them, whether by unspoken agreement or not, that they'd held back for my sake.

They weren't holding back now. Not Dad, and certainly not Mom.

It had always been me and Dad. From the very beginning. But the last few months of fighting would have made me choose Dad even if the lifetime before hadn't.

Mom was petty. Calculating. Cruel to the point that shredded any love I held for her.

But not Dad. Oh, he got mad. He yelled. But he never

sought to inflict the same kind of personal damage that she did. No matter what she said to him, no matter how vile her insults, he never spoke to her the way she deserved, the way I would have. The way I wanted to so badly in that moment that I was striding down the hall before I could stop myself.

"Kate," Dad said, and I hated his calling her that. She didn't deserve it anymore. "Don't do this. Please." And then I jumped and froze outside his door when I heard him slam something—his hand probably—against the wall. "You self-ish— Don't tell me you're sorry. You haven't been sorry for anything your entire life." More silence followed by a harsh laugh. "Right, except that."

There was a lot of yelling after that. It was all things I'd heard before, except reenergized somehow. It was as if all the fights they would have had if she'd stayed were all con-verging and breaking through at once.

"Please, Kate. Just wait a second. Think. You haven't been here, you haven't seen her."

My stomach soured the way it always did when they started talking about me. Dad's voice lowered after that. He was speaking so softly that I missed most of the next few things he said until:

"Don't you ever say that to me again."

I shrank into myself at the unspoken threat in his voice. I wasn't used to being scared of him. I'd made him mad plenty of times, but even at his angriest, I'd never been afraid of him.

I was afraid now, and I wasn't even the one he was threat-ening.

"Kate—Kate—Kate!" He threw the phone so hard, I heard it break.

My hands fisted at my sides. Things had just started to get better. Dad and I were figuring out life again—just the two of us. I was beginning to remember what being happy felt like.

With one phone call, she took it all away.

Dad would come out of his room any second. If I didn't want to have a conversation, I needed to hurry back outside and pretend that I was only just getting home.

Avoiding had kind of been the default all summer when Dad and I came even remotely close to talking about Mom. And maybe it would have worked. Maybe we could have kept dodging the subject, pretending that we weren't a family with an amputated member, ignore the phantom pains that we both still felt.

Maybe Dad and I could have.

But Mom wasn't going to let us.

Instead of backing away, instead of hiding, I stood directly outside his door so there'd be no way for him to wonder if I'd overheard him. I wanted him to know.

I met his eyes dead-on when he opened the door. "What did Mom want?"

CHAPTER 9

Dad's face was flushed red, the anger his conversation with Mom had stirred up still visible under his skin. But the moment he saw me, the moment I asked that one question, all the blood drained from his face.

I shouldn't do this to him. I shouldn't make things harder. Dad looked ill, and he hadn't even said her name to me yet. I didn't want him to have to relive the conversation. And yet, I asked him again. "Dad." *I'm sorry.* "What did Mom want?"

His eyes were wide as he stared at me—frightened, I would almost say, except nothing frightened Dad. And that seemed to be all he could do. Just stare.

But I couldn't let it go.

"She wants to know you're okay—"

I had never in my life sworn in front of Dad, but I did then. He didn't even look that shocked.

"She doesn't get to pretend she cares. Not anymore. She left us—"

"No!"

I shrank back at Dad's sudden outburst.

"Me. Not you." He rested his hand on my head. "She didn't leave you."

The weight of Dad's hand was familiar and comforting in a way that always made me feel safe and loved. But his words simmered under my skin so I shook him off. "Then where is she? Where has she been all these months? Why isn't she here yelling at you? Why did she try to—" I bit my tongue.

In a vertigo-inducing rush, I was back in my living room watching silhouettes moving along the wall in patterns that made no sense to me. And hearing her laughter, her murmuring.

The morning after she left, I'd carried my Post-it note into the hallway. My legs had moved without any direction from my brain. I had stopped when I saw Dad hunched over in one of the beautiful but uncomfortable dining room chairs that Mom had picked out.

He'd had his own note, a scrap of paper even smaller than mine. I had watched him stand, crush it into a tiny ball, and hurl it against the wall. It had bounced off and rolled under the china cabinet. Then his bones had seemed to dissolve before he fell to his knees, hung his head in his hands and wept.

I hadn't cried. I hadn't done much of anything besides back up and slip quietly into the bathroom. I'd flattened her note on the counter, but the sticky part was covered with lint from my pillow and refused to stick. I'd held it down and stared at her words until they lost all meaning. Then I'd torn it into tinier and tinier pieces, until all I had left was a palm full of yellow confetti fluttering into the toilet and swirling away.

The words themselves had been harder to flush. I could still close my eyes and see even the one she'd misspelled.

I can't do this anymore and I'm tired of trying. This isn't the life I was meant to have and it's suffacating me. I'm sorry if

*this hurts you, but I can't stay without hurting myself more.
I hope we can find a way to forgive each other.*

And she'd signed it *Katheryn*. Not *Mom*.

I wiped tears with my palms, hating that she could make either of us cry after all these months, and felt my voice strengthen. "She left *us*." Dad didn't try to correct me that time. "I don't understand how you can defend her."

Dad raised his hand again, but I stepped back, tears pooling in my eyes. He lowered it with a resignation that infuriated me almost as much as what he said next.

"I wasn't a perfect husband. I know it's easy to look at what she's done and think it was all her, but it wasn't."

"You," I said, "didn't leave. You would never do what she did." I shook, struggling not to scream. "Never."

Why did he look as if I was the one making things harder? As if I was the one who didn't get it?

"It's not that simple."

"It's exactly that simple." I pointed toward the front door. "She's the one who quit. She's the one who didn't want us."

"You can't think that way." Dad's eyes were glassy and I knew I would die if he started crying. "I didn't love her the way I should have. That's on me. But your mom—"

"She didn't love you at all! If you only knew—" I clenched my jaw so tight I thought I heard the bone crack. "Stop making excuses for her!"

"I'm not justifying what she did." And then he gave me a look that would haunt me. It was like he was trying to tell me something and not tell me something at the same time. "Not then and not now." And just as quickly the moment was gone. He swallowed. "I'm talking about your mom, here, not my wife. I don't want you to write her off because she doesn't want to be married to me anymore."

Love for one parent and hate for the other fought a vicious battle inside me. How could she not love him when even now he was trying to salvage any affection I still had for her? The outcome cloaked my voice in bitterness. "Wife. Mother. It's the same person. I can't separate the two. I can't."

"Okay, okay." Dad saw fresh tears fill my eyes. "I'm not telling you that you have to. Not right now. But I am saying that it's okay for you to still love your mom. I'm okay with you loving her."

I wasn't. Through her words and actions, she'd shown that she despised the most important person in my life. There was no fixing that. Had I ever thought there was?

I was getting what I wanted. A conversation. Something. Anything. Only, looking at Dad made me want to stitch my mouth shut. "She's not going away, is she?"

Dad wouldn't look at me, but eventually he shook his head.

My hands were empty, otherwise I would have thrown something just to hear it break. Hate was such an ugly, infectious thing. It burrowed deep inside and consumed. My hate hadn't begun that way, not even after Sean. It had started out as an ice cube lodged in my throat, an obstruction I couldn't move no matter how many times I swallowed. Then it melted, and the cold had trickled through my insides, numbing me.

I wasn't numb anymore. Everything inside me burned and scalded, and I felt like I was choking on the ashes.

"Then we'll give her what she wants. Whatever it is. I don't care anymore. Does she need a kidney or something?" That last line came out before I could even process the implication. Was she sick? Was that it? Several thoughts collided at once and I couldn't begin to sort them out. I didn't want to try.

Dad should have hugged me then. I expected him to. It's what he would have done before, but he just stood in his doorway with his arms hanging at his sides.

When I moved forward to wrap my arms around him, he stepped past me.

No physical pain had ever hurt worse.

"What is it? What does she want?"

Dad's back was to me, his voice still hollow somehow. "She wants everything."

CHAPTER
10

I blinked and my alarm was screaming at me to wake up. The idea of running made me want to kill something, so I texted Claire to count me out before passing out again.

The next time I woke up, I could hear Dad banging around in the kitchen. I pulled the sheet up to my nose and waited. For some reason, I didn't want him to know I was still home, although the Mazda was going to give me away pretty quickly. Maybe he'd think Claire had given me a ride. She did that sometimes. Either way I couldn't smile and slip into our usual talk about carburetors or whether it was time to upgrade our engine analyzer. Not after Mom calling.

When I heard the garage door and knew he was gone, I walked into a hot shower. The water scalded my skin a bright pink, but it couldn't wash my thoughts away.

I used to love her name. *Katheryn*. I thought it was the loveliest word, like those three little syllables conveyed all that was beautiful and graceful in the world. I called her Katheryn once when I was little. We were at church and I asked her to pass the hymnal, adding her name to the end of my request as if I always referred to my mom by her first name. It felt wrong the moment I said it, and all I could do was mumble an apology when she told me it was rude.

I could call her Katheryn now if I wanted—*Mom* was the word that felt wrong—but I no longer thought her name was beautiful. She still was, but not in a way I envied anymore.

The mirror in my bathroom was steamed over from my shower. I smeared my hand across the glass and searched my face, my frame, for any trace of her. Each little piece I found—the slope of my shoulder, the curve of my chin, the arch of my eyebrow, all things I would have relished once—hit me like a physical slap. Did Dad see this much of her when he looked at me? Did he also hate those little glimpses of her that seemed to shout out of my skin?

I left my hair long and loose down my back, blow-drying it stick-straight without a single wave like hers. I wasn't thinking about it getting in my way at the garage; I wanted to look as little like her as possible.

I was zipping up my coveralls over my shirt when I walked into my room.

"What is it with girls and pillows?"

I whirled, grabbing the first thing my hands encountered—a glass candleholder—and caught myself a second before hurling it. Sean was stretched out on my bed, a mint-green throw pillow clasped to his chest. I'd walked right past him without even noticing. Maybe I did have too many pillows.

"Get out of my room! Ugh. And get off my bed. You're all sweaty."

"Well, you don't look sick." He sat up and squinted at me.

I grabbed the pillow from him and smelled it. Sweat. "That's my favorite one, Sean." I tossed it back and dropped my voice. "And I never said I was sick. I needed a break. And since when do you break into my house?"

Sean climbed out from under the pillows and sat next to me at the foot of my bed while I tied my boots. "Call me next time you need a break. You know I need a buffer with Claire."

"Finally." Claire came into my room with a steaming mug in her hand. "We've been waiting for twenty minutes. I finally used the garage code when you didn't answer my texts." She held out the mug and started relaying the run I'd missed.

"Sorry." I took the mug, and a sense of wrongness crept up my skin like a spider. I raised the drink to my lips, pulling the rich scent deep into my lungs.

And I stopped.

When I was ten, I'd gotten caught shoplifting. Not by the store, but by Dad when he found me eating my stolen candy bars in my room. I came to regret my brief foray into crime many times over that summer. First, when Dad took me back to the grocery store to confess, and later, when he insisted I work off the cost of those candy bars a hundred times over. To that day I still got nauseous when I saw a Milky Way commercial on TV.

The coffee was the same.

Dad and I were strictly Dutch Bros. drinkers. There was one right next to the shop that we hit religiously.

Mom had preferred to brew her own. It was one of those little details I hadn't noticed at first. Mornings had always smelled like coffee when she was here. But not for the past several months.

I set the mug down on the far edge of my dresser like it was poisonous.

Claire put her hands on her hips. "What? I used the bag next to the coffeemaker. I even added real milk and sugar—"

Sean made an interested noise and grabbed the mug.

"—even though almond milk and Stevia taste just as good and won't immediately turn into fat."

I shook my head. "It's my mom's coffee."

Claire made an *oh* expression and pulled the mug away from Sean midsip.

"Hey!"

She frowned at him before carrying it out of my room.

Sean frowned back until he saw my face. Before he could say anything, we heard the sink in the kitchen and then Claire was back, her head peeking around the door.

"Your mom didn't make lemon muffins, did she?"

"She didn't really bake."

"Good." Claire produced a plate full of them. "I've been messing around with a recipe." She searched my face as I took a bite and chewed. The muffins were surprisingly tasty considering how healthy I assumed they were. I wasn't used to equating the two yet, despite Claire's constant efforts.

"Mmm." I offered her one, but she put it back on the plate untouched.

"Can you tell I used agave nectar instead of sugar?"

Through a mouthful of muffin Sean mumbled, "What the hell is agave nectar?"

I laughed.

Claire relaxed next to me on the bed. "Sorry about the coffee."

"Don't be. I'm just a little sensitive today."

I'd tried talking to Claire about my parents when the fighting started getting bad. Sean too, a little. And they'd tried to understand, I knew they had, but it was hard to relate when the biggest fight Claire's parents ever got in was over who got to pick the movie on date night.

Sean said his parents fought sometimes, but when I'd

pressed him to give me an example, he'd mumbled something about how they mostly fought with his older sister. I'd heard my parents fight until they went hoarse.

I'd stopped talking about it with them after that. But I needed to tell somebody this time.

I took a deep breath. "She called last night."

Claire's eyes practically popped out of her head. "Be quiet!" Claire had a self-imposed thing about language. She couldn't even bring herself to say *shut up* without breaking into a sweat. "What did she say? Does she want to come back?"

At the same time Sean said, "Are you okay?"

They both sat on the edge of my bed while I stood against my dresser. "She only talked to my dad." Sean moved to my side and leaned his shoulder against mine. Warm and solid. I moved away as casually as possible. No way could I talk about her while any part of his body touched mine.

Claire's muffin felt like a rock in my stomach. The thing about Mom leaving, the thing that I couldn't explain to my friends no matter how much I wished I could, was that I needed it to be exactly the way it was. She left. She never called or tried to contact me. She was the one who broke off all ties. She had to be gone completely, or I wouldn't be able to breathe.

Claire had the same look on her face that she got when we studied chemistry together, the one subject she had to work at. "What did she say to him?"

I shook my head. "I don't know. My dad was really uncomfortable when I asked him about it."

"Don't you want to know?"

"Shut up, Claire."

Claire spun to Sean. "Excuse me?"

"Why would you ask that?"

"But…" Claire turned back to me. "Do you think she wants to…come back?"

And what? Grovel at my feet and beg Dad and me to take her back? I'd laugh if I didn't think I might start crying.

I shrugged and decided I hadn't tied the lace right on my boot. I bent down and started retying it. Claire and Sean were arguing, but I wasn't listening.

I was trying hard not to think about why Mom decided to call. I doubted she had suddenly grown a human heart, which left me with alternatives that I could not, would not, let myself think about. Because every one of them destroyed this fragile new life Dad and I were building together.

I'd lost count of the number of times I'd retied my boots before Sean knelt next to me. "Jill, stop." His hands covered mine.

There was no pretense of being casual when I jerked away from him that time. I stood up and pretended to check my bag for my wallet and keys while I got my emotions in check. "Hey, thanks for checking up on me. And for the muffins," I added to Claire, who still looked rattled. "But I'll be late if I don't leave soon."

"You need a ride?" Sean asked.

"I drove the flip car home last night, but thanks." I was never so grateful for that wreck of a Mazda as I was right then. I didn't think I could have shared such a small space with Sean that morning.

He nodded at me and then stopped to say something to Claire that I couldn't hear. Whatever it was, she visibly softened enough to let him snag another muffin.

"You really have no idea what she wanted?" Claire asked. My stomach roiled.

"Lay off, Claire." Sean's voice held a touch of warning.

I sat next to Claire on the bed. "The muffins aren't bad. You should get your website up and post the recipe."

Claire leaned forward and wrapped me in a hug that was a touch too tight.

I broke Claire's hug, and we trailed outside to our respective vehicles. The last thing I heard before getting in my car was Sean's voice, loud and clear.

"Don't try to bail tomorrow unless you've got the trots from Claire's muffins."

CHAPTER
11

Work was work. I helped an Odyssey with daddy issues and prepped a Camry for open-heart surgery the next day. We had more than the usual amount of walk-ins too, so I didn't get around to Daniel's Jeep.

But that turned out to be fine, because he never showed up. So, yeah.

I volunteered to close again for no reason other than I didn't want to go home. I pushed it as far as I thought I could, staying away until just after ten.

Dad was snoring on the couch, the TV remote held loosely in his hand, when I walked in. I had to swallow the sharp pain that stabbed my heart when I looked at him. I hated that his life was falling asleep in front of the TV alone with take-out. I could slip into a twisting black ball of hate if I let my thoughts go where they so often did, where all the blame lay.

There was pizza on the counter. I nuked a couple of slices and grabbed a pop from the fridge. Slipping the remote from Dad's hand, I surfed until I found an old movie I liked and sat next to him, my feet curled up under me.

I'd taken a couple bites when Dad dropped his arm around my shoulders and gave me a squeeze. "Everything go okay at the shop?" His voice was thick from sleep.

I told him about it while I ate. He was half-asleep again before I finished my second slice, so I made a show of yawning and told him I was heading to bed. I waited in my room until I heard the soft sound of his snoring before I climbed out my window onto the roof.

I took a deep breath once I was up there, for once not bothering to raise any mental disgust at how warm it was. Unlike my last stargazing attempt, the sky was pricked with countless stars. The moon was directly overhead, its soft light bathing me. Beautiful.

Despite the stars, I found my eyes drifting more and more often away from the sky and settling next door. It was possible Daniel had forgotten about his Jeep or had lost track of time unpacking or had been waiting around for a window repairman. I was working on more theories when a tall shadow detached itself from the side of Daniel's house. I swear I levitated a good foot off the roof and only partially managed to swallow a shriek.

"How long have you been standing there?"

Daniel stepped closer until the moon lit his face. "A few minutes. So you do really watch the stars."

I placed my hand flat on the roof and cocked my head, waiting to see if Dad had heard me. When the house beneath me remained quiet, my galloping heart began to slow in my chest.

Daniel was watching me, a slight frown on his face. "I didn't mean to scare you."

"It's fine. He didn't hear."

"Would you have gotten in trouble if he had heard?"

"Me? No. You? Yes."

Daniel had both hands shoved into the pockets of his jeans. The pose was casual, but he wasn't. Every time a car drove past, he tensed as though he was preparing for it to hit him.

"You never showed today."

"Something came up."

It was hot and I was tired, so I let my irritation run my mouth. "Yeah, that happened to me once. Sucked."

"I'm sorry, I should have called."

I felt like a jerk, because his apology actually sounded sincere. Plus, I would have been the one apologizing if he had shown up. "It's fine. I didn't even get to your Jeep, but it's first on my list tomorrow."

Neither of us seemed big on small talk, so it was at least a full minute before he broke the silence. With a comment about the weather.

"I don't know how you can stand it out here. It's like an oven."

I made a show of looking away and hanging my head back. "It's better higher up. There's a breeze." Said breeze caught my ponytail and sent it dancing.

Another car drove past. Daniel took two quick strides, placed his hands on the cement block wall dividing our yards, and swung up. He followed it to where it bent and met my house and repeated the motion to pull himself onto the roof.

"Hey!" I said when he sat down next to me and rested his arms on his bent knees. "No joke, my dad will run you over if he hears you."

"Then you shouldn't have invited me."

My eyebrows shot up. We had radically different opinions on what constituted an invitation.

Daniel sighed. "Look, I won't stay long, all right?" He leaned back on his elbows and looked up at the stars.

Silence. I kept shooting glances at him from the corner of

my eye, wondering if I was supposed to say something. It'd been easier in the shop. During the day. I wasn't sure what to do with him on my roof. It was kind of a private place for me. And I barely knew him.

I was so focused on Daniel that I missed the car pulling up to his house. But Daniel didn't. He went still as a statue, eyes locked on the sky above him. He didn't even blink. It was the car door slamming shut that finally clued me in that his mom was home.

No wonder he preferred my roof.

When the night was silent again except for the distant hum of traffic from the 60, I decided I could do more than give him a place to hide. I could maybe help him forget what he was hiding from, at least temporarily.

I hugged my knees and nodded at the wall. "You made that look easy. You scale a lot of walls?"

He shrugged. "How'd you get up?"

I wasn't about to describe the beached whale method I employed that involved a lot of squirming and flailing about. "Pretty much the same way."

He half smiled. "Pretty much, huh? You'll have to show me sometime."

I laughed at the likelihood of that ever happening. And because Daniel no longer looked like he was going to leap off the roof. Also his half smile was kind of nice. Maybe.

A warm breeze swept over us and lifted the sweat-damp strands of dark hair on Daniel's forehead. "Cooler, right?"

"I don't think you can describe this as cooler, but it's better." Daniel tilted his head back. "So what exactly am I looking at?"

We weren't sitting that close, but I was acutely aware of him stretched out next to me. It made me apprehensive some-how, like when Dad first taught me to drive stick and I was so worried about stalling that I ran a red light so I wouldn't have to stop. "In Arizona, we call them stars."

Another half smile tugged the corner of his mouth, but he kept his eyes on the sky. And away from his house. "I thought you might know a constellation or something."

"Right there." I pointed to a spot above his left shoulder. "Astronomers call that one the Big Dipper."

He laughed, and I felt the sound tickle all the way down to my toes. I pointed higher. "Okay, that little cluster of stars... do you see it? I think that one's called Centaurus."

"What about that one?" Daniel shifted my still out-stretched hand to another group of stars. It was the first time he'd touched me, and it sent a funny buzz up my arm.

"No idea. I don't sit up here with a telescope or anything." I'd remembered Centaurus only because it was named after the centaur Chiron. Sean used to be really into Greek mythology, and since I used to be really into Sean... Something much too close to guilt buzzed through me, and I pulled my hand from Daniel's.

Daniel kept looking at the sky. There were tiny pricks of perspiration dotting his forehead and even from a couple feet away I could feel the heat his body was generating.

"I may have oversold the breeze."

"Yeah, no kidding. I thought Philadelphia was hot in the summer, but holy hell. Does it get worse than this?"

I couldn't help it. I laughed out loud. "You'll get used to it. Plus the sunrises are really beautiful, so that helps." Running with Claire and Sean so early had let me see quite a few.

"And you sit outside every night?"

"Not every night." Though I couldn't remember the last night I'd spent completely inside. Not since before my parents started competitive level fighting. Some things were more oppressive than heat. It didn't take a wild guess to assume Daniel knew that too.

"What's wrong with your house?" he asked in a quiet voice.

I felt Daniel's eyes on me until I had to look at him. I glanced at his house, quiet just then, and I decided in that moment that he might understand.

The words were dragged up from somewhere deep inside me, like I was exhuming a grave.

"My parents fought like pros. My mom could have medaled in it. She knew how to build to a screaming crescendo that would render my dad silent. She knew how to raise her voice to a volume that I could practically feel shaking the roof beneath me. She knew how to stalk him when he tried to retreat in a way that I could map their route through the house. Even up on the roof, I could hear them—not the exact words most of the time, but the vehemence, the anger, the disdain." There'd been nowhere I could go to get away from that. It had slithered up my body and held me prisoner. Night after night after night.

"And then she left." My throat closed as I spoke. "She— did something. Something that you can't fix. I woke up the next morning, and she was gone." I bit down on my tongue. Hard. Savored the pain until I was sure I wouldn't do something embarrassing. "I don't want her to come back or anything. My parents were always fighting and nothing was ever good enough for her, but it's too quiet inside now with just me and my dad." I felt my eyes start to sting, and that black twisty hate flushed anew.

I looked down at a loose shingle I'd been slowly peeling up for months and tore it free. I twisted slightly away from Daniel, needing to reclaim at least the semblance of my solitary roof again.

"Why are you out here?" I cast a brief glance at him over my shoulder. "What's wrong with your house?" It was kind of a low blow, I knew that, but I honestly didn't expect him to answer. I figured he'd leave. I wanted him to leave. I hadn't meant to say all that about my mom. I felt like I'd picked a scab open, and now that it was bleeding again, I wanted to be left alone to lick my wounds.

Daniel was smiling, but it wasn't a nice smile. It was the kind I had to wear when a customer came into the shop screaming. "I brought my mom out here because we needed to get away from some things back home. She didn't want to leave, but I didn't give her a choice. She's not real happy with me right now." He laughed, and goose bumps broke out on my arms. "But you already knew that."

Yeah, no joke. But I didn't say anything. What was there to say? I could have asked him about the prison comment from his mom, but I didn't want to invite further sharing if it meant I might have to reciprocate.

I had no idea how long we sat in silence after that. Long enough that I stopped regretting what I'd said, but not so long that I could find anything more to say. I didn't try to stop him when he finally swung down—just as smoothly as he'd swung up. But I did return the small smile he gave me when he said he'd see me tomorrow at eleven o'clock to pick up his Jeep.

CHAPTER
12

I slip into a kind of tunnel vision when I start working on cars, so I was able to let everything fade away the next morning once I got Daniel's Jeep lifted. The lug nuts proved to be a beast to get loose. I was still working on the last tire when Daniel showed up.

"Hey." I wiped my hands on my coveralls and looked over my shoulder at the clock on the wall. It was 11:00 a.m. on the nose.

"Am I early?"

"No, I just grossly overestimated my ability to remove half-rusted lug nuts. Are you good for another twenty minutes or so? The waiting room has AC and nonstop Hall & Oates. Plus a few back issues of *Field and Stream* from 2008, I think."

"I'm good."

Normally, I really didn't like people watching me work. Most people ask too many questions. Daniel didn't, even though I could feel him watching me intently, or at least watching my hands.

After a few minutes, I was mentally cursing the last lug nut, which absolutely refused to budge, so when Daniel offered to help, I didn't hesitate. I handed him the wrench and my pride was mollified by seeing the amount of effort he had to exert before the nut came off. When he moved aside so that I could loosen the caliper and remove the old pad, I saw the scabs. In the dark the night before, I hadn't noticed.

"How's the hand?"

Without having to be asked, Daniel backed up so as not to crowd me. "It's fine." He flexed his fingers in demonstration. I guess it was a good thing that old shed was rotted or he probably would have broken something.

Daniel's gaze followed me when I replaced the metal shim and installed the new pad. The lug nuts went back on without any problems.

I tilted my head toward the slop sink, and together we washed our hands. There was a foot bar in front, so we didn't have to touch the faucet to turn on the water. I stood next to him while I lathered up; when I shifted forward to rinse my hands, my shoulder brushed against his. I glanced up at him and caught his eye for just a second and couldn't help smiling before stepping back to give him more room.

I'd been expecting to feel…awkward around Daniel after telling him about my mom, but I didn't. Because I knew a little about him too. I didn't have to keep my guard up as much, and that was…nice.

When I got his Jeep back on the ground, I turned the engine on and pumped the brakes to build up pressure in the braking system.

"I guess you're all set." I turned off the engine and hopped down from the driver's seat. "Just be careful the first few times you drive it." I handed over his keys. "And don't worry if you see a little smoke initially."

Daniel gave me a look that was part smile, part confusion. "What, seriously?"

"I never joke about cars."

He eyed the Jeep, then me, and repeated the process. Each time his eyes fell on me they lingered a little longer.

"Sometimes there's a little smoke from residual oil on the rotors. It'll dissipate in a few miles, if you see any at all."

"Uh-huh."

I laughed. "I promise you're safe. I'm good with cars."

I don't know if it was my laughter or just the confidence in my voice, but he stopped eyeing the Jeep. He didn't, however, stop eyeing me.

"In that case." Daniel tossed the keys back. "Maybe you could test drive it with me until the smoke clears."

I was used to being flirted with. Compared to Sean, this barely qualified, but with Sean, I always knew his flirting was building to a big, fat nothing. With Daniel, I didn't know anything.

I could hear the sound of machinery running in the main garage. Dad definitely wouldn't sign off on me taking a ride with a guy he didn't know, and I definitely wouldn't want to explain that I knew Daniel because we'd spent a couple nights talking on our roof.

Nope, nope, nope.

The question then was, could I go and be back before Dad noticed?

I was mentally weighing the odds when Daniel took my hesitancy for something else and his back stiffened.

"Look, about the other night, I don't know how much you overheard, but I'm not a criminal and I don't hurt people. Ever."

My stomach flipped. I hadn't even been thinking about that, though I should've been. I didn't know Daniel. He could be exactly what his mother said. She'd know better than I would. Only, in the brief scene I'd witnessed, I was already more inclined to believe him over the person who'd been hurting him. All she'd done—my eyes went once again to the two scars I'd spotted before—and he hadn't even lifted a hand to defend himself. I still had a lot of unanswered questions about Daniel, but whether or not I was afraid of him wasn't one of them.

"There's a Sonic a few miles up the road. If the Jeep is still smoking by then, I'll buy."

The smile he gave me seemed to sneak up on him.

Daniel's Jeep didn't have AC so we rolled the windows down. It helped as much as sitting in front of an oven with a fan.

I flipped my hair over the headrest after we found a semi-shaded spot in the Sonic Drive-In parking lot and ordered two lemonberry slushes.

So cold. So sweet. I drained half of mine so fast I got a brain freeze. Before I could process anything but the stabbing throb in my head, Daniel reached over and slid his thumbs over my temples, rubbing in tiny circles. I wasn't expecting him to touch me, so I jumped.

Daniel drew back. "It helps, promise."

He waited half a second before placing his hands back on either side of my face; the gentle pressure of his thumbs forced the ache further and further away and replaced it with a slinking sensation like cool air ghosting over heated skin.

Only it was brutally hot both outside and inside his Jeep.

That close, I could track the drop of sweat gliding down Daniel's neck. He shifted his upper body and I pressed back against my seat, watching the rise of his chest against his

T-shirt. I traced the slight curve of his lip with my gaze the way I used to trace Sean's when he wasn't looking.

But Daniel was looking.

Seconds had passed along with the pain in my head. What was left was the heat from his hands, the tickle of his warm breath mixing with mine, and a sudden awareness of being so close that I felt blood flush my cheeks.

Daniel's dark brown eyes directly met mine until they dropped a few inches to flicker over my mouth.

"This is sort of like your breeze last night, huh?" He pulled his hands away. "I oversold it."

It took me a second to realize he was still talking about his brain-freeze remedy. I didn't think he'd oversold anything. "No, it worked. Thanks."

I couldn't stop stealing glances at him. I sipped my slush more slowly after that, though I did have to check a brief impulse to chug it again. Would he touch me again if I got another brain freeze? Would it feel the same? Would it feel better?

Was I really thinking about a guy who wasn't Sean?

"So what do you do when you're not fixing cars?"

Daniel's totally normal question brought me out of the hormone-driven thoughts I was having. I put my slush in the cup holder.

"I run every morning."

"Yeah? And you like it?"

He shifted to face me, so I did the same. "Not really." When Daniel raised an eyebrow, I explained about Claire. "It's just for the summer, then ideally she'll have all the other people from the cross-country team to run with."

He leaned forward. "And this is ASU?"

The smile that had been on my face at the thought of not having to run anymore stalled.

So yeah, I knew Daniel was older than me. Not a lot older; in ten years it wouldn't be an issue, but while I was sixteen, even a couple years mattered. And I could tell, even if he couldn't, that it was more than a couple of years.

"Ah, no. This would be Mountain View." When that name didn't register, I added, "High School." I felt like I was admitting to having leprosy, and based on Daniel's expression, so did he.

He pressed back flat against his window and squinted. "Wait a minute. How old are you?"

I'd ditched my coveralls before we left for Sonic, so I was wearing a pair of denim cutoffs and one of the shop T-shirts. I wasn't feeling super sophisticated. "Almost seventeen." My birthday was less than four months away.

Daniel's squint turned into a wince.

"How old are you?"

I felt every single one of the thirty-six inches separating us when he said, "Not seventeen."

CHAPTER
13

Can you be disappointed by the loss of something that had only begun to flicker with the promise of existence?

It had been only three days, closer to two since the first night we met barely counted, but already I'd discovered that I liked talking to Daniel. More than that, he was someone—maybe the only someone—that I actually could talk to. If my age meant that he wasn't interested in being that someone, apart from anything else igniting between us, then, yeah. I could be disappointed.

Going back to that whole I've-only-known-him-a-few-days thing, I was having a hard time figuring out what he was thinking.

The drive back to the shop was not the most comfortable three minutes of my life. I didn't say much and Daniel said even less. The only highlight was discovering that my earlier gamble had paid out: Dad wasn't pacing the garage looking for me. If we'd been even a moment later though, he would have been.

I'd just gotten out of the Jeep and handed Daniel back

his keys when the sound of "You Make My Dreams Come True" buffeted me from behind as Dad popped his head in from the main bay.

"Have I got a job for you— Oh, I didn't realize you had a customer."

I glanced at Daniel as Dad walked over, saw no obvious answer about where we stood in his expression, and made the easy decision to just go with it. "Dad, meet our new neighbor, Daniel. He and his mom moved into the Cohens' old house."

"Is that right?" Dad extended a hand to Daniel. "I'm Jim Whitaker. Welcome to the neighborhood, Daniel."

There was a moment—more than a moment—when I thought Daniel wasn't going to shake Dad's hand. He'd gone very still when Dad approached, and seemed to be having a hard time keeping his gaze from darting around the room. It reminded me of the time we found a feral cat cornered in the garage last fall. I still had the threadlike scars on one arm from when I'd tried to catch it.

Those two little lines between Dad's eyebrows appeared, the ones that always showed up when a customer would swear they checked their oil regularly and had no idea why their engine blew up. Somebody usually got yelled at when those lines appeared, but Dad just waited, hand outstretched.

Daniel's gaze lingered on me—I wasn't sure why—and then he silently shook Dad's hand.

I didn't know Daniel well enough to guess why he was being borderline rude to my dad, but I thought it was in everyone's best interest to wrap up the introductions. I drew Dad's attention to me.

"I just finished replacing Daniel's brake pads. What was it you needed?"

Daniel made it easier for Dad to shift gears by fading back

to the other side of his Jeep. The frown didn't immediately leave Dad's face, but it softened considerably as he answered.

"Thought you might want to change a battery for me."

My brows rose in response. That seemed like a trivial request, one that hardly warranted a face-to-face conversation. Normally, Dad would just add it to the board.

My interest sufficiently piqued, I followed Dad to the main bay and forgot everything else the second I saw the Dodge Stratus parked inside.

I laughed. "You are dreaming, old man." I practically sprinted back to Daniel's Jeep.

Dad was right behind me, Daniel's presence in the corner equally forgotten by him. "Since when do you run from a simple battery change?"

"Simple? Really? You actually said that with a straight face." Dad had sicced a Stratus on me once before and I still had nightmares about it. "Didn't you tell me that Stephen King wrote *Christine* after working on a Dodge Stratus?"

Dad rubbed the back of his neck. "I probably made that up."

"Dad. No." I laughed again. "No. The battery is wedged up under the driver's side bumper. I'd have to jack it, take off the tire and the inner fender skirt just to reach it."

"See? Simple, you already know what to do."

"Yeah, leave the evil cars to my infinitely more patient father."

More neck rubbing from Dad, and a little smiling. "You're always telling me you like getting your hands dirty."

Yeah, but there was getting my hands dirty and there was ripping my nails off trying to pry a battery from the cold dead hands of a Dodge Stratus.

I held my ground. Or more accurately Daniel's Jeep.

"I guess if you really don't want it—"

"I do not. I super do not." I was aware of Daniel moving up behind me and brightened. "Plus, I need to finish up here. I'm trying to talk him into retrofitting his Jeep with an AC."

Dad's flat look said he was wise to my scheme, but knew he couldn't say any more in front of a customer.

I grinned. "Have fun with the Stratus."

Dad scowled toward the vehicle in question. I knew his look was only half for show, so I took pity on him.

"Fine, I'll come help when I'm done, but I don't like you anymore."

Dad's grin put mine to shame. "You don't like me any less either."

My smile ran out of gas when it was just Daniel and me alone again. He had the strangest look on his face, like I was an alien species or something equally foreign. It was more unsettling than the look he'd given me when I told him my age. How could what he witnessed with me and Dad be worse?

"Sorry about that," I said. "If you'd ever worked on a Dodge Stratus before, you'd understand."

Except the look he gave me said he wouldn't.

"So it's just you and your dad here?"

"Right now, yeah. There's another guy who comes in during the cooler months to help when all the tourists are here." I circled Daniel's Jeep, squatting ostensibly to check each tire as I passed. "It's actually more fun when it's just me and my dad, no offense to Lou, but he doesn't appreciate the Whitaker humor." I shrugged and stepped back.

The brakes had been whisper quiet on the test drive, and even Daniel admitted that the initial smoke had been barely perceptible.

"Well, you're welcome," I said, feeling constrained by the overly polite conversation.

The noise had picked up out front as lunch-hour traffic filled the streets. I listened to it while Daniel ran his uninjured hand through his hair and then forced both into his pockets. I did not like the smile he gave me after glancing toward the door Dad had disappeared into.

I wanted to pretend I didn't know what that smile meant, but I did. I liked that his hair was so inky black that it looked like nothing, like in a picture except the artist forgot to color it in. I liked the way he was still sort of surprised every time he smiled. I really liked that he understood why I'd rather sleep on top of my roof than under it.

I liked Daniel. Or I was starting to.

Was it better or worse that he seemed disappointed too?

He pushed off from the wall and walked toward his Jeep. "I should get going. Thanks for the brake pads." When he opened his door, he paused and met my eye. "I guess I'll see you around, Jill."

Neither of us believed him.

Dad was waiting for me right inside the main bay after Daniel left. "All set?"

"Yep. He, ah, decided to pass on the AC."

Dad kept watching the door even after it closed behind me. "Don't go borrowing sugar from him or anything, okay? Something seems off."

"Borrow sugar? Like for all the baking I never do? And he seemed—" I floundered for a word but couldn't find one that felt right. "Maybe he just doesn't like Hall & Oates? Nothing off about that."

"I'm saying let's leave that one alone."

That was a new one from Dad, but not worth an argument, considering that Daniel appeared to agree with him. "I don't think that's gonna be a problem. He seems ready to leave me alone all on his own. The other day he decided to walk home and risk heatstroke rather than accept a ride. Or is that how guys play hard to get?"

"You think you're funny, but you're not."

"Lou thinks I'm hilarious," I said, referring to our very stoic seasonal employee. "Remember that time he almost smiled at my pineapple joke?"

"That was *my* pineapple joke."

I erased Daniel's Jeep from the work board. "Yeah, but I told it. I'm gonna see about replacing the ignition coils on the Land Rover before we start on the Stratus, okay?" The next song started, and "Everytime You Go Away" drowned out any response Dad might have made.

CHAPTER 14

Attempting to scrub grease out from under my fingernails was one of the more pointless things I did every day. No matter how long I worked, it always looked like I'd traced a pencil underneath. Abandoning the tiny brush, I stepped back from the slop sink and into a warm pair of arms.

I squeaked when they tightened and swung me around. And laughed when the blind elbow I threw elicited a satisfying grunting noise. I broke free and turned to Sean. "What if I'd been holding a wrench or something? I could have seriously hurt you."

"You mean I could have hurt you." Sean flattened my palm against his quite probably wrench-deflecting abs. When he flexed, I ditched the *probably* and yanked my hand back.

"My point is you shouldn't sneak up and grab me from behind."

"So I should just grab you from the—" Sean was already moving to slip his arms around me when Dad came down the hall.

"You don't want to finish that sentence, Sean."

Sean held up his hands and took an exaggerated step away from me. "Sorry, Mr. Whitaker."

Dad didn't return Sean's grin as he headed back to the office.

I twisted away, my face still warm from the moment in Sean's arms. "What are you even doing here?"

It wasn't that Sean didn't come to the shop; he did. But that was before. I didn't know how I felt about him being there anymore. I didn't feel sick though, and that was a start.

He tossed me a towel to dry my hands. "I thought we could hang out, maybe catch a movie."

I let that idea play out in my head. Me and Sean alone in his car—I could do that again. Movie theater full of people, okay. Sharing an armrest in the dark for two hours... "Um."

"Come out with me. We haven't done anything besides run for weeks. Just saying that makes me want to shoot myself. Or Claire." Sean's dimple flashed as he slung an arm around my shoulders. "We can get the trash-can-sized popcorn you claim is too small."

"It is too small," I said, trying to decide if I was okay with the weight of his arm and noticing that he smelled way too good. "So you're bribing me now?"

"If I have to."

Dad's voice echoed from the office. "Are you touching my daughter, Sean?"

Sean mouthed at me *how does he know?* but he dropped his arm. "No, sir."

I moved away, choosing the trash can farthest from the sink and Sean to throw my towel away. "Because if there's a girl anywhere near you, you're touching them." Even if he had no business being anywhere near them. Even if he didn't mean to hurt anyone.

I jumped when he spoke, not expecting him to be that close behind me.

"Whitaker. You know I don't touch every girl who comes near me."

Just my mom, then? "I don't think I'm up for a movie tonight." I was just beginning to realize how disappointed I was by Daniel's brush-off earlier. The last thing I wanted was to spend an evening tortured by the past and the person a part of me still blamed for it. "Why don't you try Claire?"

"If that's what you want. But you know if I call Claire, she'll make you come too."

He was right. Claire would make me come. But since the alternative was an empty house or evening spent on my roof with a full view of Daniel's house, I gave in.

Sean pulled out his phone. "Anyone else you want me to invite?"

"Cami," I said, because I was petty and small. And stupid.

Cami smiled at Sean and hugged Claire and me when we arrived at the theater, and without a trace of insincerity said, "Thanks so much for letting me tag along. I haven't been to the movies in forever. I don't even care what we see."

Famous last words.

Two excruciating hours later—during which time I failed spectacularly in my self-appointed quest to watch the movie and not notice every time Cami grabbed Sean's arm or tucked her face in his shoulder—not even Cami was smiling.

"Okay," she said in response to the shell-shocked expressions Claire and I were wearing as we exited the theater. "That was officially the worst movie I've ever seen. And I've seen a lot of bad action movies. Like a lot."

"This is why I voted for the animated movie," Claire told

her. "No one would have been decapitated by a shopping cart in that movie."

We all looked at Sean.

"That scene was in the trailer. What'd you expect?"

"Well, I have to go," I said. "Thanks for the nightmares I'll have tonight, Sean."

"Happy to serve. But stay—Cami was just saying we can hang out at her house."

I shook my head for so many reasons, not the least of which was the fact that my eye kept twitching when I looked at Sean standing next to Cami, but Claire answered before I could speak.

"We have to run early in the morning, remember?"

Cami looked like Claire had just stomped on her sand castle, but she recovered pretty quickly. "How about tomorrow if we meet earlier?"

My mind blanked on an excuse. "Maybe."

Claire gave me a look that belonged on a motivational poster along with a slogan like Hang in There, Baby!

Cami was great. Sean was great. I just didn't need to see them be great together. There was nothing to feel sorry about.

I took Claire up on her offer of a ride and followed her to her mom's minivan.

"That was…fun."

I looked at her.

"Okay, not the movie." Claire shook her head violently.

I kept looking at her.

"I'm sorry. I can't think of anything bad to say about Cami. I tried and the best I could come up with is that she hogged the popcorn."

"You don't eat movie popcorn."

Claire threw up her arms. "I told you I couldn't think of anything."

"I like her too."

"You do?"

"Claire, I'm not in love with Sean anymore. Cami's nice, and she really seems to like him."

"I know! Did you see the way she looked at him? As if Sean needs a bigger head." Claire cast a sideways look at me. "So you're fine with everything? I had to make sure you weren't going to bail again tomorrow. Sean is completely worthless when you don't show up." She did that thing where she looked at me but pretended she wasn't. "I doubt he would even come if you weren't there."

"Don't start, Claire."

"What? You didn't see how disappointed he was the other morning." When I didn't answer, she pressed on. "I think he's just being nice to her because she's new."

"If he was any nicer to her she'd be pregnant."

Claire's mouth pinched along with her eyebrows. "Oh, please. I've seen him flirt way more than that with the school librarian when he's trying to get out of an overdue book fine."

"Then it doesn't really matter, does it? Not to him. And not to me either."

"But I really think he's starting to come around."

"Well, he's too late."

Claire sighed as we finally reached my street. "You don't mean that. You should, but you don't."

I silently groaned. I didn't want to think about Sean like that. I wanted to think about him as my friend. As someone I loved, but wasn't in love with. I wanted to be happy if he was happy. I wanted to be able to hang out with him and not think about what almost was. Not think about why it never happened. Why so many things went so very wrong. Because that was about so much more than Sean. And if I tried really hard, maybe I could keep him away from the rest of it.

I wanted to be able to keep him, and I wouldn't be able to if I kept trudging down this same, well-worn path.

Claire was frowning and smiling at me when we reached my house. She didn't understand. Maybe that was my fault for not telling her everything when my mom left. But even months later, every fiber in my being recoiled at the thought of those words spilling over my lips. The only person I'd come close to telling was Daniel, and I was pretty sure he wouldn't be coming around anymore.

So instead I made some joke about the movie and Claire laughed. We hugged goodbye and I sent her home to her picture-perfect family where her mom always waited up for her.

And I went inside to my dark house.

CHAPTER
15

I was trapped and Claire knew it. Cami had followed through with her invitation to hang out the following night, and Claire's last-minute option was the less torturous of the two. Marginally.

It wasn't Cami's fault she liked Sean. It was my fault that I couldn't deal with watching them together. All in all I deserved to help Claire paint her bedroom for the third time that month.

"This is definitely the color, don't you think?" Claire held a paint chip against her wall. The shade in question looked identical to the one already on her walls.

"They're ripping you off, Claire. I don't care what name they call it, that is the exact color you bought before. And the time before that. And the time before that."

She gaped at me. "It's like four shades darker." She held the chip in front of my face, as if the proximity would somehow turn it into a different color.

I shook my head.

She squatted next to the paint trays and held out a roller. "I promise you'll see the difference once it dries."

I seriously doubted that.

Claire pried the lid off a paint can with an ease that spoke of way too much practice. "We should call Sean. I bet he bailed on Cami when he found out you wouldn't be there."

"Maybe we should call Micah Porter. I *know* he'd blow off plans to see you."

"Take that back!"

My eyes lit up. "I knew it! You're always staring at him in choir."

"That's because he sings off-key."

"What's the big deal? Micah's really nice and he obviously likes you. He's a little short, but so are you." I spun my roller in my hand. "Maybe we should see if he's free."

Claire snatched the roller from me, cheeks so red she looked sunburned. "Be serious. We're not calling Micah. I'm telling you I don't like him. Can you honestly say the same about Sean?"

I answered automatically. "Yes."

Claire gave me her look. The one that said *yeah right*. "Why do I have to believe you but you don't have to believe me?"

"Because," she said. "Back in junior high, *I* didn't drag you along as a volunteer dog-walker as an excuse to go past Micah's house. And *I* didn't ask Micah's mom for possible names for our future children. And *I*—"

"I never did that!" Technically. I'd asked Sean's sister. Plus I'd been nine.

"I just remembered that fake wedding album you made in fourth grade." Claire curled into a ball laughing. "I can't believe I forgot about that. You were so insane back then! Tell me you still have it."

"Are you kidding? I burned it years ago and set fire to the ashes."

"It's in that box under your bed, isn't it?"

"Noooo," I said, in the least convincing manner ever.

"Hmm" was all Claire said. "I rest my case."

"Fine, I'll call him. It's not a big deal." I grabbed my phone. "Hey," I said when Sean answered.

"What's up?"

"We're about to start painting Claire's room again."

"Same color?"

"No, this one is apparently four imperceptible shades darker." I ducked as the paintbrush Claire tossed at my head knocked a picture off her wall.

"They're ripping her off."

"Yep." I eyed Claire, making sure she heard Sean say the exact same thing I'd said.

Claire rolled her eyes, then stood there with her hands on her hips waiting.

It really wasn't a big deal, so I asked him. "Did you bail on Cami?"

"Yeah. I'm tired."

I waited for him to elaborate, but he didn't. "That's it? You're tired?"

Sean yawned loudly. "I haven't slept more than five hours a day in weeks, I'm allowed to be tired, Jill."

"I know, but...now Claire feels bad that we all ditched Cami." That was a lie. Claire was bobbing her head at me to some unheard song and mouthing *I told you so* over and over again.

"So you want me to what, un-bail on her?"

I paused. I couldn't bring myself to say yes but saying no felt almost worse. "I'm only calling because Claire wanted you to know there's a third roller with your name on it. Do you want to co—" I heard a click and held the phone out to see the display.

"So?" Claire asked, stretching out on the bed. "He's coming?"

I pushed her feet off one side and dropped down next to her. "Yeah, no. But he did hang up on me, so there goes your theory."

She shook her head while pulling her white-blond curls into a bun. "That's because you made it sound like I was the only one who wanted to call him."

It felt pointless to point out the truth of that statement.

"But that's fine, we don't need his help." She held her hands up high for me to slap, and I responded with a yawn.

"Sorry. I really am tired. And the AC went out at the garage." I took the roller she offered and started in on the top half of the wall while Claire began cutting in along the baseboards.

"I thought you looked extra flushed earlier."

Yeah. That was why. Claire was sitting and bent low over her brush, so I spelled out Sean's name in big letters then rolled over it. "You remember my neighbor?"

Claire looked up in time to catch a drip from my roller on her nose. "Nice, Jill. It's supposed to go on the wall, you know." She wiped it off with her thumb. "The guy from the roof? Yeah. Why? Did you catch him going crazy again?"

I was up on my tiptoes trying not to hit the ceiling. "I've been hanging out with him a little."

Claire made a noncommittal sound and kept edging.

"He's actually kind of cool. He's from Philadelphia. I don't know him all that well yet, but he's pretty cool so far. He's got this really cool old Jeep."

Claire stopped painting. "Uh-oh. You just said 'cool' like three times."

I kept painting. "I did not."

"Uh, yeah, you did." I heard the smile in Claire's voice

without even looking at her. When I had to bend down for more paint, she pulled the tray away. "Define 'a little.' Exactly how much have you been hanging out with Neighbor Guy?"

"His name is Daniel. And just a couple times." I leaned around her and reloaded my roller. A few more drops landed in Claire's hair but she ignored them.

"Okay, go all the way back and tell me everything."

Claire bit her tongue no less than four times while I was talking, but she didn't interrupt me, something I was supremely grateful for.

"You should have seen his face when I told him how old I was."

Claire let out a sigh that made me frown. "That's a good thing. If your age didn't bother him we'd have a whole different kind of problem."

"We're not going out or anything."

"But you want to."

"Just forget it." My arms suddenly felt like I was carrying bowling balls as I looked at Claire's two remaining unpainted walls. "Do we have to do this right now?"

"Talk or paint?"

"Both." I nudged the paint tray away with my foot.

"You always do this." Claire set her roller down in the tray. "Why did you bring him up if you didn't want to talk about him?"

"'Cause I wanted you to know what was going on, not so you could lecture me about it. *You* always do that."

"What am I supposed to do when you tell me you're hanging out with a much older guy you barely know, who may or may not be a violent criminal?"

I made a sound of disgust. "He's not a criminal, violent or otherwise."

It was Claire's turn to roll her eyes. "You know I have been on board with Jill&Sean4Ever since the beginning. You and Sean make sense to me. You and older-dangerous-guy-I-don't-know? You're gonna have to give me more than the one night on that one, okay?" When I didn't respond, she added, "Is this about Sean and Cami? 'Cause you know that's never gonna happen."

"No, I don't know that," I said, a little harsher than I meant to. "And you don't either. And it wouldn't be the end of the world. At least we like Cami."

"Yeah, but…"

"Nothing is ever going to happen with me and Sean."

"Why? Seriously, why? You don't stop loving someone overnight, Jill. It doesn't work like that."

"It wasn't overnight."

"One night we're plotting your first kiss, and the next you barely say a word to him. You aren't your mom. You don't have to give up on Sean just because your mom gave up on your dad."

I started to feel ill, listening to her. I would swear the paint fumes were making me dizzy, except Claire always bought the environmentally friendly kind that you could probably eat if you wanted to. "Is that what you think?"

Claire lowered her voice. "You won't talk about it, so what am I supposed to think?"

If Claire had spoken to me in anything less than the gentlest tone known to man, I might have been able to deflect her.

"I just woke up, okay. Sean is my friend and that's all I want from him anymore."

Claire sat quietly staring at me until I started painting again, then with a deep sigh, reached for her own brush. "Okay, but are you sure that's all he wants from you?"

CHAPTER
16

I didn't regret telling Claire about Daniel. Sometimes her borderline friend-brain comments were helpful. She'd had plenty to say about Daniel and some of it had nothing to do with Sean at all.

Over the next few days, I told myself that it made sense for me to think about him—Daniel, not Sean—given that his house was a mere pop can's throw away (ha!). I didn't overhear any fights between him and his mom. I didn't even hear his Jeep when he came home at night—always a good hour after his mom—which caused me a moment of pride at how quiet his brakes were.

But then I'd think about him in his room or somewhere and I'd wonder if any other part of his life was getting better.

Or if, like his window, it was just taped over.

And then one night he walked out his back door.

Unlike the first night we "met" I didn't try to hide. I sat up on my roof facing his yard.

Daniel leaned against the side of his house for only a few

seconds, looking up at me before scaling the wall and pulling himself onto my roof. He sat next to me a second later.

"Hey," he said.

"Hi."

"This okay?" he asked, before meeting my eye.

I hesitated. "Would you leave if I said no?"

He nodded. "Yeah."

I'd kept pretty busy all week. At the shop and running with Sean and Claire. My thighs were screaming proof of the latter. I'd almost given up on the roof that night when my muscles protested as I climbed out the window. But I'd gone up anyway. Not because of Daniel, but not entirely not because of Daniel either.

I'd thought my roof was my sanctuary, my way of escaping from everyone and everything. But it wasn't. It was kind of nice to think about sharing it with someone who needed it maybe more than I did.

Daniel relaxed when I shook my head. I didn't want him to leave.

"So we're clear, I didn't have a birthday in the last few days."

He glanced at me sideways, a smile lighting his face like the moon lit us. "We're joking about this already?"

What was the alternative? "You never told me how old you are." I almost didn't want to know. I was glad he was looking up at the sky and couldn't see my face when he answered.

"Twenty-one."

Five years. He was four years older and however many months, if I rounded down. Not that four years was any better than five. I didn't need Claire to tell me that. I suddenly understood Daniel's initial reaction to my age so much better.

"Yeah," Daniel said with a humorless laugh. "Exactly."

We both fell silent.

He noticed the unopened pop can next to me. "That for me?"

And he questioned my humor? Okay, then. "Nope." I reached into the bag by my feet and pulled out one of Dad's old baseballs. "This was for you, or more accurately, your house. Just in case."

I was still testing things with Daniel, so I wasn't sure if I'd totally misread his question until he smiled.

"Things have been quiet."

"I noticed." I also noticed that *quiet* wasn't the same as *better.*

"You been okay?"

My auto response was at the ready before I realized I didn't have to give it. I could actually tell the truth without getting psychoanalyzed or pitied in response. Really, what was the worst that could happen? Daniel deciding he didn't want to talk to me anymore? I already knew what that felt like. His situation was already worse than mine. Maybe he wouldn't even bat an eye.

So I told him the truth. All of it.

"My mom called. The last time I talked to her was one hundred and forty-three days ago, right after I caught her trying to undress the guy I'd been in love with for as long as I can remember." I hated that my throat felt thick as I squeezed out those words. I tried to smile, but had to look away before I could manage it. I had never said these words to another living soul. "In her note she said that she was suffocating but she never blamed me. Wasn't that nice of her?" I couldn't find the right place to look. My breath picked up.

"You okay?"

"Yeah. I just can't believe I told you that."

Daniel's expression hadn't changed. There was no disgust or pity on his face. Nothing that said he'd treat me differently, just that maybe he did understand.

"Actually, I can," I added, instantly changing my mind. "I

don't feel any better about it, but I don't feel like I'm choking on it all either." So I kept talking. "She only talked to my dad. I don't even know what she wants." I shook my head then stopped. "Maybe she wants a tune-up. Or Sean's number." I hated how bitter I sounded, but after Dad's cryptic words, bitterness was all I had left.

She wants everything.

If I let that go, the fear at what *everything* could be would devour me.

"Sean as in the guy you run with?"

"Sean as in the guy she tried to maul." Another deep breath. There was nothing else to say about that. Fortunately Daniel didn't need me to ask if we could change the subject.

"I've seen you a couple times running by the canals."

That startled me. There were always cars driving past. It hadn't occurred to me that he might have been one of them. "I haven't seen you."

"Yeah, I've been busy. I had a job lined up before I moved out here, but it fell through. Trying to find something else."

"And?"

He shrugged. "Maybe."

I added *chatty* to the scant list of things I knew about Daniel.

"It's too bad you don't know more about cars. My dad keeps threatening to hire a new mechanic so he can take a day off every now and then." That was a lie. We didn't have enough business to hire anyone. I was babbling.

"You wanna teach me?" he said, not really meaning it.

"Yeah, maybe." I didn't really mean it either. "So what are you going to do?"

"I used to hustle pool back in Philly. I could do that for a while."

I leaned forward. "What, seriously?" The look he gave me

was very serious and I sat back. "Sorry, I didn't think people actually did that."

Daniel had an arm draped over one bent knee. "My old man taught me."

The way he said that made me pause. "Is your dad one of the things you needed to get away from when you moved here?"

Daniel was looking down at his hand, flexing his fingers. "Here's the thing." But then he didn't say anything, like an entire minute passed and he was staring off at the back of the house across from us. When he suddenly turned and focused on me, I almost drew back.

"We don't really know each other. Not really. I don't want to tell you about my life back in Philly. There's all this stuff I'm trying to forget, you know?"

He wasn't asking me a question, but I nodded even though I had no idea what he was getting at.

"Like my dad. I don't want to talk about him." Daniel was tapping his foot, faster by the second, and he wouldn't look at me. "He was—"

"Okay." I cut him off with a hand on his forearm. "You don't have to talk about him." When he looked at me, I added, "Or anything that makes you think about him. I couldn't care less about playing pool. Honestly."

When Daniel dropped his eyes to where my fingers still rested against his skin, I pulled it back.

"You should have told me how old you were. I don't mean that like you did something wrong," he added when he saw my reaction. "It just would have been good to know."

I could have said the same thing to him. I thought the age difference was pretty obvious, but really up until that moment at Sonic, I hadn't thought it mattered. I could still fix his car, hang out with him occasionally. It wasn't a big deal.

Until it was.

Sometime later when Daniel stood up to leave, he stopped at the edge of the roof. "You said almost seventeen. How much is almost?"

"October."

His eyes were once again scanning the sky. "That's not that far away."

"Yeah?"

He was still looking up. "We're just friends, right? And you seem pretty mature for sixteen." I made a face and Daniel mirrored it. "That sounded creepier than I meant it to."

I bit both my lips to hide my smile. "How creepy did you mean it to sound?"

He laughed and shook his head. "So you're going to be around tomorrow night?"

The expression on his face made me think he wasn't sure he should be asking me that. I kind of felt the same way even as I said, "Yes."

CHAPTER
17

I didn't realize how much Hall & Oates had grown on me until Dad stopped playing them. Not right away, but after Mom called they were on less and less. There wasn't anything to dance to and Dad grew different again, quiet and heavy like when she'd first left.

Sundays were the worst. Dad always got quieter after church, introspective. We'd get home and I'd catch his gaze lingering on things that reminded him of Mom. He stood for twenty minutes in the hall closet last Sunday when he'd found the pin from her college sorority caught on the corner of one of the coats. When I asked him about it, he'd given me the strangest look, as though I was the answer to a test he'd cheated on.

Beyond that we talked and worked, but he didn't leave me any cartoons on the work board, and he didn't comment when I put on the most obnoxious music I could think of. By week's end, I couldn't take it anymore. I went into Dad's office, scanned the shelf over his desk until I found what I was looking for. I dusted it off on my way back to the garage and plunked it down in front of him as he was finishing his roast beef sandwich.

To the uninitiated, the Creeper Race Cup looked like a wrench nailed to an exhaust pipe and spray-painted gold. In reality, it was the most coveted wrench nailed to an exhaust pipe and spray-painted gold known to man.

Or to me and Dad at least.

We'd inaugurated the Creeper Races the day we moved to our house when I was eight. It was one of the best and worst days of my life.

Our old house had been a lot bigger. It had a little garden and the neighborhood was anything but cookie cutter. Claire lived around the corner too, so I didn't want to move. I didn't understand anything about money back then, but Dad explained we had to sell our old house, downsize, in order to buy the auto shop from the previous owner who wanted to retire. Dad had been working there most of my life and bringing me with him whenever possible, so I warmed up to the idea real fast.

Mom was harder to persuade.

She didn't want to move. She didn't want to buy the shop. She didn't want to give up what little she had to acquire something she'd never wanted in the first place. She wouldn't go look for new houses, refused to pack when our old home sold, and basically made everything harder. She stayed with her sister nearby the week we moved.

I remember sitting next to Dad in the moving van and him telling me all about our new little house. He kept calling it that, *our little house*, which made me feel like Laura Ingalls Wilder, impatient and excited to see everything. Dad said the little house was small and that it needed to be fixed just like the cars in the shop. He explained that Mom was having a hard time with the move but that we could help her by fixing it up before she saw it, as a surprise.

He made it into a game for us. I don't think he slept that entire week. We painted everything inside and out. He let me pick the color for their bathroom, a soft periwinkle because it was her favorite. There wasn't any garden, but we built flower boxes for the windows and filled them with colorful blooms. Dad even hung a porch swing out front in an effort to dress up the rectangular slab of concrete that jutted several feet from the door before dropping off and connecting to the driveway. It wasn't anything like our old house, but I remember thinking it was perfect when we finished.

It was Christmastime, so Dad dropped me off at Mom's sister's so we could drive around and see the lights while he added a few last details to our new little house without the overeager hands of an eight-year-old trying to help.

Mom took us to the "pretty houses" in the fancy neighborhood she liked. She pointed out her favorite, a two-story that had one of those little balconies on the front, a Juliet balcony, she called it. The owners had wrapped every inch of it in white twinkle lights. I'd smiled, pressing my face against the window, and told her that Dad could string lights like that for her at our new little house too. Instead of answering, she'd parked us in front of it and cried.

When we pulled up to our new house, she didn't say a thing about the flower boxes or the porch swing. She didn't smile at Dad when he came out, and I didn't understand why he had to pry her fingers from the car door handle.

She kept silent as I towed her through each room and pointed out all the work Dad and I had done. And when we got to the bathroom, I remember smiling so hard my cheeks hurt, thinking finally she'd be happy.

She wouldn't even come in. She just glanced around with

an expressionless face and asked Dad if he expected her to like the hole he bought just because he'd painted it.

I'd started crying and Dad scooped me up and curtly told her we'd leave her to unpack. We went straight to the shop where he sat me directly on top of a creeper, lined up his own next to mine and said the phrase that I planned to get as a tattoo when I turned eighteen: "On your mark, get set, go!"

He'd engraved those words into the Creeper Race Cup that very night above my initials after I finally won (with a helpful push).

Over the years his name covered more space on the Cup than mine, but I was on there too. And we had plenty of room left.

"What do you say?" I asked, when Dad looked from his sandwich to the Cup. "I'll even give you first creeper pick." I rotated the Cup so he could read our initials. He always took care of me, found ways to make me smile when I couldn't on my own. And I was going to be just like him.

"Aren't you getting a little old for that?"

"You know the rules of Creeper Cup say if you refuse a challenge it's considered a forfeit, and by my count..." I lifted the Cup for closer inspection. "Your lead is dwindling." I had improved as our "courses" became more intricate over the years, but not that much. Yet. And based on the way Dad snatched the Cup for his own perusal, he knew it.

Still, I thought my appeal to his competitive nature had done the trick. His eyes passed over the chipped paint and his mouth lifted.

"Which one are you looking at?"

He pointed to a year that I'd never forget.

"The one when I accidentally set myself on fire. Awesome, Dad. Thanks."

"Wasn't my fault you went careening into the rag bin."

"It was your idea to add sparklers to the creeper!"

"Your pants only got singed a little. And I thought you were more coordinated back then." He patted my head. "We know better now."

I had him. I knew it. "You grab the creepers and I'll start blocking out—"

The door chimed up front. We had a customer.

And the Cup was returned to its dusty shelf.

When Dad shut his bedroom door later that night, I opened my window. I sat on the sill and twisted my legs out, feeling like I was escaping air that had grown too thin when I finally stood and peered over the edge of my roof.

Daniel was already there. Waiting for me.

"Sorry," he said, seeing my surprise. "Figured you wouldn't want me to knock."

He meant with Dad in the house. Yeah, that wouldn't have gone well.

"You figured right." I rose up on my tiptoes and flattened my hands on the shingles that hit just under my chest. I would have preferred *never* as a date for Daniel to watch me awkwardly climb onto my roof. I took a deep breath, preparing to get it over with, when Daniel crouched in front of me and extended his hand.

"Let me help you." Daniel lifted my hand and smoothed my fingers open to grasp his. He lifted me easily too, which did all kinds of funny things to my stomach, then smiled when we both sat down.

"What?"

"Nothing. It's just, your hands." He lifted one and smoothed my fingers open. "They feel like a mechanic's."

I pulled my admittedly rough hand into my lap. "I like my hands. They say who I am and what I do."

Daniel's eyes flickered between mine. "I like that about you too." He reached for my hand again, gliding his fingers over skin that wasn't soft, but still sensitive. He found a scar that flowed from the base of my thumb to the middle of my palm and traced it. "What happened here?"

It was hard to talk with his fingers sliding over my hand.

I made a pretense of pulling away to examine the line myself, as if I'd somehow forgotten the two-inch scar.

"I tried to pry up the hood of a rusted old Nova that my dad was working on. I slipped."

"How old were you?"

"Seven." I found myself telling him about that day and the way the vein in Dad's head nearly burst when he found me messing with the Nova before nearly passing out when he saw all the blood. Twelve stitches and a new pair of coveralls later, he was showing me the correct way to open the hood.

"Not that I never got hurt in the shop again, but I was never on the wrong end of a Nova again." I smiled, then flicked my eyes to Daniel. "What about you, any scars worth showing off?"

"Not really, no."

He had at least two visible scars, the one I could barely glimpse on his collarbone depending on the way he moved, and the one on his eyebrow. But before I could ask about either of those, Daniel leaned forward and ran the back of his hand along the underside of my jaw.

"And this one?"

I dropped my chin, breaking the skin-to-skin contact.

"Sorry, too personal," Daniel said, misinterpreting my reaction.

"No, it's not. Indirectly, I guess. I crashed racing my dad around the garage on a creeper."

Daniel raised a surprised eyebrow but said nothing. In

the silence that settled between us, I realized he was giving me the choice to tell him more if I wanted to or leave it at that. I was so used to Claire pouncing on me with questions that I almost didn't know what to say when it wasn't being pulled out of me.

So I just started. I told him about moving and Mom, and about Dad turning that whole awful day into something amazing.

Talking about Mom with Daniel didn't feel like I was exposing a festering wound to someone who'd never gotten so much as a scratch. He had his own wounds—and I was sure they were a lot more than he was sharing at that point, but it didn't feel like we had to compare them that way. We both bled. How much wasn't as important.

And just like that, I started seeing stars again, brighter and more numerous than they'd ever been before.

Daniel saw them too.

CHAPTER
18

Spending my mornings with Sean and, increasingly, my nights with Daniel, was confusing in ways it shouldn't have been. Because I found myself looking forward to sunset in a way I hadn't been able to look forward to sunrise.

For the first time in years, there was someone I wanted to see more than Sean. And that shift in my heart, free as I was to make it—*free as I'd always been to make it*—felt like a betrayal.

It made no sense to feel that way, to have any guilt over one fire dying and a new one kindling, but I did. And it was harder because, when we ran in the mornings, I'd sometimes find a spark, an ember that wasn't supposed to be there. Wasn't allowed. Sean would be telling a story about teaching his grandma and her bridge club how to use Twitter, or about the latest awesomely bad movie he'd discovered, when his eyes would catch mine. We'd share this smile that was all about our past and had nothing to do with our present. His mouth would kick up on one side, revealing much more than his dimple, and I'd let myself forget that it hurt to smile back.

It was becoming…not easier, but less of a battle to ignore Sean when I was with Daniel.

Other things *were* easier though.

Coming home at night didn't feel like slipping underwater without a full breath. The nights ahead of me weren't something I had to endure. At least not alone. When Daniel and I were together, it was as if the world beyond my roof didn't exist. We didn't have to think about anyone fighting or walking out. While the world around us slept peacefully, we could escape it.

And that changed everything.

It had been a blisteringly hot day and even though the sun had long since set, the heat had soaked into the earth, my roof, even seemingly the air, and it hadn't dissipated yet.

Daniel and I were both sweating. If it weren't for him, I'd probably have succumbed to the lure of my air-conditioned house. But I'd wanted to see him more than I'd wanted the comfort of cool air.

I wanted to see him more than a lot of things. And I guess he wanted to see me too.

There wasn't even a semblance of a breeze though, so I wasn't sure how long either of us would last outside. Daniel was already faring worse than I was.

"That's because my blood is thinner than yours," I told him when he remarked on the difference. "Besides, it gets hot in Philadelphia during the summer too."

"Yeah, it does," he said. "In a way it's worse because it gets sticky from all the humidity, like you need a straw just to breathe."

I folded an arm under my head. "There you go."

Daniel sat up and nodded his chin at me. "But we didn't melt on rooftops. We had pools. Where's your pool?"

"It's in my bathroom and it's called a tub." I offered him

the half-empty, barely cool water bottle I'd brought up with me, but he ignored it. Where the warmth was pestering him, it was lulling me. "Stop moving so much. You'll cool down."

But he kept shifting constantly. I tugged my lip and looked past him, squinting into the distance, as an idea occurred to me.

"Come on." I stood and pulled Daniel up with me. For a second his stomach brushed against mine. A lot of his body brushed against a lot of mine. All of his warmth wrapped around me. I felt the tiny sweat droplets transfer from his skin to mine. My breath caught in a way it hadn't maybe ever.

No big deal. I had to repeat that a lot to myself when I was with Daniel. No big deal when his thigh would rest against mine sitting next to each other, or when his breath stirred the tiny hairs on the back of my neck when he stood behind me closer than was strictly necessary. Or like when his fingers slid down my arm once I regained my balance, but he stayed standing just as close.

I was used to the butterflies I felt around Daniel, but not the pterodactyls that suddenly swooped in and started crashing around in my stomach.

"How badly do you want to get out of this heat?" I asked, putting a few much-needed inches between us.

"Badly, but I don't want to let you—to go yet." He was smiling at me, a questioning sort of smile that made me imagine what he might have looked like as a little boy.

"I'm talking about both of us going somewhere. Maybe."

Daniel hesitated. Things between us had been…good. Easy. We hung out, we talked. But we kept it safe. Neither of us ever suggested going somewhere. All the nights that we spent on my roof had always been that—on my roof. I never actually left my house. Somehow that had seemed important. Daniel must have come up with his own rationalization for all the time we spent together, and now I was potentially jeopardizing that.

He looked away from me, frowning ever so slightly. "Not sure that's a great idea."

I walked to the side of the roof. "It's actually a brilliant idea." *Maybe.*

"Where do you want to go?"

"Not far. We can walk." I sat and let my legs dangle over the edge.

After another moment of indecision, Daniel jumped down onto the wall. Before I could roll onto my stomach and shimmy down next to him, Daniel reached up and gripped my hips.

"I got you."

I felt the muscles in his shoulders tense as he supported my weight until my feet were on the wall next to his. The pterodactyls went wild when he kept his hands on me.

No big deal. No big deal.

It didn't matter how many times I told myself that. I stopped believing it the moment I left my roof with Daniel in the middle of the night.

Big deal. Very big deal.

I stepped back as soon as I was steady.

Daniel started to jump to the ground, but I stopped him.

"How good is your balance?" I took a few steps along the top of the narrow wall. If I pressed my ankles together the very edges of my feet still hung off either side.

"What are you doing?"

"Wall walking." I wobbled. "I used to do it when I was younger and apparently much more coordinated."

"You were younger than you are now? That's hard to imagine."

Watching my feet, I kept inching forward but I caught his

grin out of the corner of my eye. "You know I'm not going to forget how old I am. You don't need to keep reminding me." When Daniel didn't say anything, I realized that I might not be the one he was reminding.

The rough cement was scratchy under my bare feet as I shuffled along the wall, and there were a few loose pebble-sized pieces that dug into my heels. Odds were good that I'd be airborne before too long. Odds were equally good that Daniel wouldn't follow me.

Every time I glanced back at him, I saw the same conflicted expression cloud his face. He wanted to come with me, but it wasn't only about want. He wanted it to be okay to want to come with me; we both did. It was a fine line we'd been walking so far; I didn't think I was the only one who noticed how unsteady things were becoming. That was one of the reasons I suggested leaving my roof. Maybe if we were moving, it'd be easier to avoid how close we were getting, since we both knew we couldn't get any closer.

I reached the intersection where the wall separating my yard from his met the two neighbors behind us, and stood waiting for him. It felt like such a loaded question when I asked, "Are you coming with me?"

He fought his smile and lost. "Apparently. Which way?"

When I pointed left, his warm fingers closed around my hips again and I startled, but Daniel only helped me keep my balance as he stepped around and in front of me. His hands left my hips, but he caught hold of my hand rather than let me go entirely.

Medium deal?

Although I felt more uncertain of my balance than I had before I'd taken Daniel's hand, I didn't let go of it. Instead I looked up at him, barely a foot between us, and watched his smile slide away. It did that more and more often when he looked at me. Butterflies filled me, head to toe. "I'm trying to imagine you at sixteen."

"I was a mess, like everyone is supposed to be at sixteen." He said it almost like an accusation.

I couldn't resist. "Would we have been friends?"

Daniel didn't hesitate. "No. I definitely wouldn't have been friends with you." He flicked a look at me over his shoulder. "And no, you don't get to pretend like you don't understand what I mean."

I stopped walking and our hands separated. "I wasn't going to pretend anything."

"No?" He stopped too. "Then why'd you ask me that? Do I wish we were both sixteen? No. Do I wish you were twenty-one or even eighteen?" He waited a breath. "Yeah, Jill. I wish that a lot."

I guess I had been kind of fishing for the answer he gave me. Not necessarily the way he gave it. I wanted the crooked smile, the teasing response. I didn't want the almost harsh honesty.

I was kind of surprised when he took my hand and started walking again, although maybe he'd finally noticed that I was wobbling like I was on a tightrope.

It was dark out despite the stars. The streetlights were on, but they didn't give off enough light to make us more than shadowed silhouettes atop the wall.

Several houses later, I pulled Daniel to a stop and pointed to one that was half a block away.

"Who lives there?" he asked.

"No one, I think. It's a foreclosure."

Daniel turned to look at me. "What are we doing?"

My confidence in my brilliant idea was somewhat shaken by the tone of his voice. "You wanted a pool. I got you a pool."

"You want to break into someone's pool?" His face caught the moonlight just enough for me to see him raise an eyebrow. The tone he used that time made me smile.

"It's not breaking in." I really hoped it wasn't considered breaking in. "And no one lives there to mind anyway." Daniel was seconds from caving, I could tell. "But we can go back to my roof if you want. Maybe there will be a breeze."

Daniel laughed once. Then again louder. We walked the last few yards to the house before stopping. "You do this a lot?"

"Nope."

"It just popped into your head?"

"Maybe you're a bad influence."

"I'm definitely a bad influence." Daniel dropped my hand and pulled his shirt off over his head before tossing it over the wall. I was suddenly grateful for how dark it was. The pterodactyls would have knocked me over if I saw him clearly without a shirt.

I flexed my toes and looked down. The pool was dark, the water rippling ever so slightly in the almost nonexistent breeze. I inhaled hot, dry air, and imagined how deliciously cool the water would feel. I'd been sweating even before we started walking, and my tank was sticking to me.

I reminded myself that no one lived there. We weren't breaking into anything. People pool-hopped all the time. And it was fine for me and Daniel to hang out as friends.

I stepped up next to him and took his outstretched hand. "On three?"

His smile was a thing of beauty. "One."

"Two." I squeezed his hand back.

We jumped together on three.

CHAPTER
19

Daniel didn't let go of me when we hit the water. We sank down together. The darkness was so complete that our hands, our fingers, our skin, were the only things that existed.

The tips of my toes brushed the bottom and I pushed off, breaking the connection with Daniel. There was a brief moment of tangled limbs as we bobbed against each other trying to tread water while we were too close.

The water that wrapped around me was warm, like bathtub warm, from baking in the sun all day, but it felt so good. Everything with Daniel felt good.

"I didn't think you were going to make it with those short legs of yours." Daniel dipped below the surface and his fingers encircled my ankle before I was yanked down with him.

I pushed up and splashed water in his face. "Short legs? I haven't been short since the fifth grade."

"When was that? Last year?" He swam to the side and pushed himself up to sit on the edge.

"The age jokes are getting old," I said. "Just like you."

He stood up. "Wanna jump again?"

It was so dark I could make out only his outline, but I could see the hand he extended, and again I took it. He pulled me up so fast that I stumbled against him. All of him. It was one of those moments where I desperately wanted him to tease me about being young, because I felt young. My heart raced and, pressed against him, I felt his heart lurch under my fingers.

And I panicked.

And I pushed him backward into the pool.

He surfaced and spun around. When his eyes found me his smile had a predatory edge to it that sent a thrill straight through to my toes. "You are so dead."

"You looked hot."

Daniel's smile grew. "So you pushed me away? You may have gotten that backward."

"Hot as in warm," I said, glad it was too dark for him to see the blush I felt rush up my cheeks.

He took a few leisurely strokes toward me. "Go on. Jump. You look...warm."

I laughed in a way that betrayed how nervous he was making me. "Not with you waiting to attack me the moment I hit the water."

"What makes you think I'm going to attack you?" He swam closer.

"Aren't you?"

Instead of answering, he reached the pool's edge and climbed out with a speed that had me leaping backward, excited and scared in an exhilaratingly mixed-up way. Daniel caught me with an arm around my waist and another under my knees. Before I could freak out about him holding me, he twisted and launched me into the pool.

Hitting the water stung and I spluttered as I surfaced. But the pool and surrounding deck were empty. I spun around.

Nothing.

The pool light was off and I suddenly felt irrationally afraid of what I couldn't see in the dark water. Arms snaked around me from behind and I was lifted up, up, nearly all the way out of the water and tossed across the pool.

When my heart started beating again, I came up laughing and choking a little. The chlorine stung my eyes and my throat. I started for him.

"Be careful." Daniel shook his head so water sprayed around him in an arc, the drops slapped against my forehead. "Right now we're even."

I could hear the anticipation in his voice. I was still in the deeper end of the pool, my legs treading water to keep me up, but I felt my toes finally brush along the bottom as we moved, circling each other. I smiled at him, showing all my teeth.

"You look crazy." Daniel laughed and lunged for me, but I pushed away, moving around behind him before he could stand.

I levered myself up on his shoulders and pushed down with all my weight, dunking him. I whooped out loud and made my escape to the other edge of the pool. "Now we're eve—"

He grabbed both my ankles when my fingers were inches from the pool's edge, pulling me back against his chest so that I sucked in a startled breath. His hands lowered to my waist and my pulse raced before he tossed me again into the deep end. His laughter filled my ears as I splashed back up. "I told you."

He waited for me to move again, matching my direction when I swam left or right, closing the distance between us with each stroke. We chased each other, splashing and dunking and, in my case, swallowing at least half the pool. We made way too much noise and didn't care in the slightest.

I got used to feeling his hands on me, his arms wrapped around me. And at the same time I'd never get used to them.

Daniel called truce before I did, releasing me when I tried to squirm around behind him. I dunked him again for good measure, then echoed his call for truce when he surfaced. I moved to the middle of the pool and was only a little disappointed when he didn't pursue me. I was too waterlogged for any more.

"Screw your roof." Daniel rested his elbows on the pool ledge behind him. "This is where we're meeting tomorrow." He sank lower and dropped his head back, eyes closed, a look of total contentment on his face.

While he soaked, I slowly swam the length of the pool, back and forth, fueled by a buzzing energy I couldn't account for. I turned over on my back and floated so that the tips of my toes peeked out of the water.

When I felt the water roll against me as Daniel pushed off from the edge, I let my legs drop and watched him glide toward me. I had a weird but not entirely unpleasant feeling that he'd been watching me.

Neither of us could reach the bottom, so we bobbed. Occasionally my foot would slide against his, or his calf would brush mine. Only once or twice at first, but then with more frequency as we drew closer until I could count the drops of water on his eyelashes.

I was treading water, but my rhythm became less controlled and I was beginning to drift higher and lower with each movement.

Daniel moved closer, his arms stretched on either side of him, skimming over the water, like he was calming the ripples I was making.

He was so close. His eyes lowered to my mouth and I forgot to swim for a second. That was the moment where he was supposed to make a joke about me still having my baby teeth or offer to buy me training wheels for my bike.

Instead Daniel breathed my name. His eyes met mine for half a second before he dipped his head.

And that's when the light flicked on.

CHAPTER
20

My stomach bungeed from my throat down to my knees, slamming into the kaleidoscope of butterflies created by Daniel's mouth inches from mine.

One profane phrase zipped through my brain as I jerked around and saw a silhouetted figure pass through the window of the VERY OCCUPIED house behind me.

The porch light illuminated a host of panicked thoughts involving me being arrested, going to jail in soaking wet clothes, and Dad never letting me get a Spitfire—never letting me anywhere near Daniel again.

It took half a second for these thoughts to flood my body with adrenaline. I swear I broke some Olympic record crossing that pool and climbing out, and Daniel was right there with me.

He jumped up and straddled the wall before leaning down to help me. I grabbed his shoulders while his hands squeezed tight on my waist, lifting me up and over the other side.

If I thought my heart had thudded before, it was nothing compared to the way it raced as I took off again. I ran along the side of the house, ducking past windows, dodging a bunch of barrel cacti, and stumbling before nearly going into cardiac arrest when hands grabbed me from the shadows of an overgrown mesquite tree.

Daniel rolled me into his chest and held a finger to his lips.

In the sudden silence, I realized stealth had not been foremost on my mind as I'd torn through the backyard to the front. "Did they see us?"

Daniel shook his head. "I don't think so. We weren't making any noise and no one called out. Hey, maybe they were breaking in too?"

Breaking in too. I was fighting a losing battle with nausea just from thinking about us in that category.

The sound of his laughter startled me. "You look totally freaked-out. We're fine. No one saw us." He raised a hand and brushed his thumb over a few drops of water that clung to the skin on my cheek.

As comforting as I was sure he meant the gesture to be, it wasn't until my own senses confirmed his words—no one was yelling and stalking around their yard looking for us— that I willed my pulse to slow. A minute later I heaved a true sigh of relief when I saw the patio light go out.

But that only replaced one heart-pounding emotion with another.

Without the pool surrounding us, I felt crazy exposed in my dripping wet clothes. Not cold in the slightest, but warm down to my bones. A sensation born from how very aware I was of Daniel. Without a shirt on.

Even when he lowered his hand from my cheek, he didn't step back.

Suddenly it was like no time had passed between that last moment in the pool and this one. Daniel shifted closer, not touching me, but I could change that with a deep breath.

I shivered a little when his hand slid up my arm, over my shoulder, and curled under my jaw. He wasn't tracing a scar.

"Jill?" he said. And it was a question, a request.

All I had to do was look up. I could feel the warmth of his breath on my skin, the heat from both our bodies. I wasn't sixteen to him in that moment.

But I was to me.

I stepped back. I half expected to hear him sigh or something, but he didn't.

I hated that I couldn't bring myself to look up at him. Had I just ruined everything? Why couldn't I have moved that half step forward instead of back? I wanted to kiss him. Wow, did I want to kiss him. But kissing Daniel wasn't something I could just want. I almost couldn't believe he'd been about to kiss me. He knew better, and he'd almost done it twice in less than ten minutes. It wasn't like he'd forgotten how old he was or how old I wasn't. Kissing me would be so much worse for him than it would for me. And then there was that whole thing that he probably kissed on an entirely different level than I would. It sent my heart hydroplaning.

"No, you're right." He ran both hands through his hair. "I wasn't thinking." And then in a quieter voice, almost to himself, he repeated it.

"Well, we have opposite problems, so we should go before we wake up all the neighbors." Without waiting for his response, I moved past him to the sidewalk, leaving the shadows cast by the tree.

"Jill, wait." He jogged up and stepped in front of me. "Hey, I—"

I gasped.

Daniel was standing directly under the streetlight, illuminating what the dark water and shadows had concealed before. The muscles I had felt, but not the myriad of scars that stood out against his pale skin in a way that blinded me to anything else. Burns swirled in ugly patterns along his ribs, recently healed gashes mixed in with shiny patches of older, scarred skin.

I breathed his name, my hand reaching out toward him.

He jerked back from me, the soft look in his eyes hardening in an instant.

I felt dizzy looking at one scar that curved around his stomach from navel to just under his armpit. "What happened to you?"

He yanked his T-shirt on and brushed his still-wet hair back, looking everywhere but at me. "I should get you home." He started walking again, stopping only when I didn't follow. "Don't be such a child, Jill. Let's go."

All the playful tenderness evaporated.

It wasn't hard to ignore the insult of his words when all I could focus on was that he'd been hurt. Badly. And more than once. "Daniel..."

He lifted the shirt back up and I flinched. "Look. See? They're old. From before I moved, okay?"

No, it wasn't okay. And they weren't that old, not all of them. My head was racing. I thought back to that first night I saw him, the way he'd held himself so stiffly. I'd thought it had just been because of the fight with his mom. Now I ached to think of the pain he must have been in.

So many scars. What could do that? He looked like he'd been half split open and no one had bothered to put him back together right. No one.

A series of stupid thoughts ran through my mind, like, how had he been able to climb onto my roof so easily? Or had I hurt him when we were playing around in the pool?

But I couldn't shake one dominating thought: *Someone hurt him.*

Questions coiled like snakes in the pit of my stomach as Daniel started walking. When I caught up to him, I brushed my fingers against his and he stopped.

"From before? This is why you moved?"

I could see the irritation when he turned to me. I'd never once seen him look at me that way. It chased away every little detail I'd ever found attractive in his face.

We were totally exposed on the sidewalk with the streetlights flooding down around us. Still, I didn't care as I searched Daniel's face, waiting for him to talk to me.

"My dad," he said with a twisted smile, "isn't anything like yours." He licked his lips. "I bet your dad taught you how to ride a bike, drive, replace brake pads? My dad taught me to be quiet. Taught me the difference between my mom crying because she was upset and when she needed to go to the hospital." He bent and picked up an empty can, hurling it at the wall behind him.

It was nowhere near me, but I flinched.

"I'd been begging her to move out with me. I told her I'd take care of her, but she had to leave him. He'd stopped hitting me when I got big enough to hit back, so I could say that to her in front of him."

I watched Daniel start to crumble in on himself as he spoke, like the bones in his body were shrinking. His next words started out as a whisper.

"She wouldn't go. She wouldn't come with me. She stood next to him like I was the one she was afraid of. Me!" He punched his chest hard enough that I winced. "I stood between him and her so many times. Let him hit me so he wouldn't have the energy to go after her. So many times... So I left her. I left her with him. I should have killed him that day. I could have."

I should have been scared by his words, by the cold and

quiet way he talked about killing his father, but I wasn't. I could hear the anguish just in the way he was breathing.

"This last time one of the neighbors called me when they heard the screaming. It was almost too late when I got there, when I got him off her." His hand slid up his side, over scars that I'd never be able to forget.

I filled in the words he didn't say. Matching up the scars I remembered. So many. But he was here. Daniel was standing in front of me.

"He nearly killed her, hit her so hard that the police didn't give her a choice anymore. But even that wouldn't have been enough. She'd have waited for him. Her bones were broken from his fists and she would have waited for him. What kind of sick love is that?"

It wasn't love at all.

"I packed everything up while she was still in the hospital. She would have stayed, so I didn't let her choose. She had no money, no place to live, and her husband was behind bars for aggravated assault with a deadly weapon. If I'm lucky, he'll be gone for ten years. If he's lucky, it'll be longer, 'cause if I ever see him again, I'll bash his skull in with that baseball bat he likes so much."

I had to close my eyes, which only made it worse as Daniel's words painted a horror I couldn't conceive of, one that made my recent confessions to him about my mom feel so unbelievably petty. But I couldn't dwell on any of that since Daniel was still talking.

"She always wanted to live somewhere warm...she hated the snow. So here we are. No snow for her, and no..." His throat choked off then and he didn't finish. He didn't have to.

I wanted to go to him, to hold him. I took a step, but I hesitated, worried I might end up hurting him if I touched the wrong place. Then a streak of white-hot hatred blistered

through me for the man who'd caused them. It birthed a vi-
olence so intense, my vision flared red.

Daniel didn't notice the emotional fracture I was feeling.
It wasn't a helpful reaction, so I tamped it down as best I
could and took another step.

He reached out, grabbed fistfuls of my shirt, and literally
hauled me to him.

I took my cue of how tight to hold on from him. Tight.
Rib-crackingly tight.

We ended up facing each other sitting on the curb, my legs
folded up between us. I listened while he talked. Not about
his dad, I could tell he was done on that account. His mom
though. With every word I could hear how desperately he
loved her. It was kind of staggering.

All I could think was, why? What had that woman done
to deserve that kind of love? The only reason I kept silent
was because I could hear him asking the same question. Not
out loud. But in every pause, every pulled-in breath. *Why?*

The small, selfish part of me turned those same questions inward. Stealing a moment that belonged to him. It
all seemed so unfair that some could love so constantly and
others so capriciously. Daniel's mom had done nothing to
deserve his love and, from the way he talked, she could do
nothing to jeopardize it. Dad had tried more than I had with
Mom, but the result was the same: she didn't love either of
us. When I tried to analyze it, put labels on her behavior,
love never came close to displacing disregard or spite.

Why did he love her?

Why didn't she love me?

We had no answers, and the lack ate at us both.

Somewhere through all of that I took his hand. I was holding it in both of mine, running my thumbs over his knuckles.
I didn't feel even the slightest bit self-conscious even when

Daniel ran out of words. Some things just fell away in the face of others.

We weren't drifting inexorably closer to each other in a moonlit pool, wanting and wondering and possibly daring. We were sitting on a cracked curb with scattered pebbles and cigarette butts littered around us.

And it was better and worse altogether.

We sat, letting dim streetlight and our words reveal scars so deep and raw that they threatened to block out every other emotion that came before and possibly after.

CHAPTER
21

I woke up Saturday morning, after crawling into my bed only hours before, to a Post-it.

It was stuck to the fridge, not my pillow. And it held Dad's handwriting, not Mom's, but that didn't stop my throat from swelling shut before I read it.

I left you the truck. Don't crash it. I'll be home from the auction Monday night. Might bring you something. —Dad

Underneath was a little sketch of a convertible peeling away. My throat relaxed and I smiled, recognizing myself behind the wheel.

Dad had told me about the auction weeks ago, and probably again yesterday, but I'd forgotten completely. I'd stayed out till almost dawn with Daniel and slept through my chance to say goodbye. Dad and I hadn't been apart for more than a day since Mom left, and unless it was self-imposed, solitude was not my friend.

My raging I-didn't-sleep-nearly-long-enough-last-night

headache reasserted itself when I looked outside and saw that Daniel's Jeep was gone.

Nausea bled through me. He hadn't meant to tell me—show me—anything about his dad; the streetlight had forced his hand. And even though we stayed together wrapped in shadows until nearly dawn, I couldn't be sure what the light of day would do to us in his mind.

I knew what it was like when someone discovered horrible things about me. It made me feel like that diseased part was the only thing about me to be seen. Feeling defined by the thing I loathed above all others…it was unbearable. I'd spent an Arizona summer on my roof trying to get away from that feeling.

I had no idea where Daniel went, except away from me.

And I couldn't even blame him.

Claire hadn't mandated running on the weekends yet—and *yet* was the operative word—but I was willing to do anything that morning if it meant leaching off some of her cheerfulness, like a parasite that couldn't survive on its own.

"You are not a parasite," she said, when I called her and shared the comparison. "Plus I just so happen to have a surplus of merriment today and I can't think of another person I'd like to parasitically donate it to."

"That is sweet and gross, Claire. Thanks."

Kind of like Sunsplash, which was where we decided to go.

Claire bounded out of her house in shorts and a T-shirt with a towel thrown over one shoulder when I pulled up. She swam her hand through the air after she hopped into the passenger seat of Dad's truck. "Let's roll."

When I failed to "roll" so much as an inch forward, Claire flipped up her sunglasses to look at me.

"Headache worse?"

"Yes." It felt like someone was inside jumping up and down on my eyeballs. "But it's not the headache." My drive over to Claire's had left me with nothing but my thoughts for company and they'd been less than pleasant.

Claire reached over me and shifted the truck into Park, then sat back with her concerned-friend face on—Claire gave really good concerned-friend face—and it was the impetus I needed to spill.

I told her about last night. Everything until Daniel's scars.

Claire's expression dissolved into frank disapproval when I got to the night-swimming part, then outright distress at our almost kiss.

"He did not!"

"No, I told you. The light came on so we ran."

"But he was going to! And you were going to! That is so... really not smart, Jill." When I let my head fall back against my seat, she continued. "There is something wrong with a twenty-one-year-old kissing a sixteen-year-old. Tell me you know that. And what about Sean?" she added with a note of hurt in her tone.

I completely ignored the Sean comment since, of the three of us, she seemed to be the only one still laboring under that delusion. "Claire. I need you to check the lecture for a minute. Can you please do that?"

"I don't know. What are you about to say?"

I squeezed my eyes shut.

"I'll try. Best I can do. But if you want to get a tattoo on your face or something, I'm not going to just sit here and smile." Claire crossed her arms and leaned back against the window. "I'm never going to be that kind of friend."

"It's not a face tattoo."

"You like him, don't you?" Claire drew her knees up. "That's worse than the face tattoo."

Sliding my hands up to the top of the steering wheel, I sighed. "I like being around him. I like that I can talk to him and not feel…" I hesitated, looking for a word that wouldn't sound like an insult to Claire, but I came up blank. It wasn't that I didn't value her friendship, but it was hard sometimes, all the times, when it came to family stuff. And family stuff had been ALL the stuff for me lately.

Before I could really start to squirm at my inability to communicate, Claire nodded almost to herself.

"I think I get it now. Not all of it," she added with slightly furrowed brows. "I don't talk to you about weight issues and stuff because you can't even begin to understand what that's like for me—and I am glad because it takes so much energy and fight, and every day I have to think about calories and food and my weight and insulin and it's exhausting." She finished in a gust of breath like even talking about it taxed her. "You've never had to safety pin your jeans because the button wouldn't reach. You've never had to wait until the late bell in a class before getting up because you knew odds were you'd get stuck in the desk. You've never had to listen to perfect strangers make comments in a restaurant about what's on your plate."

"Claire," I said, in a soft voice. "I never knew any of that."

"Yeah, because I didn't want you to, just like you don't want me to know all the stuff with your mom. And you're right. I can't relate, and even though I know you're happy that I don't have to, it must be nice to have someone to talk to about crummy mothers."

My heart gave a funny lurch and my smile was small but sure. It was… *Nice* probably wasn't the right word, but yeah. "I'm sorry I couldn't talk to you about all that," I said.

"And I'm sorry I can't talk to you about your mom. I'm even happy that with Daniel, you have someone hurting in the same way that you can talk to. But, Jill," she said, shifting back to a point I'd wrongly hoped she'd forgotten. "Anything that happens between you guys is going to only hurt more in the long run. I mean, what's the best possible scenario here?"

There wasn't one.

"You guys start, what, dating? Is your dad going to go for that?"

I didn't need to answer that.

"So then you don't tell him. You sneak around. You lie."

I shook my head. I wouldn't do that to Dad. I couldn't.

"Okay. Then you wait. Will it be better when you're eighteen and he's twenty-three? Will he wait? Will you? Because if the answer is yes, then okay. End of lecture. I won't say another word."

My headache came charging back. "Why do you have to do that? Why do you have to make everything into big-picture terms?"

"Because everything is big picture. You know that."

"No," I said. "Not yet it isn't. I tell you about a guy and you jump two years into the future and ask me what that looks like. How am I supposed to answer that?"

"When you liked Sean you could. How many times have we planned your wedding, a dozen?"

"This is different."

Claire leaned toward me. "Why? Why is it different?"

"Because it is. I just met Daniel. I'm still getting to know him. And he's got all this stuff going on, and…"

"And what? You were in love with Sean for years."

My cheeks were wet before I realized I'd started crying.

"Sean will come around, you know. He probably already—"

"No. I don't care anymore. How many times do I have to tell you that?"

"Maybe until you can say it without tearing up. And I was right there watching you watch him with Cami at the movies the other night. I see you every day running with him. I've been watching you two for months get over whatever it was that happened, and you're almost there. I can tell, even if you can't, that he's already there. So don't get distracted by something it doesn't sound like you can fix anyway."

Daniel's Jeep wasn't in front of his house when I got home late after dropping Claire off. But instead of going inside, I sat in my driveway with the engine idling and the overpowering scent of chlorine that lingered on my hair and skin. The pool from the night before had smelled sweet by comparison. Every time I closed my eyes I saw Daniel; the water droplets on his eyelashes, and I remembered that flare of panicked excitement I felt as he leaned toward me.

And then my mind lurched forward and all I could see were scars.

My fingers twitched, and pain, as vivid and real as I'd ever felt, suffused my body as I remembered each and every one.

Claire was right about that. There was nothing I could do to fix what had happened to Daniel, what was still happening to him, but that didn't keep me from wanting to try and hoping he'd come back so I could.

Just as I was about to pull into the garage, a gray Suburban stopped in front of Daniel's house. The driver got out and walked to the passenger side. When he opened the door, Daniel got out, took two steps, and crumbled onto the sidewalk.

CHAPTER
22

I flew out of the truck, barely remembering to yank the keys from the ignition, before running next door.

"What happened? Is he okay?" Heedless of the spectacular sunburn I'd gotten that day with Claire, I dropped to my knees on the graveled yard and bent to see Daniel's face. "Daniel...?"

The driver laughed. "He's just drunk off his ass is all."

I glanced at the driver before turning back to Daniel, who had rolled onto his back and was staring up at the sky with unfocused eyes. I sat back on my heels and sucked in air that suddenly stank of alcohol and cigarette smoke.

Drunk.

I hadn't ever seen it in person, up close. I hadn't smelled it before either. It started to mix with the chlorine that clung to me and the combination turned me almost as green as Daniel.

It was sobering, for me at least. Daniel was too busy trying to keep his eyes from rolling back in his head.

Driver Guy squatted down next to Daniel and patted his face. "Yo, Daniel, you cool if I take off?"

Daniel was apparently cool with anything at the moment.

"Are you kidding? You can't leave him here like this." I watched Driver Guy walk back to his car. "At least help me get him inside?"

Driver Guy unlocked his door. "Nah, I'm good."

And without another word he drove off.

A single laugh that was more a gasp than anything left me as I stared after his fading taillights.

I knelt there for at least a solid minute running through a list of possible scenarios that ended up with me successfully getting Daniel inside his house.

The list was pathetically short.

I focused on Daniel. Drunk was not a good look on him. He never opened his eyes for more than a second or two, but I could see that they were puffy and bloodshot. He didn't look anything like the guy from the night before in the pool; not even like the guy from after the pool.

I didn't ask him why. I thought that was pretty obvious, but another thought quickly chased that one away: I didn't know him well enough to make that call. We'd spent the past couple weeks together caught up in our own perfect little bubble, for the most part, isolated from people who would point out all the many reasons why our little bubble needed to pop.

Maybe drinking was what he did. I couldn't blame him, but the possibility made me less unsure about pulling away the night before.

Daniel made a noise, a groan, as he tried to sit up, and I became aware that the gravel beneath my knees was long past stinging. I stood and brushed off the pebbles, looking at Daniel's front door some thirty feet away, then at Daniel who was actually swaying where he sat. It might as well have

IF I FIX YOU   151

been a mile. Daniel outweighed me by at least fifty pounds and "drunk off his ass" meant he was dead weight.

I winced when I dragged Daniel's arm over my shoulders and pulled him to his feet. He was every bit as heavy as I'd feared, and unsteady. The friction of his skin against my sunburn was brutal as we shuffled along.

But I wasn't letting go.

When we got to the door we were both sweating. I propped him against the side of his house with my hip and my palm. "Don't fall, okay?" Daniel would end up face-first in a cactus if he went down.

I was relieved when the door opened. I had not been looking forward to playing find the house keys with the drunk guy.

Daniel's knees buckled once after we got inside and I made a grab for the back waist of his jeans and gave a vicious yank. That sobered him up and I stopped worrying he was going to puke down my neck at any moment. Mostly.

He pushed away from me when we reached the kitchen and almost went down again before he caught himself against the wall.

I reached out to help him and he jerked away.

"I'm fine." His words were slurred.

The first two intelligible words he'd spoken to me, and they were a complete dismissal. When Daniel first fell out of the car, I'd gone from panic, thinking he was hurt, before shifting to pragmatic mode to get him inside. I'd completely bypassed anything else. But I was hot and sweaty and the sunburn along my shoulders was screaming from supporting his weight. And I was so confused by my own feelings that anger seemed like the only safe one.

"You're fine? You sure about that? 'Cause I just had to

drag you inside from where your buddy—who's super by the way—ditched you on the side of the road."

Daniel's answer was to throw up all over the place.

I cleaned up the floor while Daniel slumped against the wall. I'd been out of the puke zone, but Daniel hadn't been so lucky. I found him a mostly clean T-shirt in the laundry room and turned away when he changed. I didn't need to see his scars again. I couldn't imagine the harsh lights in his kitchen making them look any better. But just the reminder of them was enough to douse my burst of anger.

I stood still and held my breath. Daniel was leaning back on the counter, discarded fast-food bags littered on either side of him. I felt something twist inside me, looking at him. He was worse than alone. The only "friend" he had—that I knew of—had just dumped him in the street. He truly had no one.

He didn't meet my eye when I took the balled-up dirty shirt from him and rinsed it in the sink. When I turned back, Daniel had a bottle of whiskey pressed to his lips.

"Stop." I moved slowly, reaching my hand up to take it. "Seriously. You need to stop."

He didn't. He eyed me and tipped the bottle back farther, his throat working with each swallow, before setting it down a little too hard. "Had to get the taste out of my mouth."

I caught a whiff of the liquor and didn't know which must have tasted worse. I said nothing, but I filled a glass of water and held it out to him.

Daniel drained the water in one long swallow; then, using the wall for balance, he made his way to the couch in the living room.

"Why?" I wasn't going to ask him outside, but he finally seemed alert enough to answer, and I needed to know how responsible to feel, since I'd been the one who forced him to relive the nightmare he was trying to leave behind. "And that guy?"

Daniel kept staring at the empty glass.

I followed him to the living room and wrapped my hand around the glass. He didn't let go when I tugged. "Do you want more? You have to let go first."

"John, his name is John…or Jake." Daniel relinquished the glass, letting me refill it at the sink. "I met him a couple times playing pool. He was doing me a favor. He could've let me drive."

"Yeah, he's obviously a great guy." I offered Daniel the water, but he ignored it, so I set it on the floor. "Hey, maybe next time he can just slow down and push you out of his car. Save him the time of having to fully stop."

Daniel leaned back into the couch and flung his arm over his face. "Don't give me a hard time, okay?"

"Hard time? I just spent the whole day defending you to my best friend. I carried you in here and I just cleaned up your puke. What kind of time should I be giving you?"

"I don't know, Jill. Just leave me alone, okay? I'm sure it's way past your bedtime."

I stood for a second nodding at him. The past week had done a number on me. I stopped thinking clearly on multiple levels. I'd been starting to forget all the very legitimate reasons to keep my distance from Daniel. The facts hadn't changed. He was too old. I was too young. Only very bad things were promised to us. He may have stopped caring for those few moments last night, but I couldn't, no matter how bad I felt for him.

And maybe that was all I felt for him. Pity. It was certainly the only emotion I could muster up in that moment. Or at least, it was the only useful one.

My skin hurt, my heart hurt, and I could still smell the acidic hint of vomit in the air underneath the cleaner I had used.

I had zero—*zero*—reason to stay there.

"I'll see you around, Daniel."

I hadn't taken a step when I felt his hand wrap around my arm.

CHAPTER
23

"Jill. Wait."

Daniel's grip wasn't hard. It wasn't even so much that he grabbed my arm as placed his hand on me. I could have pulled away and left. He couldn't have followed me in his condition.

"I didn't mean that." Daniel's stare was making me mildly uncomfortable and I got the sense that he wasn't talking to me when he said, "Why are you only sixteen?"

I drew closer to the couch so that he had to look up at me. He still held my arm and I felt each one of his fingers. "What am I supposed to say to that? This—" I gestured between the two of us "—wasn't my fault. I wish you'd stop treating me like it was."

His hand pulled me a step closer. Then two. I could smell cigarette smoke clinging to him, but underneath it was the familiar bite of citrus from whatever he wore. The mix was souring my already uneasy stomach.

"Sometimes I think about what it might be like if you were older. I move here, meet you, and you're twenty-one.

Even eighteen. We could just get in a car and drive." Then his eyes lost their focus for a moment. "I don't know how much longer I can stay," he said. "But if I go, she'll go back. And she'll wait, and wait, and wait however long it takes." Daniel's breathing was slow and steady and for a moment it was like he wasn't drunk at all.

"The first time he hit her really hard." Daniel dragged his hand up to his temple, tracing along smooth skin. "She stopped being able to see the color green. He knocked it right out of her head." Daniel's hand lowered. "She can't see me anymore. I try and talk to her and she screams like the sound of my voice hurts her. How? How did I get here? What did I do that was so much worse than him?" He tried to draw me closer, pulling on my arms.

"Daniel?" I said his name because the lucid moment had passed. And tears for him were already filling my eyes. "It's not your fault. You know that." Except he didn't look like he knew anything. "You protected her. You're still protecting her and she's—" my voice cracked but I pushed out the rest of the words that we both needed to hear "—supposed to love you."

Daniel had said his dad beat them for years, long enough to permanently damage his mom on some level. I wanted that knowledge to soften me toward her, but it didn't, not when Daniel was the one still suffering. When he finally focused on me, I could tell he hadn't heard me in the way I wanted. The words meant nothing to him because he didn't believe them.

He took a deep breath and pushed his hair back from his face. "I don't want to do this anymore. Any of it." His eyes found mine. "Except you." Both hands caught my arms and I didn't know if he was trying to draw me in or if he needed someone to pull him up, anyone.

I never knew the answer to that question with Daniel.

"Let's get out of here. Anywhere. We can drive to the Grand Canyon or Mexico."

His grip was inexorable. There was a desperate pleading note so naked in his voice that I couldn't move away even though I was so suddenly, painfully, convinced that I needed to. "Daniel, I can't," I said. "I'm sorry, but you know I can't." I didn't need to list all the reasons why. I could see them hit him one by one until his eyes went dim again and he dropped his hands before leaning back in the couch.

"Hey." His eyes wobbled a bit in their sockets before steadying. "I'm sorry I puked on you. And what I said."

He was pale and he had a slight sheen to his skin. His hair had picked up some of the dirt and gravel from the yard. The T-shirt I had found for him was much too small. And I couldn't forget what it concealed.

I sat down and plucked a pebble from his hair and dropped it into his hand. "You need better friends."

"Like you? Do I have you, Jill?" It was like part of him had completely shut down. Gone was the broken boy struggling to understand his mother's animosity. He'd boxed all that up and what was left seemed unsteady and uncomfortably intense.

"I did get you inside and—" I glanced at his shirt. "I'm still here."

"You fixed my Jeep."

"And I fixed your Jeep."

Daniel leaned into me, or maybe he fell into me. "And you smell nice."

I pushed him back. He was heavy. And didn't smell so nice. "I smell like chlorine from the water park, and I smell a little like puke because of you."

Daniel ran his eyes down to my legs and then back to my face. "You are sort of pink."

I was a lot pink. I was gonna hurt so bad tomorrow. I explained about Sunsplash, but Daniel didn't seem to be listening all that well.

"Does it sting?" He slid his hand up my forearm.

Not when he did that it didn't. "It mostly feels tight. But you shouldn't be touching me."

Daniel moved his hand up to my shoulder and rubbed his thumb back and forth. "It's redder here."

Did he even know what he was doing? I looked into his face, noticing the heavy-lidded, glazed look in his eyes. I doubted I was more than a blurry pink shape in front of him. He was probably a minute away from passing out. If that. My eyes started to sting and I squeezed them shut.

It wasn't fair what he was doing to me. Making me realize things that I really didn't want to. He was so messed up. His parents had done that to him and neither one cared that they'd damaged something so fragile. And Daniel was fragile.

He'd told me before that I was the only one he knew out here—I refused to count Jake/John—and at the time that knowledge was heady. It made me feel special to think that I was all he needed. But it wasn't true, not in the way I thought. His world had shrunk to include only his mom and me, and he'd latched onto me because he needed someone. Maybe anyone. I had people, love. Daniel didn't. All he had was me and the impossible relationship we were navigating. I knew that if his life had been different, a hair less awful, he'd have been able to stay away from me. He'd have known what I was finally forcing myself to accept. Sooner or later—and I was guessing sooner—we were going to crash. I'd already begun to brace for impact.

I dropped my shoulder and Daniel took the hint and stopped touching me. "Sorry."

I shook my head. "It's okay. It doesn't hurt that much." Other things hurt though. Other things were just beginning to throb with pain that promised to be so much worse than physical.

Daniel was muttering something and then he was touching my hair, running his fingers through the strands that weren't all the way dry yet. He was half leaning, half falling toward me again.

I leaned back but he kept coming.

I hadn't thought my first kiss would be from some drunk guy pressing me back against a lumpy couch and smashing his mouth against mine with enough force to bang our teeth together. I hadn't thought he would stink of cigarettes and taste like puke.

One of his hands tangled in my hair and the other slid up to grip my shoulder tightly, too tightly on my sunburned skin.

This wasn't a kiss in Sean's old tree house during a rainstorm, or at a bonfire, or any of the ways I wanted my first kiss to be. Daniel wasn't telling me he cared about me in that crazy intense way I craved. He wasn't telling me anything. He wasn't even looking at me.

Last night, for the first time, I dreamed about being kissed in a pool with a sky of twinkling stars watching. For the first time, I dreamed about a guy with dark hair instead of blond.

But I had never dreamed of this.

I wedged a hand between our bodies and shoved. "Get off!"

He did. He drew back all the way, freeing me to squirm out from under him. "Jill—" Daniel sank back into his corner of the couch, flung his head back and swore. "I didn't mean to do that."

I was breathing like I'd just run ten miles with Claire. Hot tears pricked my eyes. I opened my mouth. Then shut it.

Daniel's eyes were closed. His breathing, unlike mine, was even.

Beer and vomit. I could still taste him on my lips, smell him on my clothes when I left him passed out on his couch.

CHAPTER
24

Showering the next morning was an exercise in self-torture. The water spit like buckshot onto my skin, which had bloomed overnight into an angry blotchy red. The tightness had constricted so that every movement felt like my skin was going to split open.

Inside hurt too, for reasons that had nothing to do with sunburn.

I stayed in the shower until the water started spraying out frozen needles, until it was hard to focus on anything else. In my closet I found my lightest, thinnest summer dress and hissed when I slipped it on, before hurrying outside.

Leaving Dad's truck in the driveway last night instead of pulling into the garage had been a mistake, one I paid for by burning both my hand and my hip on the molten hot seatbelt buckle. I said something I really shouldn't have, especially not while heading to church. The steering wheel felt sticky when I gripped it, almost like it had started to melt along with the rest of the truck.

And then I cried like such a little girl when the AC refused to turn on.

I hit the stupid sticky steering wheel with my palms until they hurt worse than the rest of me.

I was a two-year-old having a temper tantrum and I couldn't stand the sight I caught of myself in the rearview mirror. I whacked it away and jerked into Reverse.

Down the driveway.

Onto the street.

Into the car pulling up to the curb.

I didn't swear when I heard the crunch of metal. Not out loud. Out loud I was focused on one tiny word: "No. No no. No-no-no-no-no-no."

I had never been in a car accident. Not even a fender bender. Dad had been teaching me defensive driving skills when other parents were trying to get their kids to ride a bike.

I'd hit a car.

My hands fumbled over the still lava-hot buckle as I hopped down from the truck and went to survey the damage and face the woman standing next to the vehicle I'd hit.

I heard myself saying the same asinine excuses that people told us when they brought their smashed cars in. What else could I say? I absolutely saw your car but I decided to back into it anyway? I think I gave her a card and I mentioned that I was a mechanic and could fix the—thankfully—minor damage, but I hadn't yet gotten past the fact that I'd just zipped down my driveway and plowed right into the car parking in front of Daniel's house.

I broke off midthought and stared.

The woman looked to be in her mid-to late-forties, slim and several inches shorter than me, with dark hair pulled back into a tight bun revealing a scar along her temple that disappeared into her hairline. The same eyes. The same coloring.

"You're Daniel's mom."

I'd been picturing a different woman, hollow but imposing. Ugly in a way that fit the kind of mother she was. The way my mom should have looked but didn't. Daniel's mom was all wrong too. She was slight, with delicate features and skin that might have been beautiful underneath all the heavy makeup she wore. I thought of Daniel's scars; Daniel who was big enough to avoid getting hit in the face, and the petite woman in front of me.

My insides cramped with the emotions pulling at me. I had noticed how stiffly she was moving, the bulky shape to her clothes, like she might be wearing a brace underneath. And all that heavy, concealing makeup.

But sharper than the almost overwhelming pity I felt for her was the cold knowledge that she hadn't protected her son. The memories of scars, deep and old, the ones that stretched as he grew from a little boy to a man, bombarded me. Savage, vicious, relentless. How do you survive something like that? How do you survive being rejected over and over again by the person you tried to protect? Were still trying to protect?

I had to get away before I got back in my truck and flattened her car to the ground.

"You know Daniel?"

Her voice was deep and unnaturally raspy—I immediately envisioned thick fingers wrapped around her throat, squeezing and damaging the vocal cords. Horrible. But not worse than what had happened to Daniel. A child.

I tried not to run back to my truck but the urge was almost too strong. "I fixed his Jeep. I can fix your car. Just bring it in. I'm sorry, I have to go." I yanked open my door.

There was a harsh, hoarse sound that stopped me. I didn't

realize it was laughter until I saw her face. Her eyeliner was cinched tight around her eyes and one eyelid was drooped in a way that prevented it from blinking normally. They narrowed at me.

"Whatever he told you, he's a liar."

I didn't slam my door. I pressed it closed until the latch caught. The woman behind me wasn't my mom. I didn't feel the same paralyzing urge to hide when confronted with her. My feelings were much more violent, and I let them heat my words when I turned to her.

"I don't know you. I don't even really know your son. But I saw his body and I can see what you're trying to hide on yours. I don't think he's the liar."

This tiny, frail-looking woman, the kind who made you want to protect her on sight, scanned me from head to toe. She had a smile that was almost as beautiful as my mom's. "What are you, fifteen? I guess he'll end up in prison anyway."

Her parting words and the soul-sucking heat left me wilted inside and out by the time I pulled in to the church, the same one my parents had been married in. The building itself was one of those older styles, crisp white with a steeple and a bell that rang when services were about to start. It was ringing as I hurried inside and almost ran into a woman with fiery red hair and dimples that matched her son's.

"Oh, no. Sweetie, you got roasted, didn't you?"

Sean's mom, Mrs. Addison, stopped seconds before pulling me into a hug. "Well, I can't even touch you, can I?"

"I'd rather you didn't," I said, feeling worse because Mrs. Addison always hugged me like I was her favorite person in the world. She was easily one of mine. My misery increased when I caught myself looking past her for Sean, knowing he had to be nearby.

She clucked her tongue. "What do you have against sunblock?"

"I put it on, I swear, but it must have washed off."

"Oh, honey." Mrs. Addison stroked her hand over my hair. I almost asked her to stop. It felt too nice, too much like a mom. A real one. Not the mockery that Daniel had or the pathetic excuse mine was.

She asked about Dad and I told her about the car auction, starting every time someone new came around the corner. Mrs. Addison's expression softened.

"You want me to find him for you?"

If I could have turned redder I would have, but I didn't feign ignorance, not with Sean's mom. "No, that's okay."

"So you're all alone? You can always come stay with us. Sean loves sleeping on the couch."

Sean hated that couch almost as much as he hated cross-country, but as the youngest Addison, he always had to give up his room when they had company. He'd do it for me, but I could barely sleep in my own house—sharing one with Sean would be a million times worse. Sliding past him in the hallways, catching him fresh from the shower with his hair still damp, getting squished together on a sofa while his brothers crowded in on either side...

No.

On top of that, I didn't think I could take much more of the attention Mrs. Addison would lavish on me. It couldn't be good for me, like the way they don't let dehydrated people chug a ton of water at first or they'd throw up.

"No, I don't—"

"Rick," she called over my shoulder. "Jill's coming home

with us for the night. Look." She turned me around to face her husband. "She's a roasted orphan until tomorrow."

Mr. Addison looked down at me. "What do you have against sunblock?"

I opened my mouth to explain then shut it with a sigh. "Really, I'm fine. It's one more night. But thank you." I smiled back and forth between the two of them and tried to look like I wasn't in pain. I showed all my teeth.

"You're sure?" Mrs. Addison was searching my face, her expression so full of concern and...something else that hit me right in the gut. It was the polar opposite of the expression I'd seen on Daniel's mom. One my own mom hadn't worn in a long time.

A little girl darted from behind me and I couldn't keep from wincing as she brushed my legs. And then I winced again remembering. "I'm supposed to help in the nursery."

Mrs. Addison shook her head. "No, you're going home to soak in a nice baking soda bath. I'll fill in for you. Do you want Rick to drive you? Or..." She looked to her husband and then nodded her head toward the sanctuary. "Rick, go get Sean."

"No!" They both turned at my outburst. "I don't need a ride. I will go home though. If you don't mind the nursery."

"It's already done. You go on. And come over later if you feel better or you want to feel better." Then she kissed my cheek. It hurt. It was also the best thing I'd felt in way too long.

Before Mrs. Addison could change her mind and insist that some member of her family drive me home, I bolted for the parking lot.

The truck felt even hotter driving home. By the time I pulled in to my garage, I was so miserable that I missed seeing the new car parked out front.

I gingerly climbed out of the truck, choked in a lungful of sweltering air, and was about to close the garage when someone called my name.

"Jill?"

It was a testimony to how completely awful I felt that I didn't immediately recognize her voice. I turned around and saw her close her car door and walk toward me, lovely as ever in a dark red wrap dress with her rich brown hair falling in waves down her back.

"Mom?"

CHAPTER
25

I took two steps toward her before I realized what I was doing and forced my legs to stop. Either Mom didn't notice or she chose to ignore the fact that I wasn't going to meet her halfway.

She crossed into the shade of the garage and stopped a few feet from me. Her big brown eyes filled with tears as she looked at me. "Jill…"

She was going to hug me. Pull me close to her and wrap her arms around me. I made a noise and stepped back.

I hadn't seen Mom in months. Hadn't heard a single word from her all summer. Nothing. It was like she had died. Or I had.

Despite everything, it was harder than I'd expected not to go to her. I wanted her to hold me. I wanted it bad enough that I could already see myself swaying toward her.

I started to shove all the hurt out of my head. I wanted it to be like it was, before the fighting, before she did what she did, before she left. But it could never be like that.

"No, don't," I said. "I… I got sunburned yesterday."

She lowered her arms in jerky movements, like it hurt her not to hug me as much as it would have hurt me to let her. I saw her take note of my red skin, and she nodded. "Oh, honey." Her words were the same as Sean's mom. The concern in her voice almost sounded the same too. "With your skin, you have to be really careful in the sun."

I nodded like she hadn't told me that a million times. It was so easy to slip back into the way things were, to pretend like the last months hadn't happened. Much longer than that, really.

"Did you put aloe vera on?"

I nodded again.

"What about vitamin E?"

"I just used aloe."

"I think I left a bottle under the sink in my bathroom." She took my hand and we started to go inside.

I followed along for a step or two before reality sank in again. "M-Mom…why are you here?"

"Didn't you know I called?"

I did the nodding thing again. Standing that close to her, I was finding it difficult to string more than a few words together. "But why?"

She led me back so that we were both leaning against the truck, then realized she was still holding my hand and let it go. "I've missed you. I hear you've been running?"

Cue the nodding from me.

She smiled. She was so beautiful. A lot of people think their moms are beautiful, but mine really was.

We went to the grocery store one time after she'd been sick with the flu. Even with unwashed hair, no makeup and a sickly cast to her skin, the bag boys fairly fought over themselves to see who would help carry our half-full bag of groceries to the car.

I'd kind of gotten used to it, in the way people got used to seeing the Grand Canyon. Even when you saw it every day, it was still the Grand Canyon.

"You look wonderful. Not an ounce of baby fat." Her eyes danced over my face much in the same way I knew mine were dancing over hers. "Oh, I wanted to show you!"

She reached into her purse and pulled out something small and shiny. "I got a new cell phone. It does a million things that I don't understand, but I know how to answer it when it rings." She laughed, then reached around me and found my phone in my bag. I watched as she added her number to my contacts. "There." She slipped it back in my bag. "Now you can call me whenever you want."

Whenever I wanted.

After a moment she said, "Anything else happen while I was gone? You didn't get a tattoo, did you?" She bumped my shoulder with hers while she spoke, as if instead of leaving Dad and abandoning me, she'd gone on some kind of trip and now that she was back, everything could go back to normal. Except normal didn't exist anymore.

And just like that, the spell of her being there again was broken.

"Don't. Don't do that."

"Don't do what?" Her smile was bright.

"Don't act like nothing happened."

Her smile faded but she tried again. "You're right. We've got a lot of catching up to do. I want to hear all about your summer."

Part of me wished I could pretend the way she did. Life would be so much easier if you could just wave away the parts you didn't like with a toss of your hair.

"So much has happened."

"Oh, just start at the beginning, then. And don't leave

anything out." She scooted closer to me and I could feel her happiness radiating from her like the heat from the still warm engine beneath me.

I counted the seconds it took for her happiness to wither once I started talking. It took two.

"The night after you left Dad sat up until morning. I know because I heard him calling your cell phone over and over— the one you deactivated." I watched her smile completely die before I continued. "I don't think either one of us spoke for an entire week except to answer the phone."

"That's enough." Her voice was low and firm, mine was calm and almost dreamlike.

"Why? You wanted to know what I've been doing all summer. I'm telling you. I wasn't home when Aunt Jodi picked up the rest of your stuff, but I could tell just looking at Dad's face the day she came."

"Stop it, Jill."

"He didn't cry anymore after that."

"I said stop it!"

"Why? That's what happened. You should know what you did." My calm snapped and I pushed away from the truck and spun to face her. "Why didn't you ever come see me? You never even called me."

"I wanted to call, wanted to come see you, but I couldn't."

I was nodding like an idiot and trying not to cry. I wrapped my arms around myself and held them there even though the movement pulled on my skin and hurt.

"I tried, Jill. I tried for so long. Your dad, he's not the easiest person to love."

Wrong. It was all wrong. Everything she was saying. "He's the easiest person on earth to love."

Her smile was patronizing. "I'm glad you see him that way, I really am." She took in my sweat-drenched appearance and fanned herself with her hand. "Come on." She held her hand out to me. "Let's go inside. If I'm this hot I can't imagine what the heat is doing to your sunburn."

It hurt. A lot. But not more than the idea of her in our house. Dad's and mine. She didn't belong there anymore. "I'm fine."

"You don't have to be brave for me. You'll feel better once you've cooled down. I'll even make you a smoothie, hmm? Strawberry and banana."

Strawberry and banana was my favorite. Had been since I was little. It was Dad's favorite too. "No. I don't want you inside."

That stopped her. "Jill." There was hurt in her voice. Reproach.

I felt the old inclination to obey, to cave. She was still my mom. But she was the mom who left me. In my mind, she'd abdicated her role long ago. I didn't owe her anything anymore. Not obedience, not respect, not love.

"You won't be here much longer," I said. "Just tell me what you came here for and you can get back into your air-conditioned car and leave."

"Jill!" That was about as speechless as Mom was ever rendered and I reveled in it.

"Mom!" My tone was mocking and her face crumbled before smoothing out again.

"Do you hate me so much now?"

"No." I shook my head and shrugged my shoulders. My voice was even, blasé, like I was giving my opinion on the merits of one ice cream flavor over another. "I don't hate you. I don't anything you."

I could almost see inside her head, see her realize she was losing control of the situation. So she went straight for the kill.

"I didn't want any of this. Leaving was the hardest thing I've ever done."

"Yeah, you seemed real broken up about it in the Post-it note you left."

I'd meant to hurt her with my words. Spark some semblance of remorse from her with the memory, or at least relieve some of the pressure in my chest. But she didn't react at all the way I wanted. Instead of being cowed, she advanced on me.

"I couldn't stay any longer. I was suffocating. You can't know what that felt like."

I wanted to laugh at her audacity.

"I was unhappy."

"And now you're happy? Good. Because Dad and I aren't. I'd hate to think you did this to us and got nothing for yourself in return." I was breathing heavily. Sweat was dripping off my face and my fingers were digging into my arms so hard that the skin was turning white at the edges. Painful as this situation was, I was glad to finally be telling her this. I couldn't unload on Dad. He was dealing with his own pain. And he didn't even know about Sean. But I could let it out on her. Every last vestige of hurt. She should know exactly what her happiness cost.

But instead of answering me, she pulled back. "Maybe this is a bad time. I should come back later."

She was so predictable. She wasn't happy in her marriage, so she left. I was making her feel uncomfortable, and once again she wanted to leave. Why actually deal with something when you could run away from it?

I hated that I'd learned that from her.

"No, trust me, your timing is perfect." And it was, in a sadistic sort of way. My sunburn felt unbelievably bad and it had been just hours since my first vomit-laced kiss from a guy I had started to dream about.

"I didn't want to hurt anyone," she said. "That was the last thing I wanted."

"What did you want?"

"I wanted a chance to be me. Not someone's wife, or someone's mother, but just me, just Katheryn."

She hadn't even been looking at me when she spoke, more just staring off at…something. Her dreams? I didn't know and I so didn't care. And that was fine. All of it. The sunburn would fade and peel away. Daniel and I were done before we even started. And Mom? She was going to do exactly what she wanted anyway.

"Oh, Jill. Sometimes you have to put yourself first." She put her hand on my arm and squeezed.

I was glad for the pain it caused.

"Sometimes?" I almost didn't have the energy to tell her how full of it she was. Almost. "That's all you ever did! You put your happiness, your life above everyone else's. You took everything you ever wanted! Even if it was mine!" My vision blurred for a moment and I shook my head to fling all those memories away.

My voice dropped to a low hiss. "You broke Dad. Do you know that? You broke the man who loved you, who would have done anything for you, for your happiness. You threw him away. You threw me away. I cannot imagine a more selfish, heartless person than you, *Katheryn*."

She was crying in that pretty way of hers, the one that made people want to comfort her, but I didn't care.

"I'm tired and I'm hot and I don't have anything else to say to you. Tell me what it is you want, then get out of my house."

She cried some more, but it didn't touch me. I'd seen Dad cry. Her tears were nothing in comparison.

Finally she sniffed. "I was hoping you'd have forgiven me."

"Why? You never apologized."

She shook her head and blotted the tears from her cheeks, careful not to smear her mascara. "I can't apologize for leaving, Jill. It was the right thing for me."

"And Sean?" Every part of me shook. "Was that the right thing for you too?"

CHAPTER
26

I scrutinized every minute detail of her face when I said Sean's name. I think I might have eased up if I'd seen a flicker of remorse, a tiny movement of her eyes that indicated that she understood how much she'd hurt me. But she batted my words away like a fly buzzing around her head.

"That was nothing. You know how Sean is."

All that I had left for her, the tiniest speck of an ember of affection, snuffed out.

I wanted to slap the pitying smile off her face. I wanted to scream and rage at her. I wanted to be frightening.

I wasn't.

I was small and weak. I curled in on myself and I cried for so many things. "I loved him. You knew I loved him." Through tear-blurred eyes I saw her move and then she ran her hand over my hair, petting me.

"I know, sweetie. I know."

I lowered her hand but kept my fingers locked around her wrist. "What's wrong with you? Why don't you understand that this is your fault? What you did to Dad, to me, to Sean, was wrong. You ruined us. You broke everything and you will never put it back together. Never."

I made it to the door before she stopped me, sounding much more composed than she should have, given the distraught show she'd just put on.

"Jill." She barked my name like I was in trouble. "I understand that you're angry. You're a teenager, you're supposed to be angry. And I'm your mother, so I guess I get to bear the brunt of it. I was hoping that you'd use this time we spent apart to figure out a few things, to understand me better and why things—" she made a gesture in the air "—happened the way they did. I'd hoped that we could move past this, but I can see that I was being overly optimistic."

Standing across from her in the sauna that was my garage, I looked at my mom, really looked at her. She hadn't come to me with tears of remorse and pleading words of forgiveness on her lips. She hadn't come with concern or contrition for what Dad and I had been through since she left. She hadn't come with any kind of admission of wrongdoing on her part. She wanted something from me, that was all. There was no way she'd be standing in my sweltering garage as she bypassed "glowing" and went straight to sweating otherwise.

"I need you to know that I'm not the bad guy here. I'm really not." She was babbling, her words tumbling out over top of each other.

I didn't bother asking that, if she wasn't the bad guy, who did she cast in that role? Dad? Me?

"I don't want you to hate me. That's all. I am your mom," she said. "Me, I'm the one who gave birth to you!"

This was a side of Mom I'd never seen before. She kept reaching for me, her voice breaking when I wouldn't let her touch me. She was actually wringing her hands. If I cared, I might have been concerned.

"I told you I don't hate you."

"Right, you don't anything me." She made a choked laughing noise that sounded painful. "But that's not fair. I don't deserve your antipathy. I really don't."

She was starting to freak me out. Was she sick? Was she going to ask me for a kidney or something? "Okay, tell me what you do deserve."

"I don't know. But not this hostility. You've always been Daddy's little girl. The two of you from the beginning. He never gave me a chance..."

Up until that point she'd been fidgeting and biting her lip the way I did sometimes. I don't know what happened between one word and the next, but she stopped all of it.

"I really hate him for that."

Goose bumps broke out on my arms when she said that. She was taking her time talking. I wanted her to get it over with. Tell me whatever horrible thing she wanted that had upset Dad so much. I had a momentary flare of panic that pushed the pain of my sunburn and the still stinging memory of Sean aside: maybe it was a custody issue after all. Maybe she was going to ask me to come live with her.

I was breathing faster, panting almost, as I waited for her to say it, hot, dry air filling and leaving my lungs with greater and greater speed. I would never leave Dad. She had to know that. I'd resort to something truly childish like running away before I'd let her take me from him. I'd get a job somewhere, hide out until I turned eighteen. Maybe I could still take Daniel up on his offer to drive to Mexico.

Suddenly she was standing right in front of me, close enough that I could smell her cinnamon-scented perfume. It tickled my nose and I started to back away, but she grabbed my hands and curled them in hers. She was completely calm. "I want you to come live with me."

Live with me. Hearing them out loud, those three words stole my breath. "No." I pulled my hands from her. "No."

She reached for me again. "But I'm your mom. You belong with me."

"No. I belong with Dad. You left us."

"I needed time, Jill." Every step I retreated, she advanced. "I needed to figure out what I wanted."

"And what? You want me now? Why?" My chin quivered. "I'm horrible now!"

"I want us to be a family again." She stopped and I was halfway around the truck again before I did too. She shook her hair back from her face in a motion that was graceful in a way I'd never be, and smoothed out her dress. "I wanted to tell you this under different circumstances, but..." This was the only chance she was going to get and we both knew it. "I'm getting married."

My eyes dropped to her left hand, and the diamond was so blinding I couldn't fathom how I missed it. Dad had never been able to give her a diamond. Her ring from him had been a pearl. I'd always thought it looked like the moon; it was so perfect it glowed. Who could want a diamond over that?

"You are such a hypocrite. What happened to being 'just Katheryn'?"

She frowned at me.

"That speech you gave not five minutes ago about needing to be you, not someone's wife." *Not someone's mother.*

Another frown. "Jeff is very different from your dad."

"I'll bet he is."

"Please, Jill. We can start over. If you just gave me a chance, Jeff and I, we want you to come live with us."

I bent over a little and steadied myself with a hand on the truck. "When did you meet him?" I didn't really need her to answer. I knew it had to have been before she left. Maybe her leaving hadn't been about me catching her with Sean at all. Her hesitation confirmed it.

"It happened so fast. I wasn't expecting to fall in love."

"It must have been really inconvenient, what with you already being married!" I let my voice grow louder with each word until I was practically shouting. "Jeff? Is that his name?" I didn't care what happened with her new husband, and I told her that in the crudest way possible. By then it wasn't just sweat that was dripping down my face. "Does he know about Sean? What you tried to do with your teenage daughter's friend?"

Mom's spine snapped straight and her voice lowered. "I don't know what you think you mean by that, but we both know Sean is a flirt, maybe I let him get carried away that night, but it's an ugly thing for you to insinuate anything more than that." She exhaled and placed a hand over her heart. "What happened to you? You never used to behave like this. It's cruel, Jill."

My head was going to explode. "*You* happened. You." Then, like a child, I started to whine. "Just go. Can't you just go? You and Jeff can start a new family somewhere and leave us alone…just go…please."

But she didn't. She walked over to me and looked at me with her golden-brown eyes that I'd envied all my life. "Don't cry. I'm here now. We'll get past this. I'm not going to leave ever again."

I dropped my head and let out a sob. "Why are you doing this? Don't you get that I don't want you here?"

"I think it's for the best. I told all this to your dad."

Yeah. I remembered that conversation. "You're insane if you think I would leave Dad." My tears had stopped, or more likely they'd just evaporated in the heat. I stood there like a statue while she smoothed my hair off my forehead, going back to grab a strand that was stuck with sweat to my skin.

"And you'd choose him over me?"

"Every time," I said, with as much force as possible. And then I saw her swallow.

"Even if he's not your father?"

CHAPTER
27

There was an accident at the shop a few years ago. A 2003 Chevy hatchback crashed down onto my foot when the lift malfunctioned.

I remembered the pain. The way it throbbed up my leg like a jackhammer, like an animal crunching and grinding the bones between its teeth. It wasn't the kind of pain that burst sharp like a firework only to fade away. It consumed and fed on itself, expanding and increasing beyond words like *agony* or *torture*, like it was the only thing that had ever existed and it was eternal.

Only it wasn't. The memory conjured only a shadow of the pain. It didn't seem real, like a dream that slipped away faster and faster the more you tried to grasp it. Pain.

But I had never hurt the way I did when Mom loosed her soft, poisonous words. I could feel them spreading venom through my chest, my heart beating them in burning pulses to my arms, legs, hands, feet.

"Liar."

When did I sit down? My palm rested on the oily brown

stain that spread across the concrete beneath me like a puddle of filth.

She sat down next to me. She ruined her dress. And she was holding me, rocking me. And I let her.

She wouldn't let me go when I tried to get away. When she told me about the neighbor right after she and Dad got married.

I threw up when she told me that I had his eyes.

Nothing was real after that. Not Mom cleaning up my sick or me letting her go inside without a word of protest and accepting the ginger ale she brought back. Not her soft lips on my cheek or her words—no longer poisonous—that she was going to give me some time.

Then there was only the sound of her heels clacking against the concrete, growing quieter as she left.

I don't know how many hours I sat like that.

My eyes were dry when I opened them, when I pushed up from the filthy floor and went inside. The pantry door was open. Soup cans and boxes of pasta were scattered on one shelf. My bag of half-eaten Fruity O's was lying on another next to a jug of laundry detergent and a couple rolls of duct tape. And next to that was a little box of baking soda.

I snatched it from the shelf and headed for the bathroom. The master bathroom. The one I'd helped Dad fix as a surprise for Mom when we moved in. I ran my fingertips across the creamy countertop and up the periwinkle walls.

I sat on the closed toilet sprinkling baking soda into the tub as the faucet gushed warm water. I slid off my dress and lowered myself into the water until only my nose and the top of my head were exposed. The tub was big enough that I could extend my legs completely, my toes tipping forward to rest on the far end.

I inhaled deeply and sank under the water.

No sound. No light. With the water all around me, I was floating and felt almost nothing. The water was opaque from the soda. I felt like I was in a cloud. All white and fluffy and weightless. I couldn't see any of the purple-blue paint that I'd helped roll on the walls. I wished I could stay like that forever. No pain. No nothing. Just warm and peaceful.

Even as I formed the thoughts, the pressure of my filled lungs began to build. I tried and failed to keep a bubble from escaping my lips.

Then another.

And another.

The pressure ebbed, but even that respite was brief. As soon as my lungs deflated, they ached to be filled. I sank farther down. I wasn't ready to leave that all-encompassing warmth.

I thought of the little girl who used to live behind us in our old house. Her name was something like Angie or Angel. I don't remember, because her family lived there for only a month. Less than.

I think she was four when she drowned in their pool.

I was only a few years older, but I remember my parents being really upset about it and enrolling me in swimming lessons soon after, even though I already knew how to swim. And when I finished, Dad still wouldn't let me swim in our pool by myself. Ever. I never minded, because I always had more fun swimming with him anyway. Mom never once went swimming with us. Something about the chlorine bothering her.

I used to wonder about Angie or Angel and what it felt like to drown. I'd try and hold my breath underwater as long as possible and imagine breathing in water instead of air. Not like when you choke while drinking something, but actually breathing water. Before it killed you, wouldn't it feel nice? Like this same warm floating feeling of being suspended in a tub, but on the inside too? I'd never wanted to find out before.

I thought about it then. Not the drowning and dying part, not really, but the oblivion? I thought about that.

I wouldn't be able to hold my breath much longer. Already it felt like I'd lived an entire lifetime without air. I wasn't scared. The tub was long but not especially deep. Only inches separated my mouth from the surface. I could reach it in less than a second if I wanted to. But right then, I wanted the warmth more than I wanted the air. I wanted it so much that I opened my lips—not letting the water do more than bathe my tongue, my teeth, my mouth. I wondered.

I sat up suddenly, gulping air into my lungs, my legs bent up tight to my chest and my cheek resting on my knees.

Breath after breath after breath.

I stayed like that in the tub long after the warmth left the water. Long after my fingers and toes went pruney. Long after the skylight showed that the sun had set and the bathroom became dark, too dark to tell what color was on the walls.

CHAPTER
28

Dad never let me turn the thermostat down past 79 degrees, but even with the heat pressing in from outside, I still shivered when I got out of the tub. I stood up and took Dad's old gray bathrobe off the hook. Technically, it was my robe since I'd bought him a new one last Christmas, but in my head it would always be his. I'd washed it half a million times so it was wearing thin in places, but it was also the softest fabric on the planet. Every time I slipped it on I felt nothing but a whisper drifting over my skin.

It couldn't be true. It couldn't.

She was a liar.

There was no way. I would have known. Dad would have known. He'd never have endured everything she put him through if it were true. If I weren't his. He could never love me the way he did if I was the result of her cheating. And he did love me.

I spun to the mirror and I searched for him. For Dad.

You have his eyes.

My eyes were greenish-brown. Dad's were blue. But his father's were green.

She was a liar.

Of course I would look more like her, I was a girl. But he had to be there too. I just had to look hard enough.

Something sharp bored through my heart.

Dad and I were the same. We were so much the same. I'd believe I wasn't hers, but I'd never believe I wasn't his.

She was a liar.

Walking made me realize that my sunburn overall felt better, like my skin was only one size too small instead of the ten sizes too small from that morning. In my room I pulled on a pair of drawstring pants and a T-shirt. I started to leave, then slipped Dad's damp robe back on. Better.

When I heard knocking on my front door I almost jumped out of my skin. I stood in the hallway staring at it like a bomb was on the other side. Or Mom.

Knock. Knock. Knock.

Tick. Tick. Tick.

"Yo, Whitaker!"

"Sean?" My legs went all rubbery in relief.

He looked up as soon as I opened the door, smiling at me like he'd been waiting all day to see me, sunburn and all. "Hey. Heard you weren't feeling great." He shifted a brown paper bag in front of him. "Brought you something that might help."

I ignored the bag. For one moment I ignored everything except for the fact that he was there. I stepped out the door and hugged him. I didn't know who was more surprised.

Sean's breath stirred my hair as he brought his arms up around me. "Hello to you too." He voice was low and soft, caressing. "Tell me this isn't 'cause you're on a bunch of painkillers?"

I shook my head into his chest, knowing the respite from

reality wouldn't last, not after Mom. Not after those old wounds had been reopened, leaving me raw and exposed.

I let Sean get carried away.

And that quickly, I remembered that Sean was salt.

I pulled away just as suddenly as I'd gone to him. After everything that had happened that day, I felt like a wrung-out towel, lacking the energy to force him to leave or confront him the way I had Mom. I pushed my hair back, knowing I'd have to say something, but the action exposed my sunburned arms as the oversize sleeves of my robe slid back.

With less hesitation than I'd hugged him with, Sean reached for me, gently squeezing my forearm and letting go to watch white finger marks appear and then get taken back over by my lobster skin. "Ouch."

Something pricked my eyes as I stared at him. I could only nod. I took in his appearance for the first time, the crisp white shirt and dark jeans, the way his messy, haphazard hair looked slightly less messy and haphazard. The part of my heart that I hadn't been able to wrangle away from him caught in my throat.

He saw my gaze trail over him. "I was at my grandmother's. It makes her happy when I dress up a little. She says I'm starting to look like my grandfather." He shrugged but flushed slightly. Sean idolized his grandfather, a firefighter who died before he was born. I'd seen pictures before and there was a resemblance.

Because it would make him happy to hear it, I said, "You do look like him."

Another shrug from Sean, but he played it off with a smile. "Enough about how amazing I look. Let's talk about how *you* look this good after getting deep-fried."

I swallowed my heart back after that, not wanting his

empty compliments any more than I wanted genuine ones. "Don't, Sean." I turned and he followed me inside.

Sean's smile slid away, as though he couldn't tell if I was being serious or not. "I can't notice you look good? Since when?"

I hesitated for the tiniest moment. "You know exactly when."

The muscle in Sean's cheek twitched as his jaw locked.

"Besides, aren't you dating Cami now or something?"

Sean looked at me like I'd just grown a third eye. "What? *No.* Why would you think that?"

"Oh, please."

"I'm serious. I'm not dating Cami or anyone else. I told you that when we ran into her in the parking lot weeks ago."

An ugly response was on the tip of my tongue, but I held it. "Maybe you should tell Cami that."

Sean moved in front of me, cutting off my retreat to the living room. "I did. We talked after we all went to the movies. She is one hundred percent clear on me only wanting to be her friend." His voice slowed. "I know what I want and it's not Cami."

If there was suddenly a Spitfire behind Sean and he was offering me the keys, I'd swear I'd somehow slipped back into my dream from months ago, only this felt more like a nightmare.

I slid back a step. A small step, but it was enough. "Whatever it is you're doing, stop. You have no idea how bad your timing is. I couldn't be nice right now if I tried, and I don't feel like trying."

The longest silence in the history of Jill and Sean stretched between us. And I didn't know how to fill it.

He crossed to lean against the wall opposite me, but kept his gaze on me. The brown paper bag he held crinkled at the movement, distracting us both. "Oh, here. My mom sent this." He passed it to me. Inside was a box of baking soda and what looked like a container of homemade soup. There was a little Post-it note stuck on the lid.

Split lentil. Feel better, sweetie. —Mrs. A.

The garlic and onion scent drifted up from the bag, and I imagined Mrs. Addison dicing up vegetables and adding herbs, then holding out a wooden spoon for whichever one of her kids was closest for a taste test. None of them liked split lentil, but Sean must have told her it was my favorite.

I pulled the note free, and I started to cry.

I was dimly aware of Sean prying the bag from my hands and looking inside, frowning when he couldn't spot anything obviously traumatizing, then abandoning the bag entirely when I started to curl in on myself.

Standing wasn't worth the effort, so I sank down to the floor. Sean's warmth seeped into me as he followed me down, and when I didn't move away, he gathered me in his arms. It felt so good to let him hold me. Good enough to ignore all the reasons I shouldn't let him. I could barely remember the last time he'd just held me without anything messed up between us.

His mom made him hug me at his eighth birthday party when I'd wanted to leave because no other girls had shown up.

When we were in fourth grade, I twisted my ankle at the park by my house. It was getting dark and I freaked out when Sean mentioned going for help. So he stayed. It was three blocks to my house, and he ended up carrying me the whole way. He never once complained about getting tired, although I'm pretty sure I outweighed him back then.

The last time was when we danced together at his oldest brother's wedding that past November. We didn't know how to waltz, so we mostly just tried not to step on each other's feet, laughing off disapproving looks from his stodgier relatives until the song ended.

I was so in love with him then.

I kept my eyes shut and tried to soak in the comfort from his body. So much better than a bath.

When I ran out of tears, Sean tugged up the bottom of his shirt to dry my cheeks. The gesture could have been awkward, or even comical, but it was neither of those things. It made me look into his eyes, pleading silently before I could find words. "How can we be like this? How can we still be friends?"

I jumped when Sean found my hand, tugged it into his lap, and trapped it between both of his.

"How can we not?"

I shook my head.

"My mom has pictures of us playing T-ball together." He moved one hand to the soft skin inside of my wrist. "Those pegs on the back of my old bike? I got them so I could give you rides home from school back in elementary school. Jill, you used to pee in my pool and I still wanted to swim with you more than anybody else."

I twitched when he began tracing my veins with his fingertips. "We both used to pee in your pool."

"A lot of people did, but I still liked you the best."

"You like everyone, Sean." My voice cracked. "Everyone."

"No," he said. "I don't. Some people I've never liked."

Why was it so hard? Why couldn't I just say it? I stared at him, but he wouldn't look at me. I imagined the words passing through my lips. I imagined him finally hearing them and then…

I couldn't imagine an answer that didn't end us.

I tried blinking rapidly, but two fat tears spilled over onto my cheeks. "I saw my mom today."

Sean squeezed my hand like he was trying to keep something from tearing me away.

And that's when I heard myself tell him about her wanting me to come live with her.

About her saying my dad wasn't my dad.

We were going for our second record of silence when the doorbell rang.

There was a moment of unspoken communication between us where we both had the same fear—my mom—and reacted in wildly different ways. I shot to my feet. Sean rose up almost in slow motion and backed up at the same speed.

"Leave it," he said.

But I was already peering through the peephole.

Mom wasn't standing on my porch.

Daniel was.

CHAPTER 29

I think I hated everyone on the planet as I curled my fingers around the doorknob. I hated the obvious people for the obvious reasons and the not-obvious people for reasons that slapped around inside of me.

I hated Mom for being my mom and for never being a wife to Dad. I hated Dad for marrying her. For every year of our lives that he wasted on her. For making me doubt the only thing that mattered. I'd hate him forever if it was true.

I was so tired of hating and loving and still hating Sean. I hated that he made it hard to hate him when I should. I hated the most that he brought me soup. That he didn't want Cami. That he'd been looking at me in the wrong-stupid-too-late way.

I even hated Claire. My outsides hurt almost as much as my insides because of her.

I hated Mrs. Addison for not being mine.

I hated Daniel's mom for being worse than mine.

I hated Daniel for not kissing me when he should have

and for kissing me when he shouldn't have and leaving a bitter taste in my mouth. Literally.

I half opened the door, hating both of us for making me think that fixing him would fix me.

Glancing behind me, I gave Sean the slightest shake of my head—it wasn't my mom on the porch—and watched the tight coil of his muscles release. He ran both hands through his hair and walked off into the kitchen.

One down.

"Your dad?" Daniel asked.

"Sean."

Daniel's face contorted into something painful as he looked at me, all of me, but the expression flickered like a lightbulb burning out. "Look at you."

I could only imagine what he saw. Red, puffy skin. Even redder, puffier eyes. It was as obvious that I'd been crying as it was that he was hungover.

"Yeah, well, it's been a sucky weekend."

"I'm sorry. I'm sorry." He was backing up as he spoke, turning away as the litany continued.

My apology. There it was. Sort of. The hateful part of me wanted to let him go, wanted to let him head home to drown in his own self-loathing—his expression promised as much. But Daniel hadn't given me nearly enough fuel to feed the hatred Mom had ignited and so many others had stoked. Because I didn't really hate him. And for that reason and a lot of others, I couldn't be responsible for hurting him, even after he'd hurt me.

"Daniel, wait." I stepped closer, pulling the door with me so I was half-outside, and lowered my voice. "Stop, okay? This." I looked down as I waved a hand toward my tearstained cheeks. "It's not about last night. It's not about you." And saying it, I realized that I'd barely thought about him all day.

"Why are you so good to me?" His chin locked tight. "Why? You shouldn't be. I never gave you a reason, not from that very first night. Never."

"Because you and I know it's not about reasons." Why did saying that make me want to cry again?

He didn't say anything, but he looked like I'd hit him somehow.

"Am I supposed to say sorry?" I went on. "I don't know what you want from me."

His head snapped up. "You're supposed to leave me alone. Don't help me. Don't be nice to me. Don't—"

"So I should have left you on the side of the road when you were too drunk to walk?"

Daniel was inches from my face then, and the low volume of his voice in no way mitigated the force behind it. "Yes."

I blinked at him because part of what he was saying was right. I needed to stop trying to help him. There was a line that I shouldn't be crossing—*we* shouldn't be crossing. The world went on around us; hiding up on my roof didn't make things better for either of us. In a lot of ways it was making things worse; last night had proved that. Last night... I looked away from Daniel, wrapping one arm around myself, and wished for...things to be different.

"Jill." The way his voice broke forced me to meet his eye. "Touching you like that when I was drunk..." He was close enough to touch me. Which he did, grazing my forearm with his fingers. His hand moved and hovered just over my lip. "I should have stopped when you told me to. Maybe I wouldn't have hurt you."

I doubted that last drink I'd tried to stop him from having in his kitchen had done much. "Maybe," I whispered, watching Daniel step back and hang his head.

He never saw Sean wrench the door from my hands, moving faster than any warning I could give. I glimpsed Sean's eyes, so wide there was a complete ring of white around his irises, a heartbeat before his fist slammed into Daniel's face.

It happened fast, not like in the movies where the camera pans to each person for that perfect reaction shot to draw out the moment of each hit. There was no slap or cracking as fists hit. Nothing but sneakers skidding on the concrete, grunts and the sound pain makes when mingled with breath. And Sean's spit leaving his mouth. Spit and blood.

I never thought I'd be the kind of person to freeze in a fight, to stand still like a helpless spectator, but I was; I did. Until Sean hit the ground.

And then came the sound. The crunch of Sean's nose breaking from Daniel's fist as he followed him down. And me screaming.

"Stop! Stop! *Stop!*"

I didn't think about Daniel in that moment—what must have been going through his mind, being attacked like that— or even register the trickle of red at the corner of his mouth. All I saw was Sean on the ground and the blood pouring from his nose…soaking into the fabric of his shirt. And Daniel rearing back to strike again.

I collided with Daniel before he could hit Sean again. He jerked free, leaving me to drop to my knees next to Sean. I dived at Daniel again. "Get off him!"

I don't know if it was the phrase, so similar to the one I'd used last night on his couch, or the sight of Sean jerking up and putting himself between us, but Daniel froze.

He took in the blood smeared on his hands, Sean with a protective arm thrown out across me, and something like horror touched his eyes. The muscles in his cheek twitched and he stumbled back a step.

And then his face lost all expression until it was like he wasn't even there anymore. Just a hull, a husk, something hollow and empty and gone.

He left.

CHAPTER
30

I turned away before Daniel was fully out of sight, unable to look at his retreating form any longer. When he'd hit Sean, *I'd* felt the impact. And even though Sean had been wrong to charge out and throw the first punch, it was his blood, his pain that called to mine. Not Daniel's.

I moved in front of Sean and blanched at the blood running from his almost certainly broken nose. My tone was as soft as the fingers I brushed under his split lip. "Sean, are you... Your face..."

He drew his knee up to stand, then thought better of it when the movement made him hiss. He flinched when I started to wipe the blood off his chin and nose as carefully as possible with the belt from my robe.

I was going to run out of belt long before he ran out of blood. My chin quivered. "Why? Why did you start that?"

The one blue eye that wasn't swollen shut focused on me. "Jill, I heard what he said about hurting you...that you tried to stop him."

My eyes fell shut, a rock of guilt weighing in my gut. I

let what Daniel said at my door replay in my head, listening for wording that Sean could have misinterpreted so badly.

Touching you like that… I should have stopped when you told me to.

The concrete of my porch was cool under my palm, and the warmth from Sean's hand sliding over it made me jump. "What did he do to you?" Just those few words caused beads of blood to seep up over his lip and smear, making them look impossibly red and wrong. He'd been hurt because he thought someone hurt me.

"Me? Nothing." I wasn't the one bleeding, he was. "But your face… I'm so sorry."

When I tried to dab at his upper lip again, Sean caught my wrist. Again, the same question delivered with almost zero inflection. "What did he do?" A muscle tensed in Sean's cheek, betraying that he wasn't nearly as calm as he was pretending. "He said he hurt you."

I grabbed for Sean's hand, needing to remove that fear immediately. "No. Sean, no. Nothing like that. That was—" There was no good way to sugarcoat what Daniel had done, especially when I couldn't justify it to myself. I stuck with the bare-bones facts. "What you overheard, he didn't mean it like that. It's my sunburn and…he came home drunk. I helped him get inside and he kissed me. That's all."

I looked away, remembering the things I'd relayed to Sean about Daniel before I knew him. The arguing, that he belonged in prison, the way he destroyed the shed in his yard. But nothing about him protecting his mom or the years of abuse he'd suffered as a result. Nothing about the scars left on him inside and out.

And then I sucked in a breath. For Daniel, with the life he'd had, I knew he'd reacted on instinct from Sean's first hit. He had to fight back, put the other guy down or he'd get put down himself. And then seeing someone have to protect me from him...

"I can't believe he did this." I couldn't look at Sean's face anymore, not when I felt responsible. "You shouldn't have hit him. He's not like you." Daniel didn't have the huge loving family Sean had. He didn't have a father or grandfather to inspire him or show him by example and legacy what a man could be. Daniel had abuse and disdain. He had his proffered love spit on, struck down again and again until he no longer expected anything else.

I pulled my hand free and curled it into my lap. "What you did..." I sat back on my heels and looked at the blood splattered around my porch. "Sean... I cannot believe you did this." I swallowed the rest of my words because I could believe that. He'd defended me without a second thought, had physically put himself between me and Daniel at the end even after he was beaten.

I stood and dropped down on the porch swing. The air was suddenly too thick and I felt like I was chained to two cars driving in different directions.

"I can't believe you didn't. Some drunk guy kisses you, hurts you, and you don't brain him with a crowbar? What the hell, Jill? I almost lost my mind when I overheard him trying to say he was sorry."

Daniel had looked so heartbreakingly pitiful. "You don't understand—he was reacting to you hitting him. I don't think he even registered what he did."

"Then he's a psycho."

"He's not." I lifted my head. "Sean, he came over to apologize to me. You just hit some guy you don't know, for reasons you didn't have in the first place. I told him to stop drinking, not...anything else. He stopped the rest as soon as I pushed him off me."

Even the swollen eye made an appearance then. "*Off* you? He was on top of you?"

The heat in my voice died an instant death. The air in my lungs escaped in an audible rush remembering Daniel's weight and the panicked surge of my heart. "I don't want to talk about any of that with you. I left, okay? He's never done anything like that before, and I'm never going to be in a situation again where he could. I don't want to be put in a position where I have to defend any of that, because I can't. I'm not going to try."

"Hey, I hit some guy who forced himself on you then beat the hell out of me. I need you to stop defending him for two seconds." Sean lifted his forearms and clenched his fists. "Listening to you about this guy, this—" He ground his teeth, looking for a word, and came up blank. "If your dad had been here instead of me, you'd be digging a grave right now and you know it."

I was staring at the thick bluish veins visible in Sean's arms, unable to contradict him. If Dad had been the one to overhear Daniel... "You don't understand." *I* was still trying to understand.

"You're right, I don't." Sean pushed up from the ground, using the wall behind him for support. He stopped right in front of me, one blue eye pleading with his words. "So help me."

Help him. Help Daniel. Fix them both, and me, and Dad, and Mom. Fix everything. The impossibility of any one of those tasks hit hard as I stared at the boy I used to think I'd love forever.

I shook my head. "Why did you come over tonight?" My voice was weak under the weight of all my failures. "I didn't want you here." And then more quietly, "I *don't* want you here."

Sean stood in front of me, bleeding. Bleeding for me. Because he thought someone had hurt me. And he couldn't stand that someone would hurt me.

The irony robbed me of words.

I left him there on my porch.

And as I closed the door, the only person I hated was myself.

CHAPTER
31

On Monday, my world didn't end. I kind of thought it would.

Mom didn't show up again.

Neither did Daniel. Neither did Sean.

Mrs. Vanderhoff called to say that Claire wasn't allowed to resume cross-country training until she could move without crying. Apparently her sunburn was much worse than mine. I didn't even get to talk to her.

Dad was still gone so the shop was closed.

It was just me.

I cried for a while. Then I sat for a while longer after that. When I couldn't stand myself anymore, I got up.

The gravel in the front yard crunched as I walked across it before squatting down to uncoil the hose we almost never used, ostensibly for the plants that might have existed at some point. The hose heated in my hands as the sunbaked water expelled first. I aimed it at the porch, washing away the brownish stains that looked nothing like the blood from the night before.

There was a smear against one wall. I hosed that down too.

Me, I'd already washed until I was pinker than was comfortable. Again.

I had to throw away Dad's robe.

Back inside my phone flashed with a missed call from Sean, but no message.

I almost called him back. Then I almost called him back half a dozen times more.

When he called again that afternoon I counted the rings until it hit voice mail.

No message.

Dad wasn't due home for hours, so I filled the day with trashy reality TV and turned up the volume loud enough to feel. I was watching a woman who no longer had what I'd consider a human face taking her Chihuahua to see a psychic when I felt the slight shudder of the garage door lifting. I clicked off the TV and stilled in the recliner.

He's not your father.

I flung myself out of the chair and ran to the garage, halting at the open door when he got out of his car. Dad. Too-long brown hair, grease-stained jeans, a Jim's Auto Shop tee that showed off the beginning of a paunch. He had bags under his eyes, but he smiled when he saw me.

"There's my girl."

I barreled into him and held on tight. I couldn't breathe enough of him in.

"Whoa. Miss me, or did you crash the truck?"

My face was pressed into his shoulder so my voice came out muffled. "Both."

Dad released me to look at the truck. The damage from my little fender bender with Daniel's mom was almost impossible to detect since we hadn't started any of the body repairs yet. He'd think I was teasing. "I missed you too. In fact..." He reached in the pocket of his jeans and tossed me something that glinted in the overhead light. Keys. "I'm not gonna lie, it needs work."

I read the logo and looked up at him, not really believing the word carved into the black leather fob. I'd completely forgotten his note about bringing me something. I owned a 1967 Triumph Spitfire Mark III convertible. Dad got me a Spitfire. I should be flying, grinning to the point of pain. But I wasn't.

I stood staring at the shiny key in my hand, tracing the jagged little teeth that would start my Spitfire. I was glad it needed work. Between choosing a brand-new model and a clunker, I'd pick the clunker every time. In that moment between reading the name on the fob and looking up at Dad, I saw the rest of my summer. My sneakered feet next to Dad's booted ones, tapping together from underneath the Spitfire while some awesomely bad Hall & Oates song blasted through the tinny garage speakers. Sharing takeout while arguing over engine specs. Mini road trips to salvage yards for parts. Seeing Dad smile at me the first time I brought the whole thing roaring to life, proud of me.

All of that was worth more than the car.

He's not your father.

Mom's words were a relentless rhythm banging in my head. Slamming around in my skull with greater and greater intensity the longer I watched him. My father. Not my father.

"That's all I get, huh? One hug?"

He got everything. All that I had. I felt my eyes begin to prick as I went into his open arms, holding him, and by sheer force of will I kept them dry.

"Nothing will ever mean more to me."

Dad laughed. "Now you're overdoing it."

I squeezed my fist tight around the key to my dream

car and followed Dad into the much brighter lights of the kitchen.

"All right, let me get a look at you." Dad maneuvered me around by the shoulders, twisting this way and that. "Nasty sunburn. It looks like your face had a fight with the stove and lost."

"I know." I tried to smile at his teasing, but I was suddenly so choked up I had to look away. "Are you hungry? There's half a frozen lasagna left."

"My favorite. Let me change, then we can start making plans for your Spitfire." He dropped a kiss on my head and headed for his room.

Down the hall I could hear Dad opening and closing drawers. He was whistling. Happy. Because I knew he saw our summer the same way I did. The last time I'd listened to him in his room, he'd been yelling at Mom, pleading with her. He'd told me that day that she wanted everything. *Everything* meant me. And not just me. She wanted to rend the only part of my family I had left. To say being his daughter was a lie.

The key slipped through my fingers, spinning as it fell, clinking as it hit the tiled kitchen floor.

But if it was a lie, he would have told me. He'd have warned me that she was going to spin this story about some neighbor. He'd have told me not to give it another thought. He'd have told me about his father's eyes and explained that was why mine were greenish and his were blue. He'd have said all of that to me.

But he hadn't. He'd told me it was okay to love her. Why would he do that after she told him she wanted to take me away? He'd yelled at her over the phone. He'd been mad and…and…afraid.

Maybe she hadn't told him. Maybe it was a lie just for me, to make me doubt him and cling to her. Maybe she knew better than to try and lie to him about something like that. Maybe…

I picked up the key and closed it in my fist. It could all be a lie. It could be. It could.

I nuked us both a slice of lasagna. When Dad came back he hugged me again and told me all about his trip while we ate. I was only half listening, even when he related the bidding war he got into over my Spitfire. It was so awful, looking at his face and being terrified that all of the little things I'd thought I'd gotten from him might come from some stranger. Wondering if he felt the same way looking at me, had always felt that way and I'd never known it. It had been only ten minutes and I was making myself sick.

"So, the sunburn. Are you going to try and tell me the Vanderhoffs ran out of sunblock?"

I forced a laugh and rattled off an excuse about how much fun we'd been having at Sunsplash and hadn't remembered to reapply.

Dad smiled and started telling me a story about the last time he remembered getting sunburned so badly he couldn't walk for days. "Maybe we should move to Oregon, huh? All that year-round cloud cover?" He stood up and took our plates.

"Yeah, maybe. We could franchise the shop."

Dad's laughter from the kitchen made everything hurt less. And then I killed it.

"We wouldn't even have to tell Mom. We could just pack up and go." Through the pass-through into the kitchen, I saw Dad stop in front of the fridge. "No forwarding address. New phone number. It would just be you and me and she couldn't find us." I watched him stand there, immobile, while I spoke. I leaned forward on the couch trying to see him better. When he moved, it was like a projector starting up again, sound and picture lurching back together.

"I think I'd miss the sun, wouldn't you?"

The sun visibly hated me at that moment but I smiled and nodded when he came back. Yes, the sun. That's why we couldn't go. Nothing about the fact that I might not be his, that maybe he couldn't take me if she didn't want him to. That she might try and take me away, split me in half between them.

"But if I wanted to go, if I wanted us to go somewhere away from here, could we?"

Dad came back with two bowls of ice cream and inexplicably propped my feet up on a pillow, his cure-all for anytime I was sick or hurt. He tucked me against his side in a way that actually hurt my skin, but felt good anyway. "We could go anywhere you wanted."

We watched *SportsCenter* after that, and I never once felt the urge to escape to the roof.

CHAPTER
32

The upside of Dad getting me a Spitfire was everything. I didn't have to worry about Daniel (much) or brood about Sean (obsessively). I didn't even have to agonize about Mom (ad nauseam).

Because finally I had something in front of me that I knew exactly how to fix. And I had Dad with me.

He seemed lighter too after that. I think that since he'd brought me something he'd known would make me happy, he couldn't help but be happy himself. He wasn't quite grooving around the garage yet, but that might have been because he hadn't beaten me to the shop when the Spitfire arrived. And when I say arrived, I mean it was towed. It didn't actually have four tires, or windows, or a steering wheel.

Or a transmission.

Dad's grin matched mine. "Pretty great, isn't it?"

It was better than great. It was late nights and long weekends. It was Dad and me, and Hall & Oates, and fingernails that might never be clean again. I don't think I'd ever been happier in my life.

Yeah, Daniel and Sean and Mom were still circling, but some dreams were so sweet they demanded to be savored.

And damn it, the Spitfire was sweet. Or it would be when Dad and I were done with it.

I beat a drum solo on Dad's back waiting for him to lift the hood so I could see my baby in all her glory.

Yeah, well, that was a stretch. Dad had prepped me for the gorier details, but the live show was still a bit stunning.

"Did you find her in a tub full of ice with stitches around her gut?" When Dad frowned at me, I added, "You know, because her organs have obviously been harvested and sold on the black market."

"Always with the jokes. I warned you she'd been pretty well stripped."

"Yeah, but..." I leaned in through the driver's nonexistent window. "Somebody actually took the pedals. Who does that?"

Dad rocked back on his heels, watching me as I climbed over seats and ran my hands over every neglected inch of that car. "Lot of work, that's for sure. Long days, weekends..."

He'd been hunting for a Spitfire for me since I was fourteen; we both had. We'd found some in good condition and others in better than good, but Dad always passed them by. It was because we wanted the project, the car that would require the two of us to work over every valve and hose, every bolt and seam. I wanted a Spitfire, but what I really wanted was a Spitfire to rebuild with Dad.

"But we can do it, right?" I slid out from underneath the chassis. "I mean, we can make her run again?"

"Yeah, we can make her run. Are you kidding? She'll be perfect."

The initial parts assessment was easy, since a lot of stuff was just plain gone or in obvious need of replacement. Once we really dug in, it wasn't as bad as it looked. There was a lot that could be salvaged, and Dad was confident we could find the rest without completely draining my bank account. After that it became a question of when, not if.

I pulled the calendar off the wall and laid it on a worktable for me and Dad to see. I flipped ahead and circled a date.

"This is D-day. I will not ride my bike to a single day of my junior year. So, that leaves us…" I started ticking weekends off on my hand and adding in after-work hours. Dad still had his truck to finish, not to mention the Mazda and two other cars he'd gotten along with the Spitfire. I also had to factor in the inevitable problems we'd encounter along the way, and potential delays with parts…

There was no way. Maybe Dad would take pity on me and let me drive something with four wheels to school instead of pedaling something with two. I looked at the Spitfire. However many weeks it took, it was going to be worth it.

I started to close the calendar, but Dad stopped me. He tapped the same weekends I had before school started.

"The two of us working together. Shouldn't be a problem. The others can wait."

It took me a second to realize he meant his truck. And the Mazda. And the other flip cars. He was going to put all his projects aside—the ones that actually made us money—to help me with mine.

I looked up at him. "You love me a lot, huh?"

Dad looked like he might embarrass us both by tearing up, but fortunately the door chimed up front.

"So much that I'm gonna let you take care of the oil change that probably just walked in while I go grab an early lunch."

"Fine, I will!" I called after his retreating form, grinning for all I was worth.

Only it wasn't an oil change waiting up front.

It was my freshly battered neighbor.

And we froze; Daniel unable to step forward, and me unable to step back.

He was wearing sunglasses, but I could see the dark tinge of double black eyes protruding from around the edges. I pulled my lips tight looking at him, realizing how hard Sean had hit him. There was another bruise blooming along his jaw and my sadness bloomed along with it.

"Your face..." I took a step, but Daniel immediately backed up. And that was a good thing. It hurt, like a piece of metal flying from a bench grinder and embedding straight into my chest, but it forced me to focus on everything that had happened and not just him being hurt.

I wasn't mad that Daniel had defended himself when Sean attacked, but he went so far beyond defending himself that just remembering it made me queasy.

All those nights on my roof, and that one almost kiss in the pool, that's what I wanted to remember. I wanted to blot out the night he got drunk, to dismiss it as an aberration. Before that night, I never would have believed he could treat me so callously. Not when I was beginning to think I meant something to him, when I was beginning to want to mean something to him.

It all hurt so much that there wasn't room left for butterflies. I missed the butterflies.

And I couldn't decide if that meant I missed Daniel too or just the way I felt with him, because they weren't the same thing.

I'd learned that with Sean. Even after everything with Mom had shredded my heart into teeny tiny broken pieces, I'd still missed Sean. I'd missed him enough to try and fix something that maybe was meant to stay broken.

And I knew that was messed up. All of it was.

"I'm sorry that happened." That was as much as I could give. It felt like a lot and somehow not nearly enough.

Daniel slipped his aviators off and I sucked in a breath. Sean had hit him really hard, like burst-a-blood-vessel-in-his-eyeball hard. "Why did it happen?"

I couldn't look at his face; I could not do it. It made me think of all the times it probably looked worse. And it made me think of Sean, who most definitely had fared worse in their fight. And the whole thing was awful. Even knowing why Sean had hit him and understanding why Daniel had hit back with such brutality, I couldn't unsee it.

Daniel still didn't know why he'd gotten in that fight. The reasons were little comfort to me, and I doubted they'd be any better for him, but maybe this could be the first of hopefully many things I got to be wrong about.

"Sean overheard some things out of context. He thought you'd hurt me."

"I did hurt you."

I didn't correct him. "He thought you did something that deserved being hit over. You didn't. You never have."

Daniel shook his head slightly, but didn't refute me.

A loud banging from the garage distracted us both. What was I doing? Dad could walk out any second and see us, and there was nothing casual about the way we were looking at each other.

"Can we go somewhere then? We need to talk without—" He gestured toward the garage. "Take a ride with me?"

CHAPTER 33

Daniel was waiting outside when I returned after telling Dad I was grabbing my own lunch with a friend—a friend I let him assume was Sean.

He waited until we pulled out of the parking lot before saying, "So you met my mom."

That sick feeling of shame slobbered over me. "If by met you mean backed into her car while she was parking, yeah. Did she tell you I offered to fix the damage?"

"Kind of." Daniel pulled out the card I'd given his mom. It was creased all over, like it had been crumpled up into a fist and smoothed out again. When I saw the words scribbled on the back, I understood why:

Your whore backed into my car

There was a nagging thought somewhere in the back of my mind that prompted me to be embarrassed that she classified me that way, but it didn't seem worth it. And ultimately it didn't matter what she called me, considering it was hardly worse than the things she called her son.

"I can only imagine what she said to you," he said.

"Pretty much the unabridged version of this." I shredded the card up as small as possible and let the pieces blow out the window, hoping Daniel would let it go too.

He didn't. His hands were tightening on the steering wheel before the wind could carry away the last piece.

"She doesn't think right anymore. I'm sorry."

"Don't be," I said. "Not about that anyway."

There was a very pregnant pause after that.

"I've been apologizing to you since the day we met. You'd think I'd be better at it by now."

I still felt sick, but not because of hitting his mom's car or what she'd said. I felt sick about Daniel. I didn't want another apology; I wanted not to need one. I wanted to be back on my roof where we could hide from the world and the things we'd done. I wanted the dream back instead of the reality.

Daniel muttered something under his breath. "Do you know what I thought that first night I saw you?"

I had a few unpleasant ideas.

Daniel rubbed the fist he had bloodied on his shed that night, and then again on Sean's face. "I forgot I was angry, just by looking at you." Disbelief must have been written all over my face when he finally turned to me. "You think I'm lying?"

I remembered him angry that night, and that first day at the shop, and when I saw his scars, when he got drunk, when he hit Sean... Even understanding what was behind all his anger, it was harder for me to forget as easily as he claimed he could.

"You have no idea what you looked like sitting in the moonlight. You glowed, and I wanted to be close to you, before I even knew your name. That's why I didn't go back inside right away."

"That sounds like a bit of revisionist history to me. I'm pretty sure you stayed outside to yell at me."

Daniel smiled at my attempted humor. "I'm serious. I walked out of a nightmare and there you were. It was because of you that I walked out. I don't remember if I yelled or not, I just remember not wanting to blink. And then you offered to fix my Jeep." The sides of his mouth kicked up higher.

"After which more yelling ensued."

"That wasn't yelling, that was shock and something I needed way too much." His smile grew until his whole face was happy. "I almost kissed you in my Jeep that first day."

I went warm remembering the feel of his thumbs on my temples.

Then Daniel's smile died completely. "It was like a punch to the gut when you told me how old you were."

"It wasn't fun for me either."

"And then seeing you with your dad… I don't even know all the ways I could destroy your life, and it's a good life, Jill, it is. But that's not even the problem anymore," he said, drawing my attention back to him. "After that next night, I stopped trying to stay away. I barely tried to begin with. I stopped caring that it was seriously wrong for me to be look-ing at you the way I started looking at you. We were spend-ing night after night together, and the first time I got you away from your roof I tried to kiss you."

I spun to face him. "Hey, swimming was my idea. I was the one who got you away from my roof. You say you're al-ways apologizing to me, maybe that's because half the things you try to apologize for aren't your fault."

"I shouldn't have tried kissing you that night and I shouldn't have succeeded the next."

My features smoothed and I sat back against my seat. No,

he most definitely should not have gotten drunk and kissed me on his couch.

"I never had any business going anywhere near you. You're sixteen years old and you've got so much. All I've got is poison."

"That's a lie."

"Which part? I know we pretended that hanging out was just about us avoiding our problems, but it stopped being about that a long time ago. If we hadn't had that night in the pool, it would have been something else, and maybe that time you wouldn't have pulled back." Daniel was stopped at an intersection and he stayed even when the light turned green. It wasn't until cars started honking behind us that he started driving again. "I'm not saying this right."

"We didn't set out to spend all that time together," I said. "Or to start having more than friendly feelings for each other, really it was the opposite. But you aren't poison. I don't know if you realize what you've done for me. Before you, I didn't have anyone to talk to about my mom and everything that happened. And I'm glad I got to be there for you even though you didn't mean to tell me so much. But getting drunk after telling me about your dad—"

"Isn't an excuse for what I said and did."

"No, it's not. But honestly, you kissing me wasn't the worst part of my weekend, not by a long shot."

"What does that mean?"

"It means my mom showed up and told me I was a bastard. How's that for perspective?"

Daniel looked away. For him that probably would have been great news. For me, vomit still burned the back of my throat at the possibility.

"I don't want to dredge any of that up right now, I just

wanted you to know that I wouldn't give you back, not even after everything…went wrong."

"I wouldn't give you back either." He bounced his hand off his knee. "Is it true? What your mom said?"

"I don't want it to be." A tremor rolled through me. "I really, really don't want it to be."

"I can't even hold you right now, can I?"

At some point while I was talking, my arms had wrapped themselves around my middle and my hand curled around the base of my seat belt. I'm sure it looked like I was seconds away from flinging myself out of a moving car, but that wasn't it. I wasn't holding myself back from him; I was trying to hold myself together. Period. Full stop.

"Don't answer that. This is gonna be a problem for me." He sat back and ran his hands through his hair. "The sick truth is that if your friend hadn't hit me the other night, I probably would have tried to kiss you again." Daniel slipped his glasses back on, covered the worst of the damage. "In fact, I know I would have, because sitting with you right now and after telling you exactly how much of an asshole I am, I still want to. And there is no world where that is okay. How am I supposed to go back when I don't want to?"

If it were possible to split into two totally different people, I would have done it right there.

Part of me felt like it'd be impossible to reverse back to a place where I wasn't aware of his body in relation to mine. Where I just wanted to help him and didn't want…

But the other part was still clutching my seat belt like a shield between us. Because that night after the pool, when we were hiding in the bushes and he'd lifted my chin, I remembered pulling back. And after that drunken kiss, and his hurting Sean…how could I do anything but pull back? I *was* sixteen. He *was* twenty-one. Dad *would* murder us both.

His mom would probably call the cops and get him arrested. He wasn't poison, but the two of us together...

And Sean... I couldn't even convince Claire I was over him.

The shop came into view ahead. Rather than risk Dad seeing me get out of a Jeep instead of a Jetta, I had Daniel pull in at the check advance place next door.

Daniel reached for his keys and the lulling noise from the engine died, plummeting us into silence. "I'm not going to be around for a while, a week, maybe two. I need to do something I've been putting off."

I frowned. "Are you okay?"

He shrugged off the question. "It's just stuff I should've taken care of before we moved. It'll be fine. Might be good to spend a few nights away, you know?"

"Yeah." I hated that I couldn't see his eyes through his sunglasses. I really hated that he didn't sound half as indifferent about his upcoming trip as he was trying to. I wanted to ask him more, but everything about his body language said he'd already told me more than he wanted.

I reached for the door, but it didn't budge.

Daniel leaned around me, lifting the handle just right so that it opened. "It sticks a little. Guess I should have asked you to fix that too."

The warmth from his body pressed into my side. It was as close as we'd been since... I half turned to see his face. Bruised.

I felt exactly the same way.

He didn't pull back. "That night at my house. I don't want you to think about me kissing you like that..." His eyes dipped to my mouth and a forgotten butterfly fluttered to life in my stomach. And then, before I think he even realized he was going to, Daniel bent and brushed his lips against mine.

The pressure was so light that I barely felt the warmth from his mouth until it was gone…until I could miss it.

It was just the one kiss, no more than a second or two. A kiss that you'd miss if you blinked.

Nothing like my dream.

Nothing like that night.

I didn't have to push him away. It didn't last long enough for me to even have to make that decision.

"I'm sorry for so much, Jill."

"I know." And I did.

CHAPTER 34

The rest of the week passed in a ricochet of emotions. Everything with Dad and the Spitfire was a dream that I never wanted to wake from. Everything outside the shop was... not a nightmare, but the constant threat of one.

By the time Wednesday rolled around, Claire had sufficiently recovered from her sunburn to run again. Sean had been MIA since the fight with Daniel. He'd stopped calling me, and when Claire finally got ahold of him after her sunburn healed, he hadn't said much. She and I had been talking all week, so she knew what had happened and the way I'd left things. I knew it was bad when even Claire couldn't offer a hopeful outlook.

I'd also told her about Mom and her nuclear bomb. It helped more than I'd thought possible, telling her about all that stuff. It was different than talking with Daniel. Sometimes Claire couldn't school her reactions fast enough, and the switch on her friend brain broke at some point. But it was...okay. We were okay.

We were sitting on the grass at the school track in the

early-morning light, when Claire suddenly blurted out a confession.

"I gained two pounds," she told me, somewhere between ashamed and triumphant. "My mom was worried that I was getting too skinny—can you believe that? Anyway, I promised her I would, so I did. She was really happy." Claire's chin dropped to her chest. "Only I feel kind of sick about it. I know it's stupid. I know it." She tapped her head. "But I can't stop thinking about those two pounds, like I can feel them. When I was fat I didn't care." She sighed and squinted at the rising sun that was just high enough to stretch glowing ribbons across the field as it pierced the trees around us. "I can't remember how I did it. How do you?"

"Not care? I don't know. I never thought about it. It's like me with Sean. You never had to learn not to think about him. I'm still working on that." And a million other things, but I knew my audience.

Claire nodded like my answer was the one she was looking for. "Makes you kind of wish we could trade, huh? Fix each other's problems?"

"That'd be awesome." It had been a week and a half since the fight on my porch and I was going quietly mad wondering how Sean was. I knew he was okay physically. Claire had found out that much. Apparently he'd told his parents he broke his nose catching an elbow playing basketball. He had a really good relationship with them, and it only made me feel worse that he'd had to lie to them. For me.

"Okay, I may have done something you're not going to like." Claire uprooted a small pile of grass.

"What did you—" I started, but turned to the parking lot when I heard another car pull in.

"I sort of tried to fix one of your problems for you by telling someone that cross-country training was starting again today."

The "someone" needed no further explanation as Sean got out of his car.

We started stretching in silence, Claire looking back and forth between Sean and me with a cautious optimism that I wasn't sure I shared. She greeted him with the same bright smile she'd given me earlier.

"Pretty great that we're all back together, isn't it?" Not even crickets answered her. "Earth to Sean. What's up?"

I caught Sean's eye as he stood. "What's up is that it's hot and I'm pretty sure it's still last night, so let's do this so I can go to bed." Which was the exact perfect grumpy Sean thing to say. Claire rolled her eyes at him and got to her feet.

I rediscovered something that day. Running was not my thing, I knew that, but running without Sean to complain with—and it didn't feel like he was there when he was silent—was the absolute worst activity ever. He didn't pantomime strangling Claire when she tried to motivate us to speed up. He didn't lean his shoulder into mine and gradually move me off the trail until I had to grab ahold of him or end up swimming—not that he'd ever let me get that close to falling in the canal, but it was his stupid game that I thought I hated until he no longer wanted to play.

I was beyond miserable when we got back to the school and I collapsed on the grass, panting. Seconds later, Sean thumped down next to me, resting forward on his knees. Claire had beaten both of us and was sitting on my other side, her breath barely faster than normal.

"You suck," Sean told her.

"Hey, don't be mad at me if you can't handle three miles

after a week off," she said. "I told you to run without us. I called you and everything."

"And what did I tell you?" he said, without raising his head.

Claire's face flushed slightly, but with her fair skin, it was rather impressive. "I," she said, "am your friend, so I will not repeat what you told me."

Sean found the energy to laugh and I wasted what little air I'd forced back into my still-panting body to laugh with him. We stopped when the sound blended together.

There was this moment when our eyes met and my smile was still half there. But it was like he was looking past me. Not seeing me at all.

"Come on, guys." Claire had noticed our little exchange, and her mouth was pinched in disapproval. "I don't know why you're both being so stubborn, but this—" she pointed at both of us, then crossed and uncrossed her arms "—needs to stop."

I didn't say anything and Sean took the opportunity to guzzle from his water bottle.

"Okay, so this is it now? You're just going to give up?" She gave Sean a look before turning to me. "Jill?"

I had to turn away when she stared at me like that. My eyes fell on Sean, barely two feet away but feeling much farther. His face was healed except for some light yellowish bruising and a thin, almost imperceptible line from where his lip had split—from where Daniel had split his lip. Looking at it made me feel guilty and angry all over again. Mostly guilty. But I didn't look away.

Just meet my eye once. Convince me again that we have a chance.
He didn't.

This time was nothing, *nothing*, compared to what had happened with my mom. He hadn't given up then, so why now? When I couldn't look at him refusing to look at me anymore, I shoved him. "What is with you?"

"Um, Jill? I don't think—"

"No." I waved off Claire. "He hasn't talked to me in over a week so why is he even—"

Sean let out a barked laugh and shook his head. "Except for last week, right? You know, when you called me and I took you to lunch." Sean leaned toward me and put his arm around my shoulders and addressed Claire in an overly enthusiastic way. "I dropped everything and raced right over to get her. 'Cause I'm that guy!" He flung his arm away from me and got to his feet, all pretense gone. "You're gonna have to find someone else to run with, Claire. I'm done."

"What?" Claire gave me a wide-eyed look, then pushed up onto her knees.

I was on my feet right behind Sean. How could he possibly know I'd lied to Dad when Daniel and I talked? I went after him when he started for the parking lot, motioning for Claire to hang back.

CHAPTER
35

The farther Sean made me chase him, the angrier I got, until at last I darted in front of him. He had to stop or collide into me, and the last thing he looked like he wanted to do was touch me.

His eyes skidded away from me and his chest heaved.

"Are you done?" I dug my hand into my side, pressing at the stitch our earlier run had created and the sprint revived. "I can't follow you if you decide to take off again."

Sean didn't dodge around me, but he didn't speak either. He dropped his pissed-off expression for a split second, and what was underneath it was sadness, like he'd lost something and he was only now realizing it.

But that made no sense, none of it did. Not his locked jaw or his curled lip, not his rigid posture or the waves of hostility I could feel. He was supposed to be the one apologizing, not acting like it was the other way around, like it wouldn't matter even if I did.

My eyes twitched as I searched his face. His last words from the track trickled through me and I was overcome by a wave of dizziness. I swallowed. "How did you—how did you know about lunch on Thursday?"

Sean drew back, like he couldn't stand to be near me. "Your dad called to offer me a tune-up. Shocked the hell out of me. He said I was always driving you around and I said 'not really' 'cause you weren't even answering my calls at the time. Then he said I took you to lunch last week."

I felt the blood drain from my face.

"So there I was," Sean continued, his eyes narrowed at me in a way I wouldn't have been able to conceive of a couple weeks ago, "lying to your dad and listening to him thank me—*thank me*—for always being there for you. Yeah. Can you believe it? He finally likes me."

The heat from the asphalt was wafting up and wrapping around my legs, hot and horrible, but it was nothing compared to Sean. Especially when his voice softened.

"And I couldn't figure it out. Why would you lie about me taking you? Why would you bother? You wouldn't if Claire picked you up, or another friend from school or anybody really. And then I thought, maybe it was about your mom. Maybe she showed up and you didn't want him to know. Okay, that would make sense. But, then—" Sean laughed "—the last time you saw her, you didn't exactly welcome her with open arms. I doubted she'd risk coming to the shop with your dad there." Sean affected a confused expression and huffed out a breath. "But maybe there was someone else you wouldn't want your dad to know about." He dropped his voice. "Tell me I'm wrong, Jill. Tell me you didn't lie about me—make me lie to your dad—so you could go off with him."

But I couldn't.

"Jill...?" Sean's eyes blurred as they flickered back and forth between mine.

I took a step toward him, hands rising involuntarily. "I didn't know my dad would call you. I never meant to put you in that position."

Sean was shaking his head. Not wanting to hear me, but I kept going.

"It's not like that. We didn't get to talk after everything and we needed to talk, Sean."

But Sean was walking away.

"I haven't even seen him since then. Hey. Hey!" I caught Sean by the shirt, damp with sweat under my fingers.

He rounded on me. "You think I care if you're with the psycho next door?"

My face flushed hot at his word choice.

"I don't." He practically spit the words. "I did, and I got a broken nose and a slammed door for my trouble. So now I don't care. Do what you want, but don't lie about me to your dad. I won't cover for you next time."

Hot tears scalded my eyes, but I blinked them back. "You're so self-righteous. You didn't do anything wrong, huh? It was all me?"

Sean's expression didn't flicker.

"You hit my—friend." I barely tripped over the word, but Sean's hardened look incensed me and I got right in his face. "A friend who helped his mother escape from a sadistic monster who nearly crushed her skull with a baseball bat. You hit him when he was still recovering from the injuries he got protecting her." That got more than a flicker in response. "He told someone—me—for the first time, about his dad and how he'd been beating them. You have no *idea* what that was like for him, reliving that nightmare. So he got drunk and he kissed me. He knew he shouldn't have. He apologized right before you tried to knock his teeth out." Sean's hostility had faded with each word I spoke. I should have stopped when he started flinching, but it was too late by then. The words rushed out.

"That's who you hit. A guy who was so used to being beaten that he snapped and fought back because he didn't expect you to stop." My chin quivered but I refused to cry. "It's not okay what he did to you. It's not okay that he kissed me. None of it is okay, but you act like I don't know that. I do! You never gave me a chance to say I'm sorry, or to explain or anything. You stand there and you lecture me and you go off and say the worst things you can think of, but I keep coming back. I'm here. I was ready to talk to you, to see if we could fix us. To see if you wanted to, but you don't. You want to pretend you're perfect. You're not."

And that old hurt, the one I'd tried to ignore for months, the one I couldn't bear to think about because of what I knew it would cost me, choked out. "You almost kissed my mom, Sean."

That one cut as deep as I'd meant it to. I could see it on his face. I clenched my teeth to keep in the sob, letting only rapid breaths pass through. The Sean in front of me was my friend again. The one who maybe loved me, if Claire was right. The one who'd take any pain to protect me. But when he reached for me, I jerked back.

"No! How could you do that to me?" I didn't want him to answer. I'd break apart if he tried.

I looked at his eyes, back and forth, but there were no answers, so I left without even going back for my bike.

And he didn't chase me.

CHAPTER
36

People were looking at me as I walked home, slowing their vehicles. One lady even lowered her window to ask if I was okay. I waved her off with some excuse and kept walking. It was hot and idiots honked, and I walked. One foot in front of the other, almost as fast as the tears that ran down my cheeks. I couldn't stop them from spilling over any more than I could shut out the thoughts that made them.

Sean and Daniel. Sean and my mom. Mom. Dad.

More and more cars clogged the streets. I started counting them to fill my head. Four white pickup trucks, two red compacts and half a dozen gray minivans. And one green Jetta.

I could have made a scene when the Jetta pulled up next to me. I'd run out of tears, if nothing else, but it was the sight of my bike in his backseat that made me stop.

Sean leaned over and pushed open the passenger door.

And I got in.

Neither of us spoke as Sean drove me home. We even kept silent as we unloaded my bike.

The back tire bounced on the driveway when the bike

was free, and we both stood up, the Jetta separating us. What little control I'd gained from my walk and subsequent ride home—and it was very little—evaporated when I saw Sean's hands rest on the roof of his car, all ten fingers splayed out and the knuckles turning white. He wasn't even blinking.

"I know you have to go to work, but I'll come by tonight. We need to talk." There was no question from Sean, just a simple statement of fact.

Closing my eyes, I flashed back to Sean's face that night I'd walked in on him with Mom. The way she was leaning much too close. The way my heart started to splinter before I even understood what I was seeing. The way a million tiny and not so tiny dreams died in the moment that I did.

Sean was waiting for some kind of acknowledgment, so I nodded once and walked my bike up.

We were finally going to talk about it. And afterward, maybe we wouldn't ever talk again.

Dad's truck was still in the garage when I checked the window, which given how late I was, was alarming enough to push Sean from my mind.

"Dad?" Once inside, I made a beeline for his room, thinking—hoping—maybe he was just sick. But his room was empty. His bed was even made. I was darting through the kitchen to check the living room when he came walking through the opposite entryway.

He was holding his phone. "We need to talk."

I braced myself against the fridge, almost as out of breath as I'd been after running earlier. Except it wasn't exhaustion panting through my body. It wasn't shock, or even fear, so much as dread. Like twisting in a swing, round and round, watching the ropes coil together, tightening, and shortening until there was nothing left to twist together. I'd been watching the swing twist higher and higher all summer, sometimes faster, sometimes slower, but always inexorably closer to that point when it would spin free in a rush, trying to hurl me off.

Except I wasn't a kid on a playground shouting with my friends. I was a motherless girl, standing in a tiny galley kitchen watching the fluorescent light leach away what little color was left in Dad's face. He'd been watching the swing twist too, dreading his next words even more than me.

My hand found the fridge handle and squeezed for no other reason than I wanted something to hang on to.

"About Mom."

Dad looked smaller when he answered. "She left a message. She wants to see you."

My response was a confession and an apology all in one. "She already did." I saw those three little words physically impact him, hurt him. And I had to hurt him more. "When you were at the auction. I know what she wants. And I know why." I bit the inside of my cheek, but I couldn't keep my chin from quivering as I looked at him. "Dad… Daddy…it's not true. Please tell me it's not." The idea that I might not be his, that he might not be mine, was unbearable. It was such a vile thing, this poisonous seed that she'd planted, and I'd fed without meaning to. I needed Dad to destroy it. To pull it up so I could salt the earth.

But he didn't.

His face crumbled. It was the worst thing I'd ever seen. The worst. It cauterized my tear ducts in an instant.

She wasn't a liar.

Denials screamed in my head and I was moving, staggering across the kitchen on legs that felt as worthless as Mom's wedding vows. I wrapped Dad in a bear hug, locked the tips of my fingers behind his broad back and squeezed as tight as possible.

"I knew when she got pregnant. We hadn't been able to… I should have told you."

"No. I don't care. It doesn't matter."

He grabbed my shoulders and held me away from him. He came just short of shaking me. "It does matter." I felt something rip inside at the words he said next. "She could try and take you away. Do you understand that? Do you want to come visit me on the weekends?"

"Then we'll leave. Oregon, remember? People need mechanics everywhere."

He let go of my arms.

"Dad, remember?"

He turned my palm up and dropped the keys to his truck in them. Dad's blue eyes were glassy. "Go in without me. Leave the closed sign and work on the Spitfire."

I didn't immediately comprehend what he was saying. It had nothing to do with Mom. Nothing to do with the new reality we suddenly shared. I couldn't understand why he wanted me to leave when my instinct was the exact opposite. I wanted to physically hold on to him. If there was a chance that she could take me, I'd make her pry me away from Dad if it came to that. I'd make it come to that.

I'd have sworn Dad felt the same way, except he was stepping back from me. He was sending me away. He was quiet.

My heart was beating in my throat, so that every word had to fight to push free. "You can come with me. I'm so close to starting it. The timing sprockets came in. Don't you want to take the first test drive with me?" We'd been talking about it for the past couple days, arguing over the music we'd play.

Dad shook his head. "Not today. I'll look her over tomorrow and we'll see. You go on." He brushed past me after that, disappearing into his room.

Leaving me.

Dad had never left me.

I was going to choke or hyperventilate or worse—break down in body-racking sobs—if I stayed in that kitchen, so I found myself in the truck speeding toward the shop.

CHAPTER
37

When I got to the shop, I flipped on all the lights and stared at the few vehicles in the otherwise empty main garage bay, being assaulted by a potential future where I was taken from all of it. Taken, while Dad did nothing to stop it.

Sweat pricked my forehead and neck until the heat demanded my attention. The fans whirled to life and the AC kicked on. Moving was good, so I kept at it. I dropped my iPod into the dock and vanished under the hood of my Spitfire.

I worked straight through dinner, stopping finally to inhale something from the fridge. Shadows crept across the floor as I worked, claiming more and more of the shop until they consumed the last sliver of sunshine.

Someone tapped my foot and I sat up so suddenly that I nearly knocked myself out. I fought off unconsciousness and rolled out from under the Spitfire, hoping to see Dad.

But it was Claire.

"Hey." I rubbed what was sure to turn into a spectacular goose egg on my forehead. "Make a noise or something next time."

"Sorry," Claire said. "It's kind of loud in here."

With the fans and music blaring, I was watching her lips more than actually hearing her. I walked over and turned off my iPod. "Better?"

"Much. And that explains why you didn't hear me calling you all day."

Claire always looked a little out of place in the garage. Too clean. Too bright. She was searching for somewhere to sit that wouldn't immediately destroy her white eyelet sundress. There was a wheeled stool in the corner that was half duct tape and half tattered red vinyl that she seemed to be considering before noticing the Spitfire.

"Oh, hey! It's got tires." Claire smiled at me. "It looks like an actual car now." She circled the vehicle, running her hand along the door. "When do we get to paint it?"

No part of me felt like laughing, but I did because of course she would ask about paint. "Another week, maybe two." And then my heart sank again. There was so much that could happen in two weeks.

Misreading my expression, Claire came over and rubbed a hand on my shoulder. "Don't worry about Sean. You guys bounce back, you always do. And this…" She gestured to the Spitfire. "It's going to be amazing when you're finished with it."

I turned away and pretended to study something under the hood until I could slow the panicked rush of my blood. Because that was what it was. I was frightened of the things I knew and terrified by the things I didn't. And there was too much space and silence in the garage. I started puffing my cheeks out and in with my breathing, but it wasn't helping. The engine block blurred in my vision and I blinked half a dozen times before it cleared.

And when it did, I looked again. And again. And I straightened, mentally running through all the progress I'd made that day. I'd been working for eight hours straight, so focused that I hadn't stopped to consider that I might actually be able to start it.

Drive it.

Right that second.

Before anyone else could stop me.

The key was already in the ignition when I slipped into the driver's seat.

I really didn't know. I thought, but I didn't know.

I closed my eyes as I turned it and let my grin spread when the engine purred to life.

"You want amazing?" I nodded my head toward the passenger seat. "Get in."

The wind blew all of my fear away as Claire and I peeled out of the garage. The Spitfire roared and it was beautiful. The body was still a mishmash of flat gray and the interior was little better, but split leather was nothing as we whooped and I pressed the rebuilt engine to its limit along the empty roads by the citrus groves.

We hit 60mph in under fifteen seconds. Claire's grin became a little tense as she watched the speedometer's needle climb past 80, then 90. I wanted 95 like it was life, but I let up on the accelerator until Claire raised her arms up and laughed.

Still, the top was down and our hair was whipping and tangling against our faces in the moonlight. Driving that night was like a religious experience. There were almost no cars, no people, no noise. The streetlights made the roads glow and all the traffic lights were green, just for me. I forgot about everything as pavement disappeared under my car. We laughed like idiots for exactly 11.7 miles. The noise my car made after that was less a purr and more a death knell.

I groaned out loud and the car rolled to a halt alongside a

huge stretch of orange trees. Claire gave a halfhearted "Woo" right before I let my head thud against the steering wheel.

"That sounded bad," she said.

Bad nothing. It sounded like the Spitfire'd had the automotive equivalent of a stroke. The smoke billowing from under the hood confirmed it.

"You can fix it, right?" Claire asked after I got out and popped the hood.

I let the smoke dissipate and got a better look. I answered, talking more to myself than anything. "It might be a corroded radiator sending rust into the cooling system. That would kill the water pump or possibly block the radiator. Neither means we'll be driving away tonight, but it's better than the alternative. If it's a blown head gasket…"

I checked the spark plugs, and coolant was squirting out. I slammed the hood shut and bit my lip. Hard. "There's nothing to fix. The engine is toast."

There were a million details that Dad would have checked before letting me circle the parking lot. A million things that I lacked the experience and skill to do on my own. Tomorrow, he'd said. He'd check it and we'd see. But a couple weeks ago he'd said we could go to Oregon too. Anywhere I wanted to go. Today he wouldn't even answer me.

"I'm so sorry, Jill. I know how much this car means to you."

I nodded and reopened the hood to let the lingering smoke escape. It stung my eyes and scratched my throat, making me cough and sit back down in the front seat. I cared about this car only because Dad had built it up for me when I was little, saying that any mechanic worth their socket wrench had a dream car. When I'd told him this was mine, it was better than any straight A report card I could have brought home. We'd studied engine plans, he'd drilled me on specs, and we'd hunted auctions together. He'd told me sixteen was my year. For the Spitfire. For everything.

Everything.

And now I had less than nothing.

"I shouldn't have been driving this yet." When Claire tried to console me I shook her off. "I'm serious, Claire. I could have killed us. I didn't even check the brakes. We could be wrapped around an orange tree right now if the engine hadn't died."

I saw Claire shrink back into her seat as my admission sank home.

"Aren't you going to yell at me? What I did was really stupid."

Claire didn't say anything for a minute. Then, "I'm guessing your dad is going to yell at you plenty."

The vein in Dad's forehead that throbbed whenever he got mad was likely to rip right out when he found out about this. Or maybe not. He wasn't acting at all like I'd thought he would, so what did I know?

I pulled the keys from the ignition and slid my forehead along the steering wheel, turning enough to watch the smoke thinning around the still propped-up hood. I shut my eyes and winced as though in physical pain. The engine. Dead. I'd killed my dream car, and I didn't have any more time to fix it again, if that was even possible.

Because she could come back at any time. And Dad wasn't going to fight for me.

"He told me today that it's true. What she said." I didn't need to be any more specific. Claire understood.

"Oh," she said. "Oh."

"That's why he sent me to the shop. I told him we should leave, move somewhere she couldn't find us and instead he gave me his keys and sent me away."

"Could she do that? Take you from him?"

"I don't know. Maybe."

"How do you feel?" she asked.

I fought not to roll my eyes. "I feel like my car, Claire. How do you think?"

"I mean about your dad. Does it matter to you?"

I wanted to be able to answer immediately, like a reflex, something I didn't even have to think about. But the right words didn't race out of my mouth, loud and confident. "I don't want it to."

Claire squeezed my hand. "Then it doesn't have to."

I looked at her and understood what she was telling me even as I was snapping at her.

"How is today different from yesterday?" she asked.

I shrugged and gestured at the thinning smoke still drifting from my car. "I'm not getting rid of my bike anytime soon."

Claire pinched the skin on the back of my hand.

"Hey!" I yanked it back.

"What is fundamentally different about your life today?"

I rubbed my hand. "I found out that my dad isn't—" I broke off when Claire tried to pinch me again. "Stop. What are you doing?"

"You're not answering the question."

"You keep pinching me like a five-year-old."

"Nothing is different."

"Everything is different." I pinched her back.

"Is it? Was he your biological father yesterday? Were you his biological daughter? Did he love you more before? Do you love him less today? Does knowing any of this make you want to go live with your mom?" Claire kept ticking the questions off on her left hand.

When she started in on the right hand, I stopped her. "Okay, okay."

"It doesn't have to be different unless you let it. I mean,

look at your dad. He knew, right? He's always known, and it didn't matter to him, so don't let it matter to you."

I drew in a deep breath through my nose, looking at Claire and willing my heart and my head to embrace what she was saying. I wanted the anxiety and dread to stop curdling in my stomach. I wanted her words to demolish the fear and bitterness that tainted the future as I saw it. I wanted to stay with Dad and the shop and for everything to go back to the way it was before Mom came back. I wanted her to stay gone.

And then I realized that waiting wasn't going to get me any of those things.

"You're right." I twisted around and grabbed my bag from the backseat. I pulled out my phone and sat back.

"Are you calling your dad?"

"No. I'm calling her."

"Your mom? You're calling your *mom*?" For a second I thought Claire might start pinching me again—with both hands—but she sat perfectly still.

"I'm not going to do this anymore—flinch every time the phone rings or there's a knock at the door. I can't sit here waiting and dreading every moment like it might be the last. Dad isn't going to fight." That admission was like a car crashing into my heart. "But I have to."

I found Mom's number in my contacts list. When she'd added it that day in my garage I'd never thought I'd use it. "It's ringing."

Claire looked torn between tearing the phone out of my hands and moving closer so that she could hear better. Instead she pulled out her own phone and composed a text to her cousin to pick her up ASAP. She showed it to me before sending, giving me the option of meeting Mom alone or with her as backup. I reached out and pushed Send on Claire's phone just as Mom answered on mine.

CHAPTER
38

The park where Claire's cousin dropped me off to meet Mom was deserted that late at night. I left the Spitfire where it had died—I'd have to deal with it later when I called Dad. The streetlights in Claire's neighborhood—our old neighborhood—provided enough light for me to see my mother when she arrived. She was wearing jeans and one of my old tank tops. With her hair pulled into a messy-but-totally-chic bun and barely any makeup, she looked impossibly young. The wary expression on her face only added to that impression.

She lowered herself onto the bench next to me like she expected me to attack her. I wasn't sure what I was going to say or do. My mouth was dry and it felt like a wire was pulled tight between my temples. My hands curled under the wood of the bench as I stared at the merry-go-round. I remembered this park. I drove past it all the time, but I hadn't set foot in it in years, not since we moved.

"This is a little unusual." Mom looked around the empty playground, still but for a swing softly creaking in the breeze.

"But I'm glad you called. I wanted to talk more last time after—"

"We're not going to talk about what you told me." My hands gripped the bench harder and I started blinking too fast. "I don't care about any of that, so it doesn't matter. Don't—don't bring it up again."

A car drove by. Then another.

"No, I'm sorry, but you're not going to dictate the conversation this time. I'm done feeling guilty," she went on. "I've forgiven myself and that's all that matters. I decided all that when I left, so as much as I know you want me to, I can't apologize for any of my choices. That's something you're going to have to get past. I'm getting there. Jeff is helping, the therapist I've been seeing is helping, and having you back is going to help even more." Her eyes bored into mine. "Your dad, he'll be fine on his own. I'm the one who needs you. Not him."

"No." I shook my head, because what she wanted was impossible. "I won't make things better for you, I promise. I will ruin anything good, because if you take me from Dad I'll have nothing left." I was still wearing my coveralls and I fisted the loose material above my knee, turning my knuckles white before releasing it. "Look." I held my hand out to her. I hadn't scrubbed my hands before leaving the shop with Claire, so my nails were edged with black and the creases in my knuckles and palms were marked with dark crisscrossing lines. "You don't want this. You don't."

Something happened when she looked at my hand. Her shoulders shook and her face crumbled. It wasn't pretty or dignified or calculating or any of the things I associated her with. It made me want to shrink away. And run.

"You used to cry when your hands got dirty. You don't even remember, do you? If you fell outside, even if you weren't hurt, you'd hold your little palms up and these big fat tears would start. You wouldn't stop until we washed your hands." As she spoke, she continued to gather herself until her face smoothed completely, everything back to picture-perfect except for the iron grip she kept on her purse. "You weren't even four when he started taking you to the shop. You'd cry when he'd put you down, when he'd pick you up with grease on his hands, when he'd wash your hands in the slop sink. You hated it. You hated the noise and the smell. But he took you with him every week. It was months before you stopped crying when your hands got dirty."

I didn't remember any of that. I'd always loved working in the shop, handing Dad tools, rolling tires that were bigger than I was. It was better than any playground.

Her eyes lost their focus for a second before locking on me. "You have no idea, you really don't. And I never wanted you to. Because I love you."

I was losing. I could feel it. And the reality snuffed out my resolve so completely that I shivered in the warm night air. I was little more than ashes and she was an inferno.

"I hope you never know what it feels like to pay for a single—" she swallowed "—mistake every day of your life, to see it in his eyes and feel it in his touch. He said he forgave me, but he lied. Every day he punished me. Every day. He couldn't love me anymore, but that wasn't enough, so he took your love too. I'd bring you home dolls and he'd replace them with cars. He coached your soccer team, but I couldn't put you in ballet. I never had a chance with you. And I felt so guilty all the time that I couldn't object—he made sure of that. So now I'm making sure of this."

She swept her eyes over me then around the park. "I know you're upset with me for leaving, and I can see now that I handled that situation badly, but I've been so alone for so long."

I sucked in a breath when she tried to take my hand, and she froze midair.

"Jill, he took you from me. You weren't his, so he made sure you weren't mine either. But it was another lie." She lifted a hand to stroke my head. "If you could only see the way he looked at you at first. He wouldn't touch you as a baby, did you know that? I loved you, and he couldn't stand to—"

Ripping away, I shot to my feet with a cry that made my knees want to buckle. "No." My voice was so low that I felt it rumble in my chest. I brushed away the tear that slipped down my cheek and clenched my teeth to keep any others back. I met her eyes, hating that my chin quivered. "No," I said again, and my insides, my bones, everything that held me together, failed. Inside something forever broke. "Why aren't you better?" It wasn't even a question, it was an accusation. "I wanted you to be better, even tonight I wanted it." I clamped my teeth down on the side of my tongue, harder and harder until the throbbing that filled my head dulled the one in my heart. "Why can't you love me? And not this— Don't," I broke off when she stood and reached for me. "This isn't love. I don't know how you could think it was. You're hurting me. And you're doing it to help you. That's wrong. Mom, that's wrong."

"I'm not trying to hurt you, I love you. If you just listen—"

"But you are!" I shook my head, mouth opening and closing, with tears slipping down my face. She couldn't hear it, but I did. There was an accent when Mom talked about love, like it was a language she hadn't fully learned and I knew now she never would.

"I don't know what more you want from me, I really don't."

I started forcing my teeth together, wondering if it was possible to bite down hard enough to crack them. She didn't know? She didn't *know*? "I tried to hate you when you left. I couldn't understand how you could do that to Dad, to me. Everything. It was horrible walking in on you with Sean. And not just because I love him, but because you would do that to Dad." I pressed a hand flat against my stomach and half hunched over. I was going to be sick. "And then you tell me he's not mine and he hated me and—" I had to bite down harder, biting until it reached my heart. And it didn't help. I couldn't replace or distract from the hurt.

Because it wasn't a hurt. That word was inadequate, it was deficient. Hurt was when you scraped your knee, when you got your finger slammed in a car door. Hurt was pain. It wasn't a searing, freezing silent scream, an endless falling.

I stepped away, needing to put distance between us, with her crying like she was the one who'd been sliced up and stitched back together. Tears and snot and great heaving breaths. Wave after wave of agony crashed over me until I was drowning. I couldn't breathe when she reached for my hands and squeezed.

I took strength from that gesture, but not in the way she wanted. I slipped my hands free and rubbed both my eyes dry, needing them clear when I looked at her. "But I can't hate you, and the only reason is because of Dad."

Her crying stopped, instantly, and it was only how ugly it had been that made me believe it had been real to begin with.

"He wouldn't let me. And not because of him, because of me. It would have been so easy for him to trash you to me. I wanted him to, but he never did, not once, not when you deserve it so much more than he knows. Even now he keeps trying to get me to give you another chance. Because he would rather suffer than see me hurt. That's love. And it's the exact opposite of what you've done."

Lips trembling, she lifted her chin. "I do love you. I'm trying to show you that I love you and I always have."

My voice shook like this was the last thing I'd ever say to her. "I don't know what kind of legal rights you think you have over Dad, but I'm asking you not to pursue them. I am begging you." And then I had to look at her. I had to. I looked at the diamond on her left hand, the way she kept rearranging the grip on her purse. She plucked at the strap, turning it first one way then the next. It was exactly the kind of thing I did when I was uncomfortable. And then I finally said it, the only thing I had to stop her, and I had no idea if it would be enough.

"If you love me at all, prove it. Mom, stop hurting me."

Her whole body lifted up on a sob that she caught in her hand. A second later she hugged me tight, clutching me like she'd never ever let me go.

And then she did.

CHAPTER
39

When it was just me and an empty park, when Mom left with an "I'm sorry" so insubstantial, hearing it might have been a trick I played on myself, I wandered over to the swing set she used to push me on.

I barely fit. The thick chain links dug into my hips as I swung back and forth. When it started to hurt, I got off and sat down on the merry-go-round. I was still sitting there when he showed up.

Somehow I wasn't surprised.

When I glanced up at his approach, when our eyes met, something like relief, only warmer, filled me.

My feet were trailing lazy patterns through the shredded tire mulch that covered the playground. "They didn't have this when we were little. Kind of takes the fun out of it if you can't get hurt when you fall."

"I don't know." Sean reached down and plucked a domino-sized piece of tire from the ground. "It's not exactly soft. Want me to shove you off the slide and see if it hurts?"

When I didn't give him so much as a pity laugh, Sean let the piece fall back to the ground.

"Claire?" Not that I needed to ask. Of course she'd called him.

"Yeah."

"Were you watching the whole time?" With my feet pressed into the ground, I moved the merry-go-round, back and forth, back and forth, to keep my brain as numb as my heart.

"No. Claire called me ten minutes ago. She figured your mom would have left by then.

"What are we doing, Jill?"

"Sitting." Even though I was sitting, it was like the ground shifted underneath me, tilted just off center so everywhere I looked was crooked.

"At the park by your old house? At night?" He brushed my cheek with his thumb. My tears were gone, but there was no hiding they'd been there.

Sean bent down in front of me. I wanted to take his hand and tug him next to me, rest my head on his shoulder and listen to his voice and the way his laugh colored his words when he told a joke, let everything else fade away in the warm night air.

But I couldn't. I was caught in this swinging between wanting and desperately not wanting him to tell me what had happened the night he almost kissed my mom. The night he maybe did, and I just didn't know.

The back and forth was making me physically ill. When I stayed silent, Sean leaned back. I couldn't look at him when he started to speak.

"What you said this morning. Is that what you really think? What you've been thinking all this time?"

You almost kissed my mom.

He waited for me to look at him. I didn't open my mouth, but I didn't have to. Sean's face lost all expression then. And when he started talking again, his voice was little more than breath.

He told me what I already knew. He was alone with my mom, my very unhappy mom, the night she left. It was innocent enough at first. She always flirted. He said he didn't. He made sure I understood that fact. Like it mattered somehow.

It didn't.

She'd asked him a lot of questions, and it was like his answers didn't matter. What did he think of her new dress? Her new necklace? Did he notice that she'd highlighted her hair?

Apparently my dad never noticed anything.

He'd told her about the text I'd sent explaining that I'd be late to meet him at the house.

And she'd wanted to see.

She'd sat on the arm of his chair and leaned in to see his phone, but then she'd stayed there, leaned closer.

I pulled my legs up, wrapping my arms around them as tightly as possible. I found a seam on the merry-go-round and dug my thumbnail underneath it.

Then she'd wanted to know what he thought of her perfume. She'd swept her hair behind one shoulder and bared her neck.

I tried to stop listening.

I knew that she'd started toying with the button on his shirt.

I didn't know that she'd told him that when my dad worked late, it was usually hours before he got home.

The merry-go-round shifted and Sean was sitting next to me.

He said my name twice, refusing to continue until I looked at him.

I looked. His words didn't change the past. He'd stayed right in that chair. He could have left.

But he hadn't.

When I asked him why, he didn't answer.

A dot of blood bloomed dark and red against my skin when my thumbnail tore. It was almost pretty until it smeared. Until it throbbed. Until I pressed my thumb into the hard metal seam and the hurt zinged up my arm, adding a different kind of pressure behind my eyes.

Sean was really smart. He'd tutored me in a bunch of subjects last year. He was probably going to be valedictorian. But he hadn't left that night with Mom. He'd sat there. He'd stayed.

He made me listen.

He made me look at him through eyes that blurred his features.

"I thought she told you. All this time I thought you knew, that she'd explained before she left." He squeezed his eyes shut in a grimace before opening them again. "How could you stand to look at me thinking... Jill...?"

By clinging to some things like they were oxygen and shoving others so far away that I could almost pretend they didn't exist. Because Sean was both. He was what I needed and what I couldn't stand all at once. I loved him and I didn't. Both. Completely. I had no idea what I was doing with him, only that I couldn't do it anymore.

"She didn't say a word to me after you left. Nothing."

Sean let his head drop. "Jill. Why do you think I stopped going to your house before that? Did you even notice? I wouldn't even go inside. We'd meet at the shop, or Claire would pick you up. That night I tried to pick you up at the shop, but you sent me away so I timed it out so that I would get to your house right after you, so I wouldn't be alone with your mom."

This was already worse than not knowing. He didn't trust himself to be alone with my mom. I was going to be sick.

"Your mom... That wasn't the first time that she did something like that."

The sob I kept locked inside forced my chin up as it tried to break free. I blinked so fast that the swing set across from me flickered in and out of existence. If I trusted my voice I would have begged him not to say any more. *Please don't make me imagine any more. If there were other nights that I didn't walk in on...* My body shook like it was caving in on itself.

Sean reached for my hand and I tore it free, wrapping my arms tightly around myself. I stopped blinking and squeezed my eyes shut, praying he'd leave before I had to open them again. Praying I'd never have to see either one of them ever again.

"I'm not leaving this time." He stood but lowered himself to the ground in front of me. He'd be the first thing I saw when I opened my eyes. That would hurt. Even the sound of his voice hurt.

"Jill. You know me. Think. I would never do anything like this to you. Never. *Never.*"

But he did. He had. The loop was back. Mom whispering in his ear, lips moving closer as her hand slipped to the button on his shirt. Only this time I didn't interrupt them. The button popped free, and the next, and the next. Her hand on his thigh...

Sean's words cut through the rushing in my ears. "Tell me. Have I ever flirted with your mom or hugged her or even smiled at her the way I smile at you? Jill, tell me."

The insistent tone in his voice forced my eyes open, forced me to flip back though all the memories I had of Sean and

Mom. Sean and me sitting on the floor in my living room watching movies and Mom joining us with popcorn, all the nights she asked him to stay for dinner, or offered to drive him home when it got too dark to bike home before he had the Jetta. A million other mundane memories. But nothing I could point to as flirting. At all.

In fact, on movie nights I remembered him jumping up to get us pops as soon as she sat down next to him, and when he came back he'd sit on my other side, the one farthest from her.

He almost never stayed for dinner and never at all on nights Dad worked late. I'd always thought it was because his own mom was such a good cook.

And before he got his license, even on nights when I had hours of homework ahead of me, he'd cajole me into riding along when Mom drove him home. Every time.

He saw when I came up blank, when the sob no longer battled to escape but started to sink down. There was nothing. I let the loop play again, watching him, watching Sean, and not Mom. The way he sat, the white-knuckle grip of his hands, the furrow of his eyebrows. He wasn't touching her. He wasn't looking at her. He had looked like he wanted to leap out of his skin. I'd been agonizing over the fact that he hadn't left until I showed up, but I'd watched her hand move to touch his leg as she leaned in. If I'd waited another second before dropping my bag, what would I have seen? In my weakest moments, it was another button on his shirt opening. But Sean, and all my own memories, said no. Said never.

I searched his face. I wanted to believe him. I wanted it more than I wanted my next breath.

Sean drew back and dropped his head. "Your mom was really unhappy. I know you knew that, but I never told you about any of the other stuff. It wasn't anything huge, little stuff. Like wanting me to taste a sauce she cooked, but she wouldn't have any clean spoons. Or walking out in a towel and saying she forgot I was there. Then she'd say things... things that could have been innocent, but didn't feel like it. Things she'd never say in front of you or your dad. Sometimes it was comments about your dad. So I tried to stay as far away from her as possible. And I did, until that night. You said you were going to be home by seven so I got there at a quarter after. You weren't there yet, so I was going to wait in the car, but your mom saw me through the window and waved me in. Jill, I never would have gone inside if I didn't think you were gonna be there any minute, never. And I swear I was going to bolt out that front door if you hadn't shown up then. I swear it."

There was a ferocity behind his words that was almost scary. He was as desperate to be believed as I was to believe him.

And I did. Suddenly, like a lightning strike, I did. And it was easy. It fit in a way all the fear and the dread never had. In that moment all my doubt vanished. I was blinking at him. His face becoming clearer each time. Until I could see all of him.

And Sean saw me too. "You gonna make me say it?"

I shook my head. I didn't need him to. I truly didn't.

"I never came close to kissing her. Never."

"I know." Those two words strung together left my tongue carrying a weight so great that its absence left me feeling like I would float away. I smiled at Sean, the first real smile I'd given him in months.

"So where does that leave us?"

CHAPTER
40

Sitting next to Sean on the merry-go-round made me realize how long it'd been since I'd counted the inches that separated our fingers. How long since I'd tried to number the flecks of silver that shot through his eyes.

How long since I'd stopped.

So long, and not long at all.

It felt like aeons since I'd learned to think about him the only way I could without something ugly slicing at my insides.

Only there was nothing ominous circling my thoughts of Sean anymore. He was Sean. My best friend, even more than Claire. Long before my heart got tangled up between us, he was the boy I'd spend hours playing "Need for Speed" with, the boy who used to sneak me into his brother's no-girls-allowed tree house, the boy who dressed up as Oliver Hardy to my Stan Laurel for Halloween three years in a row.

I didn't wake up one day and decide to love Sean Addison. I woke up one day and realized there wasn't a time I could remember not loving him. Until one night, with whiplash-inducing speed, I stopped.

So much of my life was tied up in Sean Addison. All the good stuff and the bad. But if the bad was gone, where did that leave us?

"I don't know." It was the only answer I had.

"Maybe I do. Hear me out, okay?" Sean leaned forward enough for a nearby park light to paint a star in his eyes. "You know I hate running, right? Tell me you know that?"

"I know."

"Right. Good." He sat forward again, his hands between his knees. "And Claire, well, sometimes I want to kill her, but I love her and—" Sean sighed before catching my eye and holding it. "Do you remember Jamie Pilther's thirteenth birthday? We carpooled together."

I blinked, trying to follow his random subject change. But I remembered every single detail about that night. Jamie was pretty hung up on Claire at the time and, as her best friend, I'd reaped the benefits by getting invited to his birthday. Most of the party I'd spent playing messenger between them:

"Does she want to hold his hand?"

"No."

"Does she want to be his girlfriend?"

"No."

"Does she want to sit next to him while he opens his presents?"

"Okay."

After the presents were opened, I'd officially resigned as messenger girl. Claire had gotten over her initial shyness and was able to talk to Jamie by then anyway. But that wasn't why I remembered Jamie Pilther's thirteenth birthday. And that wasn't why Sean was bringing it up.

I don't remember who suggested we play spin the bottle, but I do remember my eyes instantly scanning the crowded basement for Sean. Claire refused to play, but she was the only one. My hands were shaking when it was my turn. I could even still remember where Sean sat, four people to my left, and watching the bottle spin, round and round and round.

I remember it didn't land on Sean.

I don't remember the name of the guy it landed on, not that it mattered. Claire's mom arrived to pick us up before my brain had even fully registered my disappointment.

"I knew you wanted the bottle to land on me," Sean said, pulling me back to the present. It would have been pointless to deny it. "I wanted it to land on me too."

"Don't." I dragged my eyes away. "I don't want you to do this." He'd had all the time in the world since Jamie's party to say something like that, and he never had. Not even close. "I understand, okay? About my mom. I understand and I believe you. I think that's probably why I couldn't completely let you go, and I don't want to. I'll never want to."

Sean's eyes flitted down and he nodded. "Good. 'Cause I'd never let you."

"But you need to understand something too." Sean sat next to me waiting, but the words wouldn't come while he was that close. "Can you...can you go back to sitting on the ground?"

He moved and his mouth kicked up on one side. "I'm practically prostrate at your feet. Better?"

"Yes. But let me get it all out, okay?"

Sean's smile slipped.

"Jamie Pilther's birthday? That was nothing. That was my every day. It was insane how much I thought about you. Ask Claire." My smile was watery. "That night with my mom, even knowing what I know now, it opened my eyes. I waited for you to say something, to see me the way I couldn't help but see you. I waited so long, Sean. But you never did. Not really. And I know I could have said something, but it was so painfully, pathetically obvious how I felt. I knew you knew. I didn't get it then, but I do now."

"No you don't." The merry-go-round moved slightly as Sean sat down next to me, his hand slipping to my jaw to turn my face to his. My eyes followed more slowly, too slowly to see him move into me, dipping his head and fitting his lips over mine.

Kissing me.

Kissing me.

Kissing me.

CHAPTER
41

Kissing me.

Kissing me.

Kissing me.

All the thinking parts of my body stalled the moment Sean's lips touched mine. My heart revved in my chest and my hands clung to his wrists. His hands were firm on my jaw and his kiss eased into something so soft, so tender, that I tasted salt from a tear sliding down my cheek.

Sean tasted it too and pulled back. His eyes were searching mine and I felt his breath against my lips.

"Why?" I whispered. "Why do you have to see me now? I kind of hate you for that." Somebody's car alarm went off up the street. The blaring sound made me jump. Sean didn't seem to hear it. I sucked my lips into my mouth and tasted him.

Sean Addison kissed me.

He'd taken my face in his hands and kissed me. It was so perfect too. I would never have dreamed a moment better than the reality.

All of which made me kind of hate him.

"I wasn't lying before when I said I wanted the bottle to land on me. I kind of did, even then. Not like now. If we were playing now, I'd reach over and stop the thing myself." He met my eye. "I wouldn't need a bottle."

No. I closed my eyes. He had to stop saying things like that.

"But we were what, twelve?" he said, either not noticing or ignoring my growing discomfort. "I just remember thinking you looked really pretty in that green dress and that I wanted to be the one who kissed you." He shrugged. "But then you and Claire were all giggly later at school and I didn't think about you like that for a while. And yeah, I knew you liked me. A lot. I guess I figured that wouldn't change."

But it had. I didn't need to say why. I swallowed. My throat felt like an entire bag of popcorn was stuck in it.

Sean fell silent, which was good because I couldn't hear anything except my heart still thudding impossibly loud in my chest.

"I know that wasn't fair to you, and I'm sorry. You have no idea how sorry."

And then, because I apparently wanted to torture myself further, I asked him, "When?"

"When did I know? About you?" He waited for my nod. "Actually, that was Claire." He smiled at my look of confusion. "Do you know when she started in on me about running with you guys?"

I shook my head.

"It was right before Christmas. She caught me in the hall one day. 'Hey, wouldn't it be fun to go out for cross-country?' She said she'd make up a schedule for training over the summer and not to worry about it interfering with work or it being too hot because we'd run while it was still dark. I stopped listening to her after that because there wasn't a single thing that she was saying that I would ever consider doing.

"But then she said, 'It'll be the three of us. You, me and Jill.' And I heard myself agreeing. Even though I think cross-country will be the official sport in hell, and the idea of running before the sun rises still makes my brain cry even now that I've been doing it for weeks." We both smiled, and then Sean was looking at me with such wonder that I forgot to breathe. "But I didn't think about that. I thought about seeing you, every day, all summer. And I knew."

"Sean." I dragged his name out with almost no air left in my lungs. "That was seven months ago."

"You think I don't know that?"

"Then why?"

He looked away. "That's when your mom started…noticing me more. It messed up my head. I wanted to be around you but I really didn't want to be around her. So I waited. And then, after she left, it was different. *You* were different."

"Sean, I am so sorry that she…was like that with you. I can't even imagine." I didn't want to. Instead my brain raced back over those months, stopping on the moments with him that stuck out, that might have clued me in, but I couldn't find them. Not a single one.

"You never acted differently. How was I supposed to know that you were finally noticing me?"

"For the record, I've been noticing you since we were twelve. I've just been an idiot for the past five years." He wasn't being funny. None of it was. Part of me wanted to scream at all the wasted time. And another, much smaller part of me was glad that he'd had a few months to know what I'd felt for years.

"And your neighbor moved in." Sean tried to rein in the flicker that twisted his features. "And no, I don't want to start in on any of that. You say I was wrong to hit him, then I have to believe you."

I was too stunned by his acknowledgment of being wrong to say anything except, "Thank you."

Sean seemed surprised at himself too. "Yeah."

"And I'm sorry too. Lying to my dad about you. I never thought he'd call you, but I shouldn't have done that."

Sean shrugged. "It wasn't even about that, really. And none of that matters, not him or your mom." He wove a couple of his fingers underneath where my hand was pressed into the merry-go-round between us.

I pulled away.

"If you could see inside my head these past months." I stood up and fought not to shudder. "It hasn't been good, and you were tangled up in all of it. That doesn't just go away. I can't snap back to being in love with you because you want me to. I wish I could."

"Hey." Sean's hand was warm on mine as he stood and drew me toward him. And then he hugged me. It wasn't exactly like the hundreds of hugs he'd given me before. The arms he slid around my waist held me just differently enough that I could imagine how a completely nonfriend kind of hug from Sean would be. And that only made the knot in my throat bigger.

His chin rested on my head and his breath blew out over my hair. "I didn't mean to hurt you. Not ever." His arms tightened for a second before he pulled back enough so that I could see his eyes. It was probably the closest I'd ever been to him before. I could see all the flecks of silver. "Breaking your heart means I'm going to try and fix it. You know that, right?" I couldn't stop the extra beat my broken heart made at the way his eyes moved over my face. It was almost exactly the same flutter I'd felt watching that bottle spin at Jamie Pilther's birthday.

Sean gave me his half smile, the one that felt like it belonged to me—and maybe it did—and leaned toward me. He kissed my forehead. "You said you wish you were still in love with me. You used to love me when I wasn't even trying. Can you imagine what it's gonna be like now that I am?"

I laughed and he let me go. Reluctantly.

I sat and pulled my legs up and without needing to say anything, Sean started pushing. I watched him moving like a flipbook, catching a shot of him every time the merry-go-round rotated. The pattern sped up until Sean leaped on and we lay head to head, my legs in one direction and his in the other, staring up at the night.

"Probably not the greatest night to declare my undying love for you, huh?"

I curled my hand up over my shoulder, searching for Sean's and letting my eyes drop closed when the tips of his fingers laced through mine. Without a word. Without a glance. He just knew.

"What did she tell you this time?"

The fingers in my free hand curled, scraping across the metal tread of the merry-go-round. "Typical mom stuff. My not-real-dad couldn't stand the sight of me as a baby and the only reason he spent any time with me as a kid was to punish her. So, you know." I shrugged like I didn't care what she'd said, but the truth was lodged in my throat as I turned my head away from Sean.

After a long minute, Sean simply said, "Well, okay."

I looked back. "Okay? That's all you have to say?"

"Pretty much. I mean I always wondered if your mom was stupid or just evil, and now I know. She's both."

Air whooshed out of me. I hadn't known how much I'd needed someone else to say that. "You think?"

"Oh, yeah." Sean curled an arm behind his head. "And to be clear, she's not taking you for any amount of time. I don't care what we have to do."

I shouldn't have felt like smiling at him, but I did. He so clearly meant it. I almost asked him what we would do just to hear how far he'd be willing to go. But, with Sean, I already knew the answer.

"No," I said. "I've got more than sixteen months' worth of fighting in me, after that I'll be eighteen and it'll be no one's choice but mine." My almost smile slipped away and the knot in my throat rose infinitesimally higher. "But I don't think she was lying about my dad when I was little. She was telling the truth about my paternity, and the rest makes sense. It does."

"Jill..." Sean flipped to my side and wrapped an arm around me. "I love you like Claire loves her treadmill, but I've got nothing on your dad."

Sean was warm where his side pressed against mine and he made things so easy when I tried to make them hard. I squeezed his hand. "I'm really glad you came."

"I'm glad you let me. Do it more often, will you? Oh, and that," he added when I shifted closer. "See how well we fit?"

I let my head tip onto his shoulder.

Above us the stars looked like they were glowing water ripples, like stones skipped across the sky.

It was a good fit.

CHAPTER
42

It was late when Sean drove me back to the shop to pick up Dad's truck. Not curfew-breaking late, but near enough. Just as we passed Pep Boys, I knew something was wrong. The lights were on at the shop even though I'd turned them off.

I went a little pale when we turned into the parking lot and Sean's headlights illuminated Dad standing in the open garage bay.

"Did you call him?"

I shook my head. I'd turned my phone off when Mom showed up, but when I turned it back on, the screen lit up with missed calls. Lots of missed calls. Most from Dad.

As soon as he parked, Sean reached for his door, but I stopped him. "You sure? 'Cause I don't mind getting yelled at." He looked back at Dad standing directly over the spot that had previously held my Spitfire. "And you are about to get yelled at."

"It'll be worse if you're there. And I need to tell him everything."

Sean touched my hand as I opened my door, squeezing

it. "Hey." He waited for me to look back. "He loves you. I do too."

I couldn't dwell on that look and those words, but later I was going to let myself think about Sean and... Yeah. "I'll call you."

Sean's headlights passed over us as he backed out, leaving me to walk the dozen or so feet to the garage in relative darkness. I used every shadowed step to fortify myself for what I had to say.

Everywhere my eyes touched, a memory lay fresh on the surface. And the memories weren't of me crying over dirty hands or wishing I could take ballet; not one. They were of racing creepers with Dad on slow days; eating calzones with one hand so we wouldn't have to break for lunch on busy ones; Dad holding me up to stand on a bumper and inspect an engine; the first day I walked into the shop and saw my name on the board by itself, not alongside Dad's as his helper; realizing no matter how many hours I spent sliding across the floor in my socks, I'd never be able to moonwalk as well as Dad.

And he was my dad. His nose had the same little bump on the ridge that mine did. He used to skate his finger down it and pretend the bump caused his hand to fly off my face, making me laugh until my belly hurt. And they were the same. My bump and his. It didn't matter that his came from when he used to wrestle in high school and mine came from what amounted to a sperm donor.

"Dad?"

He was holding a piece of paper in his hands. The crease said he had folded and unfolded it at least a dozen times. He folded it again before answering. "You took the Spitfire."

That ill-fated joyride with Claire felt like a lifetime ago. "I know I shouldn't have, but—"

He gestured in the direction Sean had driven off and my obviously missing car. "Anybody hurt?"

"No."

"And the Spitfire?"

"Hurt." I didn't wait for him to ask for details. Halfway through describing the leaking coolant, he cut me off.

"We'll talk about that later." He took his paper in both hands and stared at it. "This morning, about what your mom told you, I didn't get to—"

"It doesn't matter."

"It does."

"Not to me." Claire said it didn't have to matter unless I let it, and she was right. Me and Dad. Nothing else mattered as long as it was the two of us. I'd always thought that, but I didn't *know* it until that year. Mom leaving the way she did, why she did; all of it had torn everything else away. It had poisoned Sean for me, given me a connection to Daniel that ended up hurting us both. Even my relationship with Claire had suffered as I'd withdrawn from her and just about everything else.

But I'd still had Dad. He'd still had me. When Mom had said she was going to take me from him, had tried to tell me he was never mine, I'd fractured head to toe. And I'd existed way too long in that fragile fearful state, knowing a sharp blow, a misplaced step, would shatter me.

But it didn't matter. Only one thing did.

"Why did you send me away today?" My voice was that of a little girl. I heard it and felt it, the smallness, the vulnerability. "You said she could take me and you couldn't stop her. Why didn't we leave? Why didn't we go to Oregon or anywhere that she couldn't find me?"

I noticed his hand tightening around the paper he held. The skin between his brows furrowed. "I tried to forgive her. I tried. But when you were born, you looked nothing like me. So I stopped trying."

I listened to Dad go on about the utter ruination of his marriage and the role he'd played, the one I'd never known about and still couldn't fully blame him for. Not even after he confirmed some of what Mom had told me.

"I wasn't a good husband when I had the chance, when it might have mattered. I needed today to think about what taking you from her would mean, because I stopped wanting to punish her a long time ago. How could I, when she gave me you?"

With that one sentence my world straightened. The ground was solid under my feet and I felt whole, loved by the person I needed most. He could have stopped then. I didn't need another word; even if every other accusation she'd leveled against him was true, she couldn't break us. Nothing could.

"It was…hard when you were born." Something twitched in Dad's eye. "I didn't want to love you, but I couldn't help it. I still can't."

I couldn't hold back anymore. I charged across the garage and into Dad, knowing he would catch me. He rocked back a few steps, laughing into my hair and hoisting me into the air. And there was my hug. The one he wouldn't give me in our kitchen earlier. The one that he'd held back because he didn't know if he had a right to take me from her again when he blamed himself for so much.

The paper he'd been holding slipped from his hand and fluttered open on the ground. The print was patchy in places since we were always running low on ink, but I could read it plainly. And I started to ugly cry.

Not because I needed more proof; I didn't. But it felt

good, better than good, knowing it was right there in black and white.

A flight confirmation for two one-way tickets to Portland.

Dad pulled back, holding my shoulders. "Jill, it's okay now."

I nodded because it was, no matter what happened next. "When the Spitfire broke down, I called her. I wasn't going to wait for her to show up again. I tried to make her understand that it's you and me, Dad. Always and forever. But I don't know what she's going to do." I bent down and picked up the paper. "But I want to stay here, to fight here."

Dad let me go so suddenly that I wobbled. He took the paper from me and tore it into pieces, smiling the whole time. "I came looking for you after I printed this." He dropped the shredded pieces onto the table. "But when I got here, your mom…she called me. Jill, she's not going to fight us."

Something fluttered in my chest, and I remembered that last hug she'd given me. For a moment I forgot everything she'd done to Dad and me and Sean. For one soaring heartbeat, I let her love me. I closed my eyes. "Say it again."

He touched his forehead to mine. "She's not taking you away from me. It's over. You're stuck with me now, kid. Oil changes and cold pizza and—"

"Everything I could ever want."

CHAPTER
43

Nothing about Arizona weather was subtle. Five months of summer meant it wasn't just hot outside; you felt the skin cells on your body die as the sun burned them away. Rain was no kinder, except we didn't call it anything so mundane as rain. It had its own season—monsoon—and it overlapped with the last two months of summer, bringing with it torrential thunderstorms, flash flooding, dust devils and the more frightening haboob dust walls that could average 30mph.

By the end of July, the air had lost its burning sting in favor of sticky heaviness despite the still-blistering sun. I could almost see steam rise up from the earth each time the rain hit.

It wasn't unusual for the retention basin down the street to flood high enough that some of our neighbors took kayaks and inner tubes to the makeshift pond.

Driving became something of a combat sport. All the rain brought oil and grime to the road surfaces, making them slick and slippery. Add in near-zero visibility and flooded underpasses, and business at the shop picked up considerably.

It felt wrong to be happy about that, but I was.

And the much-needed influx in business wasn't just from the monsoon season. Claire and Sean and I passed out flyers until we had more paper cuts than skin on our hands. It wasn't until that first week of August, however, that I realized we were going to make it. Not just the shop, but me and Dad.

Each day after that last visit with Mom felt surreal. We weren't going to get a letter from a lawyer or another call from her. I'd wake up in my bed—which I'd begun sleeping in on a trial basis—and I wouldn't believe that she was truly gone.

And it was hard wanting to smile and cry about that. Because she was my mom. She would always be my mom, so it would never be as simple as hating her and not.

I wanted to talk to Daniel about it like I wanted air. I was panting for it. I missed him. But it bothered me that maybe I didn't miss him enough.

He'd gotten home two days ago. I saw his Jeep, but not him. The past couple nights I'd thought about going up to my roof to see if he might slip out and join me, but I never got farther than peering out my closed window. It wasn't a good idea to be that person for him; it wasn't fair to either of us. And it wasn't like he was seeking me out either. Maybe it was better that way.

So instead of escaping to my roof at night, I went during the day.

I normally sat on the flat spread of roof that covered the back patio, but this time I sat closer to the edge, letting my bare legs hang free as I leaned back on my palms and watched the sunset.

There was still a sliver of golden sun peeking through in the west. The deep purple sky was shot through with vibrant pinks and oranges. They never looked quite real. Even after nearly seventeen years, there was something sublime about Arizona sunsets. It looked more like a child's paint set splashed across the sky, only it was too perfectly painted.

Of course I looked at Daniel's house, but I looked down at mine too.

Only two people lived there. I dragged my hand across the shingles, feeling the rough surface scratch against my palm.

I didn't startle when Sean poked his head up over the edge. I'd watched his Jetta pull up and knew Dad would have told him where I was.

A month ago, the idea of sharing this space with Sean would have horrified me. Back then, he was one of the main things I was trying to escape. But I didn't feel the need to hide from him anymore. I wanted him with me. After that night on the merry-go-round, the idea of watching the sunset with Sean—or doing anything with him—was about as far from horrifying as it could get.

He knocked on the eave, making me smile. "I brought you something. It's part of my get-Jill-to-love-me strategy."

Then he chucked something at my head.

His phone. Then his keys. Both of which narrowly avoided hitting me in the face.

"This is you trying to get me to love you?"

Sean grinned. "Nah. This is me throwing stuff at you that I don't want to drop. But it's cool, I can multitask." He tossed one more item at me.

When I caught the closed bag, the rich, buttery scent danced up my nose as I opened it. I loved movie popcorn. Sometimes I'd even buy it without going to a movie. Even cold it was delicious.

And Sean had brought me a bag. "What movie did you see?"

"No movie. I figured you'd like this more than flowers."

It'd be really easy to fall for Sean again. Too easy.

So far, his multitasking was impressive.

"Does the grin on your face mean you're inviting me up?"

I smiled bigger. Yes, I was.

Sean stopped several feet from the edge where I sat. "Why don't you come back this way."

I patted the roof next to me. "It's nice right here."

Sean took a step, a small one, then stayed where he was. "Nope. Can't do it."

"Sean." I shifted around on my knees and set the popcorn aside. "Are you afraid of heights?"

"Yes," he said. "Come over here and comfort me."

I laughed. "It's a one-story house."

"Sometimes it's the principle of the thing. Now come here. I'm cold and frightened."

"Why did you come up here, if you don't like heights?"

"Because I was highly motivated."

Sean didn't even blink when he said that, which made me feel decidedly not cold or frightened.

I walked over, and the second I got within arm's reach, he pulled me to him. He didn't let go of me even after we sat down, as though he thought one or both of us could plummet to our deaths at any moment. I pulled back. "You do know you'll have to climb down at some point."

"I do," he said. "I have a plan. You go down first, then you catch me. Good plan, right?"

"I could always get my dad to catch you."

"Wouldn't work." He shifted to reach across me and place a hand on the roof by my hip. "I'd lose my incentive to jump."

I laughed and pushed him back while my heart fluttered not unpleasantly.

"Besides, it was the only way I could think of to see you today."

"I see you practically every day."

"I know, and I already have to work at that."

I cocked my head at him. "It's not really that hard when we do everything together."

"Shall I enlighten you?" Then he laughed and my toes curled. "Some of this is mildly embarrassing, so try not to mock too much."

And then he told me.

"Your bike is destroying my backseat, but I keep it covered with a blanket so you'll let me keep driving you home."

I tried to lean around him to see if I could make anything out from where he was parked, but Sean mirrored my movement and caught my hand.

"Sometimes I let the air out of my tires so you'll help me change them." His thumb started tracing the veins at my wrist causing my pulse to speed up. "See my bumper? I deliberately backed into a tree two days ago. For you. Well, for me really, because I'll get to be with you when you fix it."

I made a face.

"I told you it was embarrassing."

"No, it's not that." I squirmed a little in his hands. "But did you have to wreck your car?"

Whatever Sean was expecting me to say, that wasn't it. His dimples went into overdrive. "That's what bothers you about what I just said? Wrecking my car? Here." He lifted my hand and placed it on his chest directly over his heart. "I'd drive it into the canal if that's what it took."

"Don't do that. You can't imagine what kind of damage water does to a car."

"I'll put sugar in the gas tank."

"That's not funny."

"And the next time I get a flat—"

"Please don't say it." I squeezed my eyes shut.

"—I'll. Just. Keep. Driving."

"Sean." My eyes shot open. "We will not be friends anymore if you do any of those things."

"Promise?"

And I felt it. That match strike, engine catch, firework thrill in my heart. It wasn't that desperate need that had smothered me in the past, keeping me anxious and half-sick most of the time. It was like a flower blooming. It made me feel strong and warm and happy.

I felt the gentle beat speeding under my palm and knew my heart was pounding just as fast, and not only from car-related anxiety. I felt it in the fingers that locked with mine and the breath that ghosted over my lips.

When Sean kissed me, I waited for that same wrongness to flare up, the one that reminded me of Mom holding his shirt, the one that said *stop because this will hurt.*

But it never came.

Instead, I thought of him coming to the track after working all night to run with me, because of me. I thought of him bringing me movie-theater popcorn even when he wasn't going to the movies, because he knew I loved it. I thought of the way he'd held me when I told him about my mom. The way my pain had hurt him like it was his own. Not just that night at the park, but always.

I thought of everything that had ever made my heart soar, and it was all Sean.

And I kissed him back.

His arms encircled me and his lips pressed against mine with the sweetest pressure. It wasn't a long, drawn-out kiss. It was his lips on mine, his breath mixed with mine, and it was a moment that I would have lived in for eternity.

When he pulled back and took in my face, his lit up with a kind of wonder that I couldn't help but laugh at. Sean's dimpled smile did that funny thing to my heart again, only this time it didn't scare me.

But the screaming from Daniel's house did.

CHAPTER
44

Sean and I jerked apart. He spun every which direction, but I knew exactly where to look even before her next scream had words.

"You killed him!"

Glass breaking, piercing and shrill, shredded the night. I rose up on my knees to see a table lamp in Daniel's front yard surrounded by a sea of glass, glittering against the dull gray gravel.

I scrambled over the peak of my roof and down the front side, my bare feet skidding and just barely stopping me from sliding off the edge. It only took seconds, but unnamed fear clenched me so hard in those strangled heartbeats that I barely registered catching my hand on a stray nail. It tore right through the fleshy part of my palm.

It didn't hurt until I saw him, framed in jagged glass beyond his broken living-room window. Daniel stood immobile while his mom was a blur of fists. Her words barely had form. Shrieks and incoherent sobs slapped at me as she struck him.

"You killed him!" she screamed, over and over before folding in on herself.

A phone lay forgotten at her feet. When Daniel reached for her, she shrieked as if she were on fire and attacked again, slapping him hard enough that his head snapped to the side, and our eyes met through the broken window.

I had nothing with me this time. No pop can to throw, no coupon for his Jeep. I couldn't fix anything. I watched Daniel turn back in time to catch another slap.

I'd only seen Daniel once with his mom, and then only in silhouette. They were flesh and blood this time, less than twenty feet away, bordered by broken glass like some sort of sick stage play. I saw the way the pained expression slipped from his face.

Then she spit at him. "It should have been you."

When Daniel failed to react, impotence smothered me until I wanted to scream as she drew back her hand again. Maybe I did scream. Because he caught her wrist only inches from his face.

She had to see what I saw, the break. The moment Daniel was done. The moment he stopped trying. She attempted to pull her wrist free, but he held on. He didn't need to yell like she did. His voice held a kind of quiet anger that was impossible to miss.

"He'd have killed you a dozen times over if I hadn't gotten big enough to distract him. I let him bust my hand with a hammer the last time you burned his dinner. He didn't deserve what he got?" He lifted his head. "It was *my* jaw he broke when he lost his job, *my* back he burned." Daniel pulled up his shirt, and even twenty feet away, I could see the round, puckered flesh dotting his shoulder. "What did he deserve for that?" He pointed to the massive scar that spanned his torso. "I was ten when he pushed me out the upstairs window, do you remember? I hit the porch light on the way down. He wouldn't let you take me to the hospital until you cleaned up all the blood. What's that worth?" He threw her hand back and she stumbled. Her black hair had fallen free from her bun and the strands snaked around her face, concealing her features, but they did nothing to disguise the contempt in her voice.

"We would have been fine if you'd stayed away."

"He would have killed you if I'd stayed away! And for what? Because you forgot to record a show he liked? Maybe you were wearing the wrong color. What did you do to deserve a dozen broken ribs and a bat bashed into your face?"

"No!" she screamed, jumping at him again. "You were the one who made him mad. If you'd just left us…"

I was moving then, skirting the edge of my roof until the wall appeared below me. When I flipped onto my stomach to slide down, Sean was there. Sweat broke out across his forehead, and not from heat, as he followed right behind me. Concrete from the wall touched my bare feet, then gravel a second later as I jumped to the ground. I started to run but an arm wrapped around my waist and pulled me back.

"Jill, there's glass everywhere." Sean looked at my bare feet.

But she was still yelling, hitting him.

"I'll go," he said, already moving toward the house.

"Give me your phone," I said, and Sean tossed it back to me, but the sirens we heard halted both of us.

Blue and red lights flashed from around the corner, illuminating dozens of neighbors in their yards, and more than a few in Daniel's.

Everything after that was a blur of moving bodies and blaring noise. We watched two officers emerge from the car, jump through the window and start wrestling Daniel's mom to the floor. Neighbors recounted events for latecomers, and later for the officers.

"He didn't do anything," one said, while another quickly nodded.

"It's true. She attacked him. He never retaliated."

I dropped my eyes to Daniel's mom, who was on the ground with a knee in her back still screaming obscenities at her son. It took forever to haul her out of the house. When she passed me, her black eyeliner was smeared all over her cheeks.

Daniel's face. It was painful to look at as he watched them load her into the backseat. He still wanted to protect her, even as she intoned over and over again that they should keep him away from her.

Daniel tried to go after her. "Wait," he said. "She's not right. You can't—" An officer halted him, but he called to her. "Mom, I'll be right behind you."

His face was worse when he noticed what I did: she fought less and less the farther away she was from her son.

Behind me, a neighbor was watching too. "She said he killed someone."

I shook my head, knowing there was no way that could be true even as part of me called out for the justice of it. But could the rest be true? I'd barely been listening to Daniel's mom. It hadn't been the content of her words that I'd focused on, so much as the scene playing out in front of me, but I did now, keeping my eyes on Daniel as the officer spoke.

Daniel's father was dead.

CHAPTER
45

I curled my knees to my chest, hugging them tight against the premonsoon breeze. The clouds had spread overhead and blotted out the stars. Only a tiny break showed that the moon was up and slowly being swallowed by the encroaching clouds.

The night was quiet. No gossiping neighbors in their yards, no sirens, no screaming. Even Sean had gone home.

I'd been up on my roof for what felt like hours. Waiting.

Earlier, he'd given me no reason to expect him. No look or indication that he'd want to talk with me—*need* to talk to me. Nothing beyond that fleeting moment when our eyes had met and I'd exhaled more air than my body could possibly contain, knowing he was okay.

The wind kicked up and my hair flew around to whip my face. A clap of thunder sounded. By my guess, I had about eight minutes before the clouds split apart.

Eight minutes wasn't enough time.

I was watching the last glimmer of the moon disappear as the storm clouds took full possession of the night sky, when I heard him.

The back door of his house squeaked open. His head was turned in my direction before he even stepped out. It was as dark as it ever got, but I thought I saw his shoulders lift when he saw me. Two long steps, a burst of energy on the last, and he was on the wall. Seconds later, he was next to me.

And I couldn't blink for fear that I'd waste what little time I knew we had; time that really didn't have anything to do with the coming rain.

Lightning flashed in the distance, throwing the planes of his face into relief for one second, two. My heart broke for him in those seconds.

His jaw was locked, his eyes lowered. His dark hair fell forward to skim his cheekbones. More thunder. Louder and closer this time. I wasn't even going to get my eight minutes.

"He's dead."

"I know," I said. *Altercation.* That was the word the officer had used. It sounded so civil for what amounted to one prisoner beating another to death.

"I went to see him last week."

A boulder hit me square in the stomach. The officer had said Daniel's dad died that morning, and Daniel had been home for a few days already, so he hadn't been there *there* when it happened, but maybe...maybe he'd said something? Or his dad had?

"I'm not sorry he's dead," Daniel said.

"I'm not either." And more than that, I was relieved Daniel felt the same way. I could still taste the bile that had risen in my throat when Daniel had confronted his mom with the physical marks his dad left on him. If he had to deal with guilt on top of that... I'd want to kill his dad all over again.

I didn't want to ask him any more questions because there were no good answers, but they spilled out anyway. "Why did you go see him?"

"I found out she was calling him, from almost the second she got out of the hospital. Maybe even before."

My eyes shut.

"It didn't matter that I got her away, moved her halfway across the country, because he still had a hold on her. I could take her to the other side of the world and she'd still write to him, talk to him." His voice was so full of pain that it hurt me. "She'd wait forever."

My head and heart lurched in opposite directions. He'd gone to the monster that had destroyed his childhood—and was still poisoning any possible happiness with his mom— to plead for her. I shuddered, knowing this man I'd never met—and now never would—would have never acquiesced, not if half of what I'd heard about him was true.

"I asked him to stop. No more calls, no more letters. To let her go."

I didn't need to ask what his dad had said.

The answer had been no.

Horribly, unthinkably, no.

I could imagine that fight through a pane of Plexiglas, the heated words and hotter tempers. I could see the guards dragging his father off as if I'd been there. And even though Daniel didn't say, I could all too easily see his stoked temper inciting the wrong inmate—or five in Daniel's father's case—and sparking the last deadly encounter of a brutally executed life.

It had taken his dad more than a week to die from his injuries.

And I couldn't be sorry about any of it.

I kept looking at Daniel out of the corner of my eye. I didn't want to stare, but I was looking for anything, any shift of his body, that meant he wanted to say more. But he didn't shift. He barely moved.

So I did.

I stretched out my legs, half curling one under me. "It's going to start pouring any second. It'll be like we're under a waterfall. But we can go inside—I don't think my dad will mind." I knew he wouldn't. Any other night, yes. But not this night. I put my hand flat on the roof between us, intending to stand up and urge Daniel physically as well as verbally to come inside, but his hand shot out and pressed mine down. It stung, since that was the hand I'd caught on a nail earlier, but I didn't react.

"Stay," he said. "Please."

Daniel hadn't moved save for his hand. Hadn't turned his head to look at me. It was as though the rest of his body was locked. But I stayed. Of course, I stayed. Even now, his fingers were curling under mine, prying my hand up from the scratchy tiles, lacing our fingers together. His hand was so warm compared to mine. And his grip was just shy of painful, but I squeezed back just as firmly.

I didn't bother with my sideways glances anymore. I openly stared. He was bouncing his head slowly, nodding it in small, rapid movements. Even in the dim light, I could see the scratch marks on his face from where she'd attacked him. His mom. They looked deep enough to scar.

I prayed they wouldn't, that nothing in his life would ever scar him again.

When I reached out to brush his hair from his face, Daniel turned into my hand. A moment later he was clutching me to him, his hands locked behind my back.

It wasn't a remotely romantic gesture.

His dad was dead. A man he'd spent most of his life cursing, maybe even wishing dead. I didn't know if he felt relief or anger. Maybe he didn't know. I think he'd been so focused on the burden of keeping his mom safe, showing her what life without abuse could be like, clinging desperately to the hope that she'd wake up one day and not hate him for trying to save her, that suddenly being freed from all that was its own kind of burden. One that he couldn't share with anyone.

But he was, in a way, sharing it with me.

And that was why I clung to him as tightly as he clung to me. Why I didn't press him to say a word. Why I thought of my mom and wondered if there could be an emotion somewhere between love and hate. Why I let the promised rain drench us both when it began to fall.

CHAPTER
46

Sean, Claire and I got home from the hardware store a couple days later, laden with paint cans and drop cloths. It felt like overkill for such a tiny room, but Claire was adamant, and I really wanted that periwinkle color gone from Dad's bathroom. As first steps went, it was small, but it was a start, and Claire was ecstatic that I wanted her to help me take it.

She could barely see around the massive and scarily comprehensive box of painting supplies she was holding, but Sean noticed Daniel almost as soon as I did.

He was leaning against the front of his Jeep, both hands in his pockets as he squinted at me in the bright sunlight. I didn't need to see the oversize duffel bag at his feet to know why he was waiting for me.

"We're gonna head in and get set up." Sean brushed my arm, then took Claire by the shoulders and steered her toward my house.

It was so much the perfect thing for him to say that I almost kissed him on the spot, but that didn't feel like the best way to let Daniel know what had happened while he was gone. I didn't regret my choice, but I did regret that it might hurt Daniel.

I walked toward him. "You're leaving." I tried to keep my voice steady. I'd known he would leave. I just hadn't expected it to be so soon.

"I wanted to see you before." He cocked his head, looking at me and then toward Sean's Jetta. "Guess I'm a little late."

Daniel and I had missed from the start, and the lack of rancor in his voice told me he knew that too. It was a near miss in my case, maybe for him too, but we'd avoided true heartbreak.

And we cared enough about each other to be glad.

"You look happy," he said.

"I feel happy. I'm trying not to scare it away."

His smile was bittersweet. I knew better than to ask Daniel if he was happy, but I hoped he'd find it in his future, wherever he went.

I moved so that the sun split around my body and shaded his face. "Will you go back to Pennsylvania?"

Daniel shook his head and looked at the houses across the street. "There's nothing there for me." He tried to say it as if it didn't matter, as if he was talking about some restaurant that he didn't like instead of the only home he'd ever had. But I could see the effort behind his indifference in the way he kept his eyes traveling up and down the street, like he was just casually looking around when I knew his movement was because he didn't want me to see his eyes.

"And your mom?" As far as I knew, she hadn't come back since the police took her away.

"She's got sisters there. I don't have a reason to keep her away anymore."

I heard the way he referred to them as his mom's sisters, like he had no claim on them, even though they were his family as much as hers. There was a lot he'd never told me about his family, but he'd told me enough, both then and now. Either they didn't want him, or he didn't want them. I hoped for his sake it was the latter.

The sun was hot against my back. The rays cut through the thin cotton of my shorts and caused my skin to prickle all the way down the back of my thighs. There was no evidence of the torrential rainstorms from the past few nights. The sun had sucked up every last drop of water, leaving only a slightly muggy weight to the air, a humidity that made my clothes stick to my skin.

Needing to get away from the direct heat, I moved to lean against the Jeep next to Daniel, shifting so that my shorts, and not my bare legs, touched the metal. "If not Pennsylvania, then where?"

"Not sure. Somewhere cool." He smiled and flicked his eyebrows up once at me.

"Coward," I said. "Summer is almost over. You already made it through most of the worst part. It'll be cool and even a little chilly in nothing flat." I snapped my fingers.

Daniel laughed like I'd meant him to, but it only made the hollow in the pit of my stomach grow.

"I was thinking I might head up north." He told me about some friends he had in Alaska.

"Summer in Arizona and winter in Alaska." I laughed. "You're insane."

"Yeah, well, anywhere I end up after this will seem—"

"Boring?"

"I was going to say easy."

A coolish breeze blew up from behind me, signaling that summer truly was dying, and tossed my hair forward around my face. Daniel stepped toward me.

"Will you miss me?" he asked with an intensity that made me realize how important my answer was to him.

He'd seen me with Sean, so I thought he understood what I meant when I nodded. I would miss him, if the ache in my heart was any indication. But aches wouldn't scar, aches wouldn't shatter, aches would heal and leave something that I could think about, with, if not quite happiness, not sadness either. That's what Daniel would leave with me.

He was watching my face, waiting for more than a nod. "I already do," I said. I hugged him and felt his arms hold me just a hair too tightly.

He stepped back when I released him. "Will he mind if I kiss you goodbye?" Daniel nodded toward my house. Toward Sean.

He'd definitely mind. And it was good for me to realize that I wasn't interested in kissing anyone else but the guy who'd brave heights, five a.m. runs and my paintbrush-wielding friend just to be near me. So when Daniel leaned down, it was an easy decision to shift to the left and brush a kiss on his cheek.

He smiled. "Probably for the best, huh? I am going to call you in a few years," he said, still smiling but not looking at me. "I'll be too late, but I'm going to call anyway."

A part of me couldn't help thinking that he'd always been too late.

"The stars are supposed to be really beautiful in Alaska," I said, trying to bring back the lighter feel that had always been better for us. "You'll get to see the aurora borealis."

"I'll never look at the stars without thinking of you."

I looked away. I couldn't give him a part of my heart to take with him, and it wasn't fair for him to leave part of his with me.

"Or a tire jack."

I smiled; relief and gratitude rolled into a final goodbye. "Be safe." I wanted so much more for him, but that was all I trusted myself to say. I bit my lip when he opened his door, but then he stopped and in a second had me wrapped in a hug tighter than before. Just as quickly he let me go and climbed into his Jeep. My heart caught along with the engine, and our eyes met one last time before he drove away.

Sean was sitting on my porch swing when I walked up to my house. The sudden flutter in my heart lifted the corners of my mouth when I looked at him—when I looked at him looking at me. My smile bloomed full when I realized that for the first time, we were looking at each other in the exact same way. The way that told me his heart was fluttering too.

"Just so we're clear," he said, when I curled up under the arm he offered me. "I expect you to hit the next guy that tries to kiss you, present company excluded."

"Deal," I said. "As long as I'm the only one who gets to call you Sean-y."

I held my eyes shut for a moment, prompting Sean to ask, "You okay?"

I hesitated for only a heartbeat before nodding. I did feel okay. Moments like this made me feel better than okay.

Daniel was gone, but he was free for the first time in his life. Dad and I weren't going to lose each other. Ever. And when I thought of Mom—which I did, a lot—I let a few not horrible memories wade into the sludge. The good would never make up for the bad, but knowing everything meant I no longer needed to scream in her face until I went hoarse and then throw things at her until I couldn't lift my arms anymore. Sean said that was progress. Not that either of us labored under the delusion that she'd be reentering my life in any capacity, but it was better for me not to actively hate her.

Deep breath.

There was nothing special about the afternoon that the three of us spent painting Dad's bathroom, not in any sort of tangible way that someone watching my life could point to and say, "There!" But it felt important nonetheless because of what it meant to me.

When Dad came in with takeout from Claire's favorite Greek restaurant, I took another deep breath and filled my lungs to the point of bursting, letting my chest expand until there was no room inside me for anything but air. And Claire. And Sean. And Dad.

* * * * *

ACKNOWLEDGMENTS

Growing up, I wanted to be Laura Ingalls Wilder and Anne Shirley (also Indiana Jones), so writing stories was always something I aspired to (along with teaching and possibly discovering Atlantis). Like my literary heroines, I had my Pa and Matthew, my Ma and Marilla, my Mary and Diana, and many others who helped me make this book a reality.

My literary agent, Kim Lionetti. You have made every moment of my first foray into publishing better than I ever dreamed possible. I couldn't have signed with a better agent.

My editor, Natashya Wilson. Thank you for believing in this story and these characters, and pushing me to make them the best they could be (and for all the covers of Coldplay's *Fix You*!).

Art director Gigi Lau, who designed this beautiful cover, and my publicist, Siena Koncsol, for making sure readers discovered *If I Fix You*. And the entire team at Harlequin TEEN, including Bryn Collier, Evan Brown, Ashley McCallan, Rebecca Snoddon, Olivia Gissing, Amy Jones, Shara Alexander, Lauren Smulski, Kristin Errico, Nancy Fischer, Jean Delaney, Katie Gowrie and Peter Cronsberry. I can't thank you enough.

The best critique partners on the planet, Sarah Guillory and Kate Goodwin. I would not have finished this book or any other without the two of you. You read everything I write and somehow still want to read more. You make my writing better, my characters more alive and my stories stronger. I still save all the best Fresh Prince GIFs for you.

The people who read early versions of this book and offered invaluable feedback, including Nicole Green, Susan Gray Foster, Mónica B. Wagner and Lindsey Sprague.

My best friends and sisters, Mary Groen, Rachel Decker and Jill Johnson. Mary, more than anyone, you have been my sounding board, my brainstorming partner and cheerleader through every single page of this book. Thanks for wall walking with me when we were kids and for using your Muay Thai expertise to choreograph the fight scene for me. Rachel, thanks for encouraging me to make the hard cuts in the beginning of the book (you were right) and for climbing onto roofs in the middle of the night to take pictures for me. I will never stop bugging you to finish your novel. Jill, thanks for letting me use your name and for marrying my brother so I could officially claim you as my sister after being friends since the 7th grade.

My brother, Sam Johnson. Sorry this book isn't about a vampicorn named Brian.

My uncle, Ken Johnson. Sorry I couldn't start the book with "'Ouch!' cried the badger."

My aunt and uncle, Rick and Jeri Crawford, thanks for loving and supporting me ALWAYS.

My nephews and nieces, Grady, Rory, Sadie, Gideon, Ainsley, Abigail and Dexter. I will always tell you stories.

My friend Matt Torpey, who spent countless days with me in a forest green Jetta. I miss you.

And most of all, my parents, Gary and Suzanne Johnson. Every day of my life you made sure I knew you loved me, were proud of me, and believed I could work hard enough and smart enough to do anything. I don't think better parents will ever exist.

QUESTIONS FOR DISCUSSION

1. In *If I Fix You*, Jill explores fixing cars, fixing relationships and fixing herself. What does the author show about each facet of this theme? What does she show about both forgiveness and letting go? Point to examples in the story.

2. The morning after Jill's world falls apart, Sean is waiting on her porch to explain. Where does their communication go wrong? If Jill had understood what happened, do you think she and Sean could have picked up where they left off? Support your answers with details from the book.

3. Sean and Daniel have contrasting family situations. What does each bring to his relationship with Jill, and what does she learn from the time she spends with them?

4. In what ways is Claire a good friend to Jill? What impact does their friendship have on choices Jill makes in

the story? Are there ways in which Claire could be a better friend?

5. The author shows several contrasting parent-child relationships in this book, including Jill and her father, Jill and her mother, and Daniel and his mother. How are the relationships different, and how, if at all, are they similar? Do you think Jill would be better off knowing about her parentage, or not?

6. Cars are important to Jill and her father. What does the Spitfire symbolize in the story, and how does it impact Jill as a character? Point to examples in the book.

7. Cami has a small but important role in the story. How does her presence impact Jill, and how does it illustrate another facet of the theme of friendship?

8. Jill gets very sunburned at one point in the book, just before a key scene happens. Why do you think the author added the sunburn? How does Jill being sunburned affect the scene and the story? How might things have gone if Jill had not been sunburned? Discuss.

Turn the page to read an excerpt from
THE FIRST TO KNOW
Abigail Johnson's next book
from Harlequin TEEN!

CHAPTER 1

The swing was so smooth and effortless I barely felt it. Adrenaline slammed though my body as I hit a screamer into right center, knowing it would find the gap. It had to. I dropped my bat and bolted for first, picking up speed as I rounded to second. I had at least a triple. I made the split-second decision to ignore the stop sign from my coach, kicking up dust as I passed third and charged for home. We needed this run to go to extra innings. From the corner of my eye, I saw the second baseman pivot and rear back to throw home. My heart rate skyrocketed and I slid, taking out the catcher staked over home plate.

She fell onto me in a cloud of orange dust that choked us both. We were still in a heap on the ground when the sound of the cheering crowd shifted from one side to the other—from our team's fans to theirs. The Hawks swooped out of their dugout in a flurry of teal and black and tackled their rising catcher in a massive hug.

Only one of my fellow Mustangs came and offered me a hand up: our shortstop and my best friend, Jessalyn. I brushed her off, despite my eagerness to get away from the celebration going on around me.

"Way to go, Dana."

"I was safe," I told her, yanking off my batting glove to check my nose. I'd hit the catcher's knee pretty hard.

"Actually, you weren't. Otherwise Coach would be screaming at the umpire right now instead of—"

"Dana!" Coach was descending on me with a look that sent Jessalyn retreating to our dugout. His eyebrows were practically touching his hairline and his face was blotchy red from the blood roiling just below the surface. "What are you doing? Huh? What the hell do you think you're doing?"

"I was trying to win."

"For us or them?" He got in my face, so close that I felt exactly what it meant when someone was spitting mad. My own anger receded under his frothing fury. "Are you wearing teal?" He jutted his chin toward my uniform. "Is that the color you're wearing?"

"I'm wearing red," I said, but so quietly he made me repeat it. "I'm wearing red."

"I gave you the stop sign because you were never going to beat that throw. Damn it, Dana!" He turned away, hands on hips, and then faced me again. "You don't get to decide what rules to follow. They—" he pointed at my teammates, who were watching me get chewed out from the dugout "—all know that."

My temper flared again, but I held in my response.

"That's it? You got nothing to say?"

Nothing that would make him stop yelling at me any faster. Silence was my best bet. I'd had more than a little practice getting yelled at by coaches, especially this one.

"You're not starting on Tuesday—"

My head jerked up. "What?"

"—and I'm benching you for the first three innings."

"You can't—" When he walked away, I was right on his heels but skidded to a stop when he rounded on me.

"What? What can't I do?"

It took everything in me to bite my lip. I clamped down so hard I tasted copper. I wasn't responsible for us being down by one with two outs in the bottom of the seventh. And I sure hadn't made a lineup that put Amanda Watson at bat after me. I'd had to take the chance. Amanda was the least consistent batter on our team. She either hit moon shots or struck out, the latter being more often the case when the pressure was on. But I couldn't say any of that, not if I wanted to play at all the next game.

He was in my face again. "You think Selena would have pulled a stunt like that? No. Because Selena listened to her coach."

My eyes stung at the mention of my sister, whose gaze I could feel from the stands. Every time I messed up, he compared me to her. I rotated my jaw and looked at my cleats. Selena had led her team to the state championships as a senior two years ago, something I was determined to do my junior year. And I couldn't do that by risking wins with unreliable players. Why was I the only one who saw that?

"I was trying to win," I repeated, half through my teeth.

"Yeah. All by yourself." He thrust my discarded bat into my hands and went to join the rest of our pissed-off team as they lined up to congratulate the Highland Hawks on their win.

After the less-than-sincere—at least on my part—congratulations were given and I'd sat through our coach's spiel about how well we'd played—not well enough, or I wouldn't have had to try to save the game—and how we won and lost as a united team, I ducked out before anyone else could yell at me and headed around the bleachers.

"Hey, slugger."

My scowl evaporated at the sound of Nick's voice and became a smile when I turned to see the hulking Samoan guy
who'd been one of my closest friends since junior high. Since
then, he'd grown a lot bigger, a lot cuter and, frustratingly
for me, a lot more shy, too. It had gotten so much worse since
we got partnered together in biology that semester. I thought
he was developing more than friendly feelings for me, but
with Nick it was hard to tell, which made it really hard to
tell if I was developing any feelings of my own. Still, he'd
come to my game, so maybe he was trying to be bolder. He
even spoke to me first, though I could tell he was regretting
his choice of the word *slugger* based on the way he lowered
and shook his head.

"I should have just said Dana."

"Nah, slugger's a classic. So, the first game you got to see
this year ended with me losing. Awesome."

"I thought you were great."

"Thanks," I said, not really meaning it. "I didn't see you."

"I had to come late, so I only caught the last inning."

"Even better," I said.

He smiled, ducking his head a little. "It was only the first
game, right?"

"Said like a guy who doesn't play sports." I stopped walking when Nick slowed. Then I mentally shook myself in an
attempt to beat back my venomous mood. "Sorry. I'm the
worst loser on the planet." I also wasn't looking forward to
the car ride home with my endlessly disappointed dad and
the shining sibling I'd never live up to. At least Selena would
have to head back to her dorm eventually. Dad could berate
me all night if he wanted.

Nick recovered from my semi-insult and kicked his foot
to dislodge a cricket that had landed on his shoe. It was mid-
March in Arizona, which, in addition to being the start of

softball season, meant the weather was losing its cold bite. That was all the invitation the crickets needed. They weren't at summer-level swarming yet, but the chirping was an ever-present sound outside, and it was already hard to avoid the little hopping bodies, try as Nick might.

"Aren't you going to ask why I was late?" he asked.

I hadn't known he was coming at all. I'd told him in class that I was playing, but that was all. "Everything okay? Did something happen with your grandmother?" Nick's newly widowed grandmother had recently moved in and was still grieving deeply.

"She's actually doing a little better."

"Oh, good." I squeezed his forearm, and he half jumped like I'd touched him with an iron.

"Yeah, so, that's not why." Nick slid the backpack from his shoulder and unzipped it for me to see inside.

"No way." I grabbed the sides of the bag and stepped right up to him. "Why didn't you text me?" I looked up when Nick didn't answer and found him staring at me.

"I thought it'd be worth it to see your face." He swallowed. "And it was."

Nick's skin was as rich a brown as my glove, but I thought he was blushing. Still, I couldn't dwell on the cute-but-shy thing he had going at the moment. I had eyes only for the white rectangular box he'd brought me. "I'm still pissed about losing, but a lot less now."

"Have you figured out how you're going to do it?"

I nodded. "Selena finally agreed to help, despite her massive reservations." I took a deep breath as I put the box in my duffel bag. "I think this will be the best thing I've ever done, and she's convinced it'll be the worst."

"You know if it doesn't work out, you don't have to tell anyone."

Right. But it had to work out. "I guess tonight's the night." I couldn't help bouncing on my feet a little. "Okay."

"And you can call me if you have any questions or anything." He reached out like he was going to pat my arm or something but pulled back before touching me.

That was fine. I'd need to get used to taking the lead with us, if we ever became us. I hugged him. "Seriously, thank you, Nick. I wouldn't be doing this without you."

It had been only a couple weeks since our biology teacher had started class by sticking his rolled tongue out at his students. A few people laughed at the continued display; the rest waited for the inevitable explanation. When at last Mr. Rodriguez raised his arms and gestured for us to imitate him, he was quick to point a finger at Nick.

"Thank you, Mr. Holloway—no, no. Keep your tongue out. You too, Miss Fields." He shifted his finger to me. "Here we have a perfect display of a dominant phenotype for tongue rolling." He pointed back at Nick. "And a recessive phenotype for tongue rolling. I'm assuming you cannot roll your tongue, Mr. Holloway?"

Nick shook his head while a slight flush marched up the back of his neck.

"Then my original statement stands. Now, what is a phenotype? As you all should know from last night's reading, it's simply the collection of observable traits, like a widow's peak." He pointed to his own hairline. "Or freckles or any number of characteristics that are physically demonstrable, like our tongue rollers here—feel free to close your mouths now," he said, addressing the half of the class who still had their tongues out. "What I'd like you all to do with your partners is complete a chart listing several phenotypes, note which are dominant and recessive, then *felicitaciones*! You're going to have two children and, from your original data, determine the phenotypes of each child." He began passing out packets. "Refer to chapters eight and nine of your textbooks if you need further reminders about phenotypes, genotypes, alleles, gametes and the marvelous process of meiosis. I'll be circulating the room to answer questions. Now learn, students, learn!"

I leaned into Nick, who still hadn't fully recovered from being singled out. "I think our kids are screwed. Between my attached earlobes and your flat tongue, what can they possibly accomplish in life?" I got a pity smile for my lame humor, but Nick made eye contact for more than two seconds. "Though maybe there is something awesome hidden on my dad's side that they could inherit. He was surrendered at a hospital as a baby, so we have no clue about his birth family."

Nick nodded. "I never knew that about your dad but I guess that goes for me too."

Nick had grown up knowing he was adopted—his family had their own mini holiday, Nick Day, celebrating the day they brought him home—and had never shown the least bit of discomfort talking about it. The opposite, really. Score me for bringing it up. I had Nick's full, unguarded attention. He turned to face me.

"Did I tell you I recently took one of those online DNA tests to try to figure out more of my heritage? I'm obviously Samoan, but turns out I'm 8 percent Eskimo too. I even found a few fourth cousins floating around the country."

I'd forgotten to care that he'd been holding my gaze for longer than his usual few seconds. "Wait, like actual blood relatives? A DNA test can tell you that?" My heart rate spiked as the possibilities began darting through my brain.

"Yeah. A lot of people are doing them now, so you never know who you'll find. Cool, huh?"

I'd almost kissed him that day in biology class. Instead I'd pumped him for every speck of info on the company he'd used and started planning something I'd hopefully get to finish that night. The knowledge now made me hug Nick tighter despite the duffel bag smashed between us.

From over his shoulder, I saw my mom heading toward us. I pulled back a scant second after he'd worked up the nerve to hug me back, noticing that I'd transferred a good amount of orange dust from my uniform to him in the process. I left him beating dust from his spotless white T-shirt and quite possibly ironed jeans with a promise to text him once I'd succeeded—which I absolutely would. I wasn't about to lose twice in one night.

Mom didn't care about dust and gathered me into a hug while whispering a disparaging comment about the umpire's vision before releasing me.

"Tell that to Dad." He was still in the dugout talking to a couple of the girls before making the final shift from Coach to Dad again, a distinction he and Selena had established back when he'd coached her softball team. Honestly, I never noticed much of a difference.

"Oh, I will."

That made me smile, because she would. My parents often had loud, passionate disagreements that, to an outsider, might seem like fights. But they didn't see the way Mom would goad Dad even after she'd made her point just to watch the heated color infuse his pale skin, or the way Dad would bait her until she slipped into her native Spanish because she had even less of a filter in those moments than normal.

"Who was the boy and when do I get to meet him?"

I tightened the grip on my duffel. "That was Nick, and you've met him a dozen times."

"Not since you started hugging him like that."

I so wasn't having that conversation. "Where's Selena?"

Mom gave me a knowing look at my obvious subject change. "Ask him to come to dinner. He's not a vegetarian, is he?"

To my mom, being a vegetarian was slightly less offensive than being a Dodgers fan. "He's not a vegetarian. And he's still just a friend."

"Hmm," Mom said, which meant we'd be revisiting the topic later. "Selena's waiting for us at the car."

"Where's her car?"

"She got in early, so we drove together."

Great. I get both her and Dad the whole way home.

As soon as we were within earshot, Selena started. "I can't believe you ran through a stop sign." Her shoulder-length brown hair, a shade darker than mine, swished as she shook her head. "I get that when the adrenaline is flowing, it's hard to stop, but, Dana, you don't get to make that call. When I was playing…"

I tuned her out. Selena had this way of seeming to support and motivate me that undercut everything I did, and it had only gotten worse since she left for college. The University of Arizona was only a couple hours from Apache Junction, so she still tried to make most of my games—largely, I was convinced, to remind us all of her glory days as a Mustang. She was no doubt relaying one of her many victories, where she single-handedly played every position and hit so many home runs that the other team's coach begged her to transfer schools, or my personal favorite, Dad crying when she told him she wasn't interested in playing college ball. Those were all slight-to-gross exaggerations. Dad never cried; he'd just looked like he wanted to.

"Got it. I'll play better next time. Hey, weren't you telling me that you need Mom and Dad to help you with some school project tonight?" I moved my duffel bag in front of me and widened my eyes at her. Selena could be an annoying braggart when it came to softball, but she was also the only person on the planet who could read my mind with only the slightest cue.

"I was," she said, without missing a beat, then forestalled Mom's inevitable question. "It's an extra-credit thing. I'll tell you about it when we get home. I'm sure Dad's gonna want to talk about that last out first."

I groaned. "Can we just not? Let's talk about something lighter, like teen-pregnancy statistics. Besides, it was a bad call."

"You looked out to me," Selena said.

Blood heated my face, but Dad was there before I could respond.

"That's because she was." He unlocked the trunk, not looking at me. "The umpire called it."

I came up alongside him, wishing he could be a little more my dad and a little less my coach the next time a close call cost us a game. "You know, you used to get thrown out of games all the time for arguing when you coached Selena. This would have been a perfect opportunity."

"Not all the time," Selena said, though I was positive she was calling a list to mind same as I was.

"More than once," I said, before turning back to Dad and waiting with raised eyebrows for his response. "There was that game against Chandler. You almost took a swing at the umpire."

"I was never going to hit him," Dad said. "Back then I was more of a…" He searched for the right word.

"Calentón," Mom said, smiling.

I thought it was more than Dad being hotheaded, but I didn't get to protest before he went on.

"I told you to stay, you didn't, and we lost. And even if

you'd been safe—run through a stop sign again and I'll bench you for more than a few innings." He opened the front passenger door for Mom, a practice he'd apparently started on their first date and was still doing more than twenty years later.

"You're not serious." But the look he gave me said otherwise. "Fine. Am I supposed to apologize to my dad or my coach?"

"What was that?" he asked, though we both knew he'd heard me.

"Nothing."

He sighed, coming around to where I stood. "What is this attitude?"

"Why didn't you fight the call?"

"Because you were out. Hey—hey." He called my attention back when I looked away. "I'd have fought for you if you weren't. Same as I did for your sister." He lowered his voice so that Mom and Selena on the other side wouldn't overhear. "You are one of the best players on the team. You could be as good as Selena if you worked harder."

Except Selena never had to work the way I constantly had to. And she'd never cared enough to see how much better she could have been if she had. That was maybe the one bone of contention between her and Dad. So I worked twice as hard to be half as good, and it still wasn't enough.

"Take the loss and work harder next time. We've got the whole season ahead of us, and you're no good to me or anyone else on a bench. I need you." He clapped a hand on my shoulder and squeezed. I nodded and worked my mouth into a small smile for his benefit. He needed me. I wanted more than that, but I'd settle for *need* just then.

I cradled my duffel in my lap during the car ride home, feeling the shape of the box within. And I smiled for real.

CHAPTER 2

My plan went off without a hitch. Selena was calm and cool, explaining that she needed family DNA samples for a criminology class she was supposedly taking. Selena was still technically undeclared, but she'd expressed enough middling interest in pursuing a sociology degree that neither of our parents questioned this. I think they both took it as a sign that she was finally committing to a career path. Mom happily swiped the toothbrush-like swab on the inside of her cheek. Dad was equally willing, joking about taking Mom on the lam if they connected him to any unsolved murders. They had no idea what we were really doing—what *I* was really doing.

After that, Selena passed me Dad's swab and was officially done with the whole thing.

"I'm officially done with the whole thing," she said, when we were in my room afterward.

"Fine." I didn't even look up from the DNA Detective website open on my laptop. "But don't come back to me when I'm about to give Dad the birthday present to end all birthday presents."

Selena peered over my shoulder, chewing on her thumbnail. "You really think you'll find someone he's related to?"

Arizona's Safe Baby Haven Law allowed newborns to be anonymously handed over at hospitals or fire stations without having to provide personal information, which meant Dad's birth certificate was basically blank. But none of that would matter if we found even a single DNA match. "Yes." I turned sideways in my chair. "Nick found a bunch of fourth cousins when he took his test, and he sent me links about other people who were orphans just like Dad finding half siblings and even parents."

"What if it tells us something he doesn't want to know, something *we* don't want to know?"

I frowned. "What, that he's related to some douchey celebrity? The whole point of doing it as a surprise is that if we don't like what we find out, then we trash it and he never knows." I couldn't believe I still had to convince Selena about this. She knew as well as I did how much it would mean for Dad to find his own relatives. That was part of the reason he and Mom got pregnant with me. They wanted to make sure Selena had a sibling, someone she was directly connected to. Dad didn't have that. There was such a huge contrast between Mom's sprawling Mexican clan back in Texas and Dad's blank unknown. We didn't see Mom's family all that often, but they were still there, and I always felt like I was a part of something. Dad didn't know what that was like. This was a chance to give him a family that consisted of more than the three of us.

"I needed your money and your criminology-class excuse, both of which you gave me. If you want out now, that's fine. Go ahead and give Dad a tie for his birthday."

Selena dropped her arms in obvious irritation before fishing her car keys out of her bag. "Fine. I have to get back to my dorm." She hesitated at the door. "Just don't tell me if he's 86 percent more likely to get colon cancer or something. Good stuff only, okay?"

I gave her an exaggerated eye roll. "But if it's good?"

"Then, since I paid for half of this, my name better be on the birthday card too."

Under my breath, I said, "A little more than half," before turning back to the computer and filling out the final field on the registration form.

Selena strode back to my side and blocked the touch pad before I could click Send. "I paid more?"

Oh yeah. "I'm a poor high school junior who has to constantly put money into your old car."

"And I'm a poorer college sophomore who gave you that old car for way less than it was worth."

"It was my idea, and I'm doing all the work. Plus, now you're making me go through the potentially traumatic results all on my own." Not that I expected them to be traumatic. When Selena still didn't seem convinced, I glanced at her hand covering the touch pad, then up at her while simultaneously clicking Enter on the keyboard.

She dropped her hand. "Fine. Was that it? Is it done?"

"I mail the sample back in the morning and the results come in six to eight weeks."

"Six to eight weeks. That seems fast."

Not to me. Plus, Dad's birthday wasn't for another two months after that. Nick told me it could take time to hear back from any potential matches I found and contacted, and longer still if I needed information from any of them to track down closer relatives. Still, I couldn't stop the excitement buzzing through me. Family for Dad. Family that I found— with Selena's help, but that I made happen. That would be worth more than all the softball games she ever won him.

★ ★ ★

I turned out to be right: six to eight weeks did not go fast. As we approached the six-week mark, it became impossible to focus in Biology, my last class before lunch. Not even Nick working up the nerve to ask me out—something he'd started but abandoned the last three days in a row—could completely hold my attention.

He sucked in a deep breath. "Dana, I was wondering if... I mean...do you..." A sheen of sweat broke out on his forehead and he gave up yet again. "Can I borrow a pen?"

So close, I thought, passing Nick a pen. I could have asked him out, but I really needed him to find that initial bit of courage. Otherwise I'd end up running all over him in a relationship and that wouldn't be good for either of us.

Glancing at the clock again, I didn't have any more time to give Nick in the hopes that he'd try again before class ended. "Hey, so if I leave early, can you cover for me with Mr. Rodriguez?" I was already packing up my stuff and eyeing our teacher, who was helping a student in the back row. "I need to be home when the mail is delivered or else my dad might get it first. Just tell him I went to the bathroom if he notices I'm gone." And then I slipped out the door, mouthing *thanks* to a dumbstruck Nick as I did.

Our house was only a few miles from Superstition Springs High School on the outskirts of Apache Junction, tucked into a development of identical midsize homes that were distinguished from each other only by the cars parked out front. In our case, Mom's red mini SUV and Dad's silver hatchback. We had a corner lot, which meant we had twice as much backyard as our neighbors and could practice a little without having to drive to a park. That had been the number one selling point of the home, the trade-off being that it had only three smallish bedrooms, one of which we converted into Mom and Dad's office because the large bay window afforded it the most natural light. It also gave me a perfectly unobstructed view to spy through. I slowed as I drove by, banking on the hope that they'd both be too consumed in their work to look up and recognize my car. Sure enough, Mom was fastidiously writing code on her computer, while Dad was filling his with design mock-ups for whatever website they were currently working on—I could never keep track. It was a good business, one that allowed Dad to set his own hours and still coach our high school softball team while giving Mom's analytical mind the challenge she craved since she had to code whatever designs he came up with. A right brain and a left brain working together in near-perfect harmony.

Neither glanced up as I drove by, but they would if I pulled into the driveway, so I had to be insane and park around the block, skulk/sprint through neighbors' yards and duck behind the bougainvillea bushes in front of our house. Then I spent the next twenty minutes crouched and pulling pink petals out of my hair while waiting to accost the mail carrier before she reached our house.

I'd never felt more excited in my life.

As soon as I heard the distinctive sound of the mail truck, I started disentangling myself from branches, emerging from my hiding spot just as Dad stepped outside. I didn't know how he missed me diving back into the bushes, and I really didn't know how he failed to hear my strangled breathing as I watched him share a greeting with the blue-clad mail carrier and then slowly walk back into the house with a stack of envelopes. The DNA test results were addressed to me, but I hadn't wanted to risk Dad seeing my name along with the DNA Detective logo in the corner and asking questions— and he would ask questions—so I could only hold my breath and wait while he stood in the entryway, shuffling the first letter to the back, then the second, and on and on while I tried not to have a heart attack. But then he tossed the stack on the table and closed the door behind him. I leaned my head back against the stucco-covered wall, my heart jack-hammering in my chest.

After that day, I started leaving Biology earlier and earlier, as soon as attendance was taken, so that I could be home before the mail in case it came early. But the real problem was Dad. Twice more that week he beat me to the mail, which meant two more near heart attacks for me. Not good. Plus, while Nick might have had trouble expressing his feelings for me, he was a lot less reticent when it came to his thoughts on me skipping out early.

Nick had a perfect attendance record. He'd even come back to school after having his wisdom teeth removed during lunch hour. He understood why I was leaving early, but he really, *really* didn't want to be a part of covering for me. So far, Mr. Rodriguez's move-around-the-room-as-you-will policy had kept my absence from being noticed, but Nick was growing increasingly unsettled by the prospect. It probably didn't help that he abandoned several more attempts to ask me out. Each class, it was worse, the sweating, the nervous glances, the bouncing leg under our shared desk. I made a huge mistake one day when I pressed Nick's knee still with my hand. He made the most insane noise, somewhere between a yelp and a gasp. Needless to say, the entire class—including Mr. Rodriguez—turned in our direction. Nick's face was on fire, and I was too distracted by the need to beat the mail to play off Nick's outburst convincingly. For the rest of class, Mr. Rodriguez watched us too closely for me to slip away. I was almost as agitated as Nick by the time the bell rang and I could race home. Thankfully, the results didn't come that day either.

When the mail truck started down our street on Wednesday, Dad heard it as soon as I did. He looked out the window, pushed back his chair and stood up. Mom was softly head-banging to the heavy metal music pounding through her earbuds, oblivious to anything else. I started counting steps while watching the approaching truck. Five to the hall. Ten to the front door. He was going to beat me again.

I pulled my phone out and called home. Seconds later, I heard it ringing inside and, through the windows, saw Dad head back to the office to answer it.

"Dana?"

"Hi, Dad. I think I left my History homework on my desk upstairs. I can come by before lunch is over if it's there, but could you check for me?" As soon as he moved to the stairs, I slid out of the bushes and waved at the mail carrier while directing Dad to search every random spot I could think of in my room. "It might have fallen behind my desk—can you pull it out and check?"

He put the phone down but I heard his grunt of effort as the mail was placed into my waiting hands.

"I'm not seeing it anywhere. Are you sure you left it? Dana?"

I was only half listening as I sorted through random bills and magazines. "Did you look under the bed?"

He said something about my messy room, but I didn't hear it, because the second letter from the bottom was from DNA Detective.

The envelope shook in my hand along with my voice. "It's here."

"Look more carefully next time. And you're cleaning your room the second you get home today, do you understand me?"

I hurried to put the rest of the mail in the mailbox. "I will. Thanks for checking. Love you, Dad."

"You too."

For once I didn't care that he didn't say it back. Mom always said he had a hard time verbally expressing love since he'd had so little growing up without a family, but just because he rarely said the word didn't mean he didn't feel it. I did know he loved me, and once he opened his birthday present, I'd get to feel it full force.

As soon as I was around the corner, I tore into the envelope. I skipped the geographic-ancestry and health reports as fast as I could shuffle the pages, until I had it: the possible-relative list. At first the onslaught of information was overwhelming. On the left were default symbols indicating the gender of each potential relative; next to that was the percentage of DNA Dad shared with each person, followed by the predicted relationship. Most were listed as third to fifth cousins, but I barely saw them.

The top result had a 47 percent DNA match, with the predicted relationship listed as "father or son."

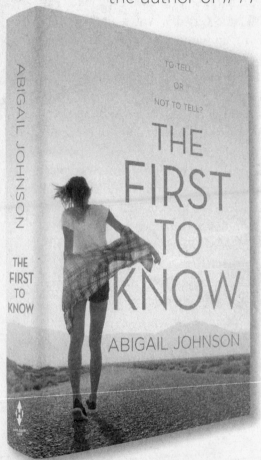

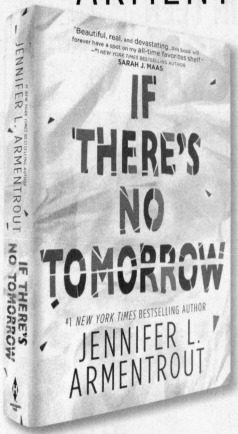